The Ardent Witness

The Ardent Witness

Danielle Maisano

www.victorinapress.co.uk

The Ardent Witness
Danielle Maisano

© Danielle Maisano, 2019
First published in Great Britain in 2019
by Victorina Press
Adderley Lodge Farm,
Adderley Road,
Market Drayton, TF9 3ST,
England

The right of Danielle Maisano to be identified as author of this work has been asserted by her in accordance with sections 77 and 78 of the copyright, Designs and Patents Act 1988.

Typesetting and Layout: Heidi Hurst
Cover Art and Design: © Lauren French

All rights reserved. No part of this book maybe reprinted or reproduced or utilised in any form or by any electronic, mechanical, or other means, now known or here after invented, including photocopying and recording, or in any information storage or retrieval system, without permission in writing from the publisher and/or the author.

*British Library Cataloguing in Publication Data
A catalogue record for this book is available from the British Library.*

ISBN: 978-1-999-6195-7-2 (paperback)

Typeset in 11pt Minion Pro
Printed and Bound in the UK by CPI Antony Rowe Ltd

For Alex, because I'd be lost if not for you.

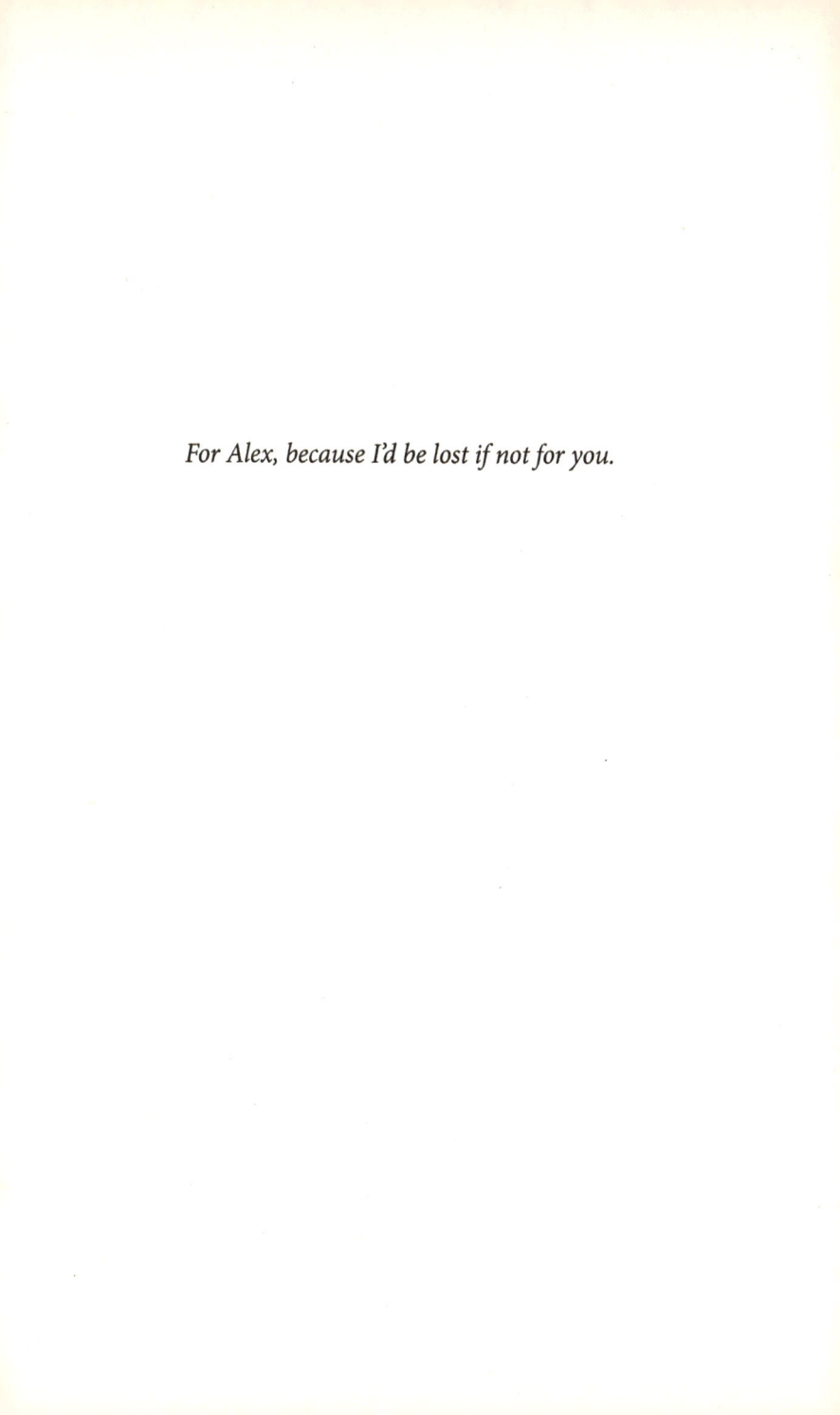

This is a work of fiction. Names, characters, businesses, places, events and incidents are either the products of the author's imagination or used in a fictitious manner. Any resemblance to actual persons, living or dead, or actual events is purely coincidental.

Chapter One

October 7, 2011
Togo

The door of the examination room creaked open. With her graying hair and white smock, far too large for her tiny figure, the *matron* approached the table where I sat. She moved without a hint of urgency and picked up the top booklet from the pile. Squinting from behind her oversized glasses, at least three decades out of style, she stood for a moment and thumbed through the faded yellow pages of the *carnets*. Patience, Lily. It wasn't her fault. It was my own damn fault for still showing up on time, expecting things to be any different. But she wasn't looking to catch any mistakes in my work. It was more of a symbolic gesture, a means of exerting her authority. A necessary act, like so many things here that reinforced a hierarchy never to be disturbed. When again she picked up the top booklet from the pile, the *infirmier's* voice came roaring once more from the examination room. The *matron* dropped the booklet and retreated down the hallway. That was it, then. Another false start.

It was almost noon and the heat was radiating from the open doorway, suffocating us between the stuffy cement walls. The forty or so women who lined the narrow wooden benches had been waiting just as long as I had but they seemed not to notice it so much. Their eyes were empty. Unmoved by the heat and the unnecessary amounts of time that had passed. They held immense reserves of patience. If I could have spoken to them directly, the whole job could have been finished by now. But most of the women here didn't speak much French. They spoke a language I'd never heard of six months ago and, aside from the basics, I understood only one word of it. *Anasara*. It meant white. All morning the word had been scattered throughout their conversations. It meant most likely I was the topic of those conversations, but beyond this it was unclear whether that was a good or bad thing. I tried not worry about it too much. All in all, I must have been quite the anomaly. At twenty-six I was probably older than half of them. A young woman living in a foreign country. Unmarried. Without children.

At least there were the children. The older ones watched me with a frightened curiosity. A few of the braver ones made attempts to touch my skin or hair and then scurried quickly back to their mothers. It was a game we'd played all morning and it had helped to pass the time. But by this point, the time for games had passed. The hours upon hours of oppressive inactivity had drained us of any desire to do anything but stare blankly at the gray cement walls full of tattered old posters, meant to elicit both fear and hope at once. Ghastly diseases next to smiling, happy families. And then there was the heat. It only intensified the scent of sweat and sickness that hung around like a bad feeling you couldn't quite shake. They said it gets easier. They say a lot of things. Time will tell. Wait and see. I had no other choice but to wait.

After only a few moments the *matron* reappeared from the examination room. Once again, she picked up the top booklet from the pile.

"Mawata Koffi," she called out, but no one rose in recognition so she called out the name again, this time more forcefully. "Mawata Koffi!" Still nothing. "Koffi, Mawata!" She tried reversing the order. Some of the women shrugged and shook their heads while others whispered, repeating the name. Her shoulders sank in annoyance as she stared again at the name in the booklet. It was too late into the afternoon to hide the frustration and exhaustion of a thankless job; its years of wear and tear were permanently etched into the lines of her thin, wrinkled face. She walked over to the entrance and peered out into the dusty courtyard, her small frame outlined in the blinding sun. She yelled out the name again, this time with a volume surprising for such a tiny woman. A voice called back from the courtyard. The *matron* continued yelling as the woman appeared with baby Mawata, strapped to her back with a stretch of brightly patterned *pagne* that matched her mother's dress. The woman was clutching a bag of fried *beignets* in her hand. She smiled sheepishly at the other women as the *matron* chided her in words I didn't understand but whose sentiments were clear. Now, finally, we could begin.

Mawata's mother untied her from behind her back. She moved quickly in an attempt to apologize for wasting time, but no one else seemed very bothered by it. It was expected to happen in one form or another. Little Mawata's fancy dress was hastily swapped for a cloth bungee diaper and she was placed hanging from the scale that was sturdily attached to the wall. The dial moved sporadically then settled on a number. These first few moments were vital as the scale adjusted to Mawata's weight while, at the same time, she slowly processed this strange new state of being.

"*Cinq kilogrammes!*" I called to the *matron*, just as little Mawata's eyes widened and her feet kicked the air in panic. I signaled to her mother we had finished, and she rushed to scoop Mawata into her arms just as the child started to scream in anger. I walked over to the *matron* and she showed me where she had marked the chart in Mawata's booklet. The baby was on the small side for a four-month-old, but still just within the normal range. We called the next child up, a newborn, only weeks old and too small to be hung from the bungee. Carefully, the mother placed the baby in my arms and I laid him gently on a scale much like the kind from the sterile white doctor's offices of my youth. It was the only thing in the entire place that reminded me of any medical facility I had ever seen before. The baby was just under three kilograms. The *matron* shook her head as she wrote the number down in the book. He was small, far below the normal range. She addressed the woman in the unrecognizable language. Her eyes were stern and her words sounded harsh, but this language always sounded that way. The young woman was embarrassed. She looked down as she docilely answered her interrogator, unable to meet our eyes. She couldn't have been more than twenty. After a moment, the *matron* paused to translate.

"*J'ai dit*," she said, with obvious frustration. "I told her that she must feed the baby every time he cries. Day and night. The more she feeds him, the more milk will come."

"Tell her also, she must be sure that she is eating enough. It is important for her to take care of herself, too. It's difficult at first, but it will get easier," I added.

The *matron* nodded and repeated my advice to the woman, who said nothing, her eyes still fixed on the ground. I placed the baby back into her arms.

As we carried on with the rest of them, the *infirmier* began to call the women and their children into the examination room to receive their vaccinations in between seeing his other patients. Sporadically, they shuffled into the room down the hall where the wild screams of traumatized babies could be heard as they unexpectedly encountered the pinch of the needle. As soon as it was over they were hurriedly placed at their mother's breast in hopes a feeding would make them forget the pain and stop crying. The whole operation took little more than an hour. A chaotic climax to a morning of dull anticipation.

"I wonder," I said to the *matron,* once the women had dispersed and we packed up what was left of our baby-weighing operation. "Maybe it would be better to do the consultations in private?"

"In private?" From the look on her face I might as well have suggested we do the consultations on the moon.

"I just think maybe the women would be less embarrassed. They might find it easier to speak up or ask questions if they're having difficulties. Like the woman, earlier—"

"There's no room." She shrugged and went back to shuffling papers.

"What if we did everything at once in the examination room, when the *infirmier* calls them in for the shots?"

"We would have to wait for him to finish with all of the other patients. It would take too long," she said. I couldn't argue with that.

"Maybe we could clear out the storage room and make a little space in there?"

"Oh Lily," she said with a dismissive tone that implied resigned amusement. "You must not forget to tell the *infirmier* you are leaving before you go," she reminded me as I picked up my bag. "Last time you forgot."

"Of course."

Last time I hadn't forgotten. It had been a small rebellion against another one of those symbolic gestures. This one, I suspected, had more to do with him being a man and my being a woman than it had to do with being polite. I couldn't get away with it every time so, reluctantly, I tapped on the door, which was left open a crack, and peeked my head in. The *infirmier* motioned for me to enter and I took a seat in the back of the room. He was just finishing up with his last patient, an elderly man whose eyes looked on, enduring and heavy, as the *infirmier* counted out plastic packets of pills from his desk drawer.

"Take one every day for seven days," the *infirmier* said in French, holding out the pills. The old man rose from his chair frailly to retrieve them. "Even if you feel better, you must still take them." He nodded but the *infirmier* continued. "You must not think, 'I feel better now, I don't need the pills, I will stop or I will give the rest to my brother because now he is ill.' If you do this you will become ill again, and then you will need even more pills. Twice the pills, you will have to pay for!"

The old man continued to nod, eagerly. He grumbled a humble word of thanks to the *infirmier* and turned to me with a toothless smile and a slight bow and was gone.

"*Les gens du nord…*" the *infirmier* sighed, shaking his head. He was a young man, no more than thirty-five. Being from Lomé, he had the countenance of a New York City doctor sent to the backwoods of Kentucky. He did little to hide his displeasure at being assigned to such a place.

"*Tu es fini?*"

I nodded.

"*Tu es fatigu*ée?"

Yes, I was tired, but his question was more of an accusation than an observation. He was tired, the *matron* was tired. We were all tired.

"*Non,*" I lied. He gave me a haughty grin, as if he didn't believe me.

"Monday morning I will take you to meet the inspector at the Lycée," he said. This was good news. I had been waiting for this meeting to be set up for a few weeks now. "He will introduce you to a teacher that can help you to start a health club for the students." He paused. "You still want to start a health club?"

"Yes," I said. "You think it would be a good idea?"

"Yes. For boys and girls?"

"That's what I was planning."

"I think you should start with the girls first," he said.

"That way you can talk more about certain things. It's a bad problem here, the girls becoming pregnant and not finishing school."

"But don't the boys need to know these things as well?" I asked, unable to hide my aggravation at his placement of responsibilities.

"Yes." He paused a moment and smiled again, that same arrogant grin. As though he knew exactly what I was thinking in my pious questioning of his opinions. "But with boys there, the girls will be too embarrassed to ask any questions. They may not even come. Start with the girls, the boys can follow later." I nodded. Never think you know anything. I was learning that I would never learn. I stood up to leave. "I can take you on my moto?" It was less than a quarter of a mile down the road. I said thank you but no.

The main road through the village was empty on my way back. Most of the people had already turned in for *repos*, that quiet time during the day when everything shuts down from noon to an undetermined hour. When the sun let up a bit and the heat became more bearable. Lazily, I walked past the tiny collections of clay rooms and thatched roofs, deserted in the blinding midday sun.

When I reached my compound, I opened the rusty iron door to see the two elderly women that lived in the set of rooms adjacent to mine. They were sat underneath the refuge of their shaded porch, exactly as they had been that morning. I greeted them in the local language. Neither of them spoke a word of French. Luckily, there was a young girl that lived with them and took care of them who could translate for us. I occupied the set of rooms at the far end of the big cemented courtyard. It was a rather grand compound for such a village, right at the foot of the small but proud little mountain that anchored us to our place here. The mountain itself was still very green from the rains. It gave everything a hidden and enchanted feel that made it seem even more faraway and otherworldly than it already did.

Inside my set of rooms it was dark and cool, with lingering traces of the crispness of morning air. Grabbing a bucket and some soap, I wrapped myself in a sheet of *pagne* and went back out to the cement shower attached to my porch, where there was a spigot for water. I filled the bucket and then I scooped the water out and poured it over my body. It was cold and at first I winced with the shock of it but after a few splashes the icy water felt refreshing. When I returned to my room, I lay down on the bed but it was too hot under the mosquito netting. I struggled to pin the net up but even that gave little relief. With luck, the exhaustion would win over the discomfort of the heat and I would be able to sleep. Outside it was quiet aside from the scattered cries of pygmy goats from behind the compound. Soon I drifted off.

I awoke some time later to a faint but persistent tapping at the screen door and the murmur of voices. Children's voices. But children didn't knock here. They hung about and whispered and peered in and laughed, but they didn't knock.

"Lily!" A voice called out, accompanied by more tapping. Gladys.

"*J'arrive!*" I sat up. My skin was still moist, but now it was from the heat and the sweat. I quickly found some clothes. Gladys was standing just beyond the screen of the front door with her two young boys, Jean and Usman, peering inside anxiously at her feet.

"I have come to say good evening!" Gladys said in heavily accented English.

The boys repeated her greeting and headed immediately over to climb across my new couch. Their hands, coated in dirt, made faint brown impressions on the wine-colored fabric of the foam cushions. "How is your work?"

"Oh, it's very good."

"You are tired?"

"No, I just had a little rest."

"Would you like for me to bring you some food?"

"Oh, no thank you," I said trying to shake off my sleepiness and match her enthusiasm, which was never easy, even without having been forced out of a dead sleep. I would have invited her to sit down but she always declined. So I stood there, awkwardly, as she looked around, her eyes harmlessly inspecting my home as she took in every detail of the empty space. She'd helped me to get the place in order when I'd first arrived and so on each visit she took a moment to ensure it was still holding together, sending her daughter over if something wasn't quite up to her standards. Too many cobwebs in the corner, a broken window screen, a dusty floor. Though her Ghanaian phrasings were sometimes difficult to understand, I had almost cried with relief when she first introduced herself and that loud and lively voice had called out to greet me in barely understandable English. She had been the first villager to show up at my door to welcome me. She wasn't like the other women I'd met so far. There was nothing timid about Gladys.

Her cheerful eyes fell back on me, pleased that everything appeared to be in order. She had a lovely smile. It made her appear more beautiful than she might have seemed otherwise, dressed in a ragged t-shirt with an old piece of *pagne* wrapped around her waist.

"Tomorrow, at the market, you will buy yams and in the evening, we will make *fufu*."

"Perfect," I said.

"*Aye!*" she cried, looking behind me. The boys had begun to ruthlessly pull piles of magazines and books from my shelves. At the sound of their mother's voice they stopped immediately. Eyes wide, they looked from me to Gladys, trying to ascertain the severity of their crimes. "Fati, she is coming. I will take them home now."

"Oh, they're all right," I said. In Gladys's absence the boys pretty much enjoyed free range of my house and all its western curiosities. Books, magazines, even my iPod and camera, from time to time. I had decided early on it was better that way. The less mystery I made of myself, the faster they lost interest. Before Gladys could protest there was a faint tapping on my door.

"*Bonsoir* Lily," Fati said, giving a slight bow as Gladys unlatched the screen for her daughter. "*Comment* ça *va?*"

"Ça *va bien. Et toi?*"

"*Bien, bien.* And your work?" She continued with the polite and habitual enquiries. Her French was very good. Much better than mine.

"*Bien*," I repeated. "And school?" She nodded again, clutching her notebook to her chest.

"I must go," Gladys said. "I will take them?" She motioned toward the boys, who were now happily distracted by a copy of *Adbusters,* arguing excitedly and pointing at pictures.

"Oh they're fine," I assured her.

"Okay, good night! See you tomorrow!"

Once Gladys was gone, I invited Fati to sit down and she shooed the boys off the couch to make room.

"What will you eat tonight?" she asked, glancing over at the wooden counter across the room, which held a small gas stove and served as a kitchen. My eating habits were still very much a curiosity to her.

"Oh, I bought some *soja* earlier from the woman near the *dispensaire*." Fati wrinkled her nose at this.

"Only *soja*?"

"Yes."

"It's not enough."

"For me, it's enough," I said and she shook her head at the thought of a lonely meal of fried tofu. She must have decided it was futile to argue with me, for she left it alone and said no more about it. I sat down in the chair across from her and picked up my book. Fati opened her notebook, but she was struggling to stay awake. Her eyes, barely open, stared blankly at the pages. She was just starting her second year at the Lycée and that was no small feat for a young girl from such a small village. Gladys was behind that, no doubt. Gladys made no secret of the fact that she had expectations for both her daughters. For Fati, she was set on the idea that she should continue her education beyond the Lycée.

Gladys's husband was an elder and highly respected

in the village. He'd lived there all his life, as had his family before him. But Gladys was an outsider, raised in a small village in Ghana, just across the border. She'd met her husband at the funeral of a distant relative in Togo. She spoke the local language; it was similar to the Ghanaian dialect of her home, and she'd made it far enough in her education to be able to communicate in English very well. But at seventeen Gladys left Ghana before she could finish school and followed her husband to Togo. After the birth of her third child, Usman, her husband decided to take a second wife from the village. It was common practice in the region but Gladys was a proud woman. She hadn't considered such a thing might happen to her. It also didn't help that the woman was much younger and less educated. Dim by comparison. That was when she decided that neither Fati nor Adiza would ever suffer the same humiliation.

While I was thankful for the liking Gladys had taken to me, I never doubted it was as much for Fati's sake as it was my own. She was hoping my good fortune in being an independent and educated young women might rub off on her daughter. So, she sent Fati over in the evenings to study for as long as Gladys could manage things at home without her. Sometimes Fati studied and sometimes she slept in the chair, notebook open, eyes closed. Either way I left her alone. Her days were an endless and exhausting blur of chores and schoolwork, and I welcomed the company. In a way, she was easier to be around than her mother. There was none of the chaotic intensity that emanated from Gladys. There was something more familiar about Fati, something intangible. It came across with a look sometimes: there was a seriousness in her eyes, a weight that never left them. Even when she laughed, it was always there. She saw beyond what others could see. She understood people. Perhaps she'd even lived a life before this one now. But then my musings were interrupted by footsteps shuffling slowly up the cement porch accompanied by giggling voices.

"Adiza," Fati said. We exchanged a sorry smile as she stood to open the door for her sister. There would be no reprieve for poor Fati tonight.

"*Bonsoir*," Adiza said as she entered with the casual confidence of a fifteen-year-old. She did not in any way mirror her sister's reserve. She was accompanied by Brigitte, the young girl who helped to care for the old women on my compound. Adiza addressed Fati in their local language as Brigitte wandered over to the kitchen area to see if there was anything to eat. She held up the bag of *soja*.

"*C'est quoi*, Lily?" she asked, knowing exactly what it was.

"*Soja*," I answered.

"*Il faut me donner un.*" A month ago, I would have given Brigitte a piece and everyone else after that out of necessity. But I had quickly grown wise. And hungry.

"It's for my dinner," I said. "If I give you one, everyone will want a piece. There is not enough." Brigitte shook her head.

"But I'm hungry."

"Don't give her any," Fati quickly interjected. "She's lying. She has plenty of food." Both Brigitte and Adiza laughed and raised their voices to Fati, chiding her for going against Brigitte's claims. Fati ignored them. Adiza had apparently delivered whatever message she had come to deliver. She scooped up the young boys and headed off, taking Brigitte with her. Fati waited for them to go.

"You must not pay any attention to them," she said once they were gone. "Remember, I told you, Brigitte's family has lots of food and lots of money." Fati was right; she had already explained all this to me before. Brigitte came from the wealthiest family in the village. Of course, wealth had acquired a new sort of relativity to me here.

"I know," I said, shaking my head as well to show that I shared in her indignity.

"I must go help with dinner. Tomorrow we will walk to the market together?"

"What time?"

"Nine."

"*D'accord*," I agreed. Nine meant any time after ten at the earliest.

"*Au revoir, Lily.*" With that Fati disappeared.

Brigitte and the women were busy pounding the *fufu* for dinner in the courtyard. The wooden pestles banged the giant basins in a rhythm I had grown accustomed to. Like the sound of crickets at dusk, it was expected and ever-present. The night came quickly here. I heated the *soja* in a pan on the stove and added some black-eyed peas I had bought for breakfast. It was bland but I was getting used to it. I poured myself a glass of wine. At least the box claimed it was wine. Maybe, maybe not. I was getting used to that as well though.

I sat down alone at the small kitchen table and picked up the letter I had received months ago. It spoke of things and people from the past. I read over the letter again. If I were in Detroit tonight, what would I be doing? If I allowed myself to settle on it for more than a minute or two, it became overwhelming. The pit in my stomach, the ache in my chest. That life was over. For now, at least.

The evenings were the most difficult part. When the excitement of each new day had settled and I was alone with my thoughts. I had to find distractions in the quiet darkness. In my bedroom, I dug out the old black Moleskine from underneath a pile of workbooks and training manuals. I flipped through the first few pages, reading over words in my handwriting, but it seemed to me now that someone else had written them.

Is this what you expected? I crawled back under the mosquito netting. It wasn't, but how exactly—well, that part was more difficult to define. I could have said it was the poverty, but that word was beginning to lose its weight with me. It was too loaded. For poverty wasn't so much the one defining attribute but more the layers that encapsulated the thing, the thing I couldn't define. It was the patience in their eyes. The eyes of the women. That was part of it. It was the arrogance of the *infirmier*. The detached indifference of the *matron*. They were all a manifestation of the thing, and yet they all took me farther away from understanding the thing itself. From putting a name to it. A reason. A meaning.

Chapter Two

A little after dawn, I awoke to the cries of pygmy goats mixed with the sound of the morning *fufu* being pounded in the courtyard. I lingered in bed and tried to recover my sleep, but it was futile. The heat made it impossible. Reluctantly, I gathered my bucket and shower materials and went outside. The old women were still seated on their benches. For all I knew, they hadn't left them all night. They waved back with the usual subdued smiles. A little before ten there was a tapping at my door.

"*Bonjour,*" I said, unlatching the screen for Fati. "*Tu es prête?*"

"*Bonjour,* Lily." She gave a slight bow but did not enter. "*Non, pas encore! J'arrive toute suite,*" she assured me. "I'll come back in ten minutes."

"*Pas de problème,*" I said.

"You are ready?"

"Yes, but don't worry, I'll wait." Around ten-thirty she reappeared at my door. This time she was wearing skinny black jeans and a stylish pink tank top with black netting over it. Her eyes were lined in kohl and she wore shimmering pink lipgloss. While our Saturday morning walks into the market had become a tradition over the last few months, it was still a surprise to see her looking so different, so American.

"*Tu es jolie!*" I said and we started down the dusty road into town.

The road was busiest on market days. Motos zipped past us along with bush taxis, loaded full of people and piled high with baskets of goods, mostly yams. They wove indelicately past the rocks and travelers on foot. We passed groups of women, striking in their traditional garb. While teenagers took a more modern approach, most of the villagers still dressed elegantly in their finest *pagne* for market day. Some of the women greeted me by name as we walked. The children were less formal as they called out the *anasara* song: a simple rhyme in French that all the children chanted when they saw a white person. The less inspired ones simply cried out *anasara*. Each time it happened Fati reprimanded them, which was her right as their elder. I tried to reassure her that it didn't bother me. She just laughed and sighed, "*Oh, les enfants…*" and shook her head.

"I spoke with the *infirmier* yesterday," I said as we walked past the Lycée. "He is going to introduce me to the inspector on Monday. I think I'm going to start a health club for the students there, to talk about things like HIV and family planning…" I was learning to use this term, family planning, as a more creative way of saying contraception. "The *infirmier* said that unwanted pregnancy is a very big problem here."

"*Oui, c'est vrai,*" Fati said.

"You think it would be a good idea, then? You think

the students would come? Girls you know? Your friends?"

"It's a very good idea."

"The *infirmier* suggested I should start with the girls only first. He said they'd be too shy to ask questions if the boys were there. That they might not come, even. But I think it's important to educate the boys too. I won't have time to do two clubs right now—it'll have to wait until spring. What do you think? I know the *infirmier* is from the south and he can be a little…hard in his opinions of the people here."

"*Oui*," Fati said. "The people here, they don't like him. You know he doesn't speak any of the local languages? For three years, he has lived here! At least you *try*." I laughed. She was quiet for a moment. She was giving the matter serious thought. "But with the club, I think he is right. It is difficult here. The girls don't talk in school as it is. They will be embarrassed, especially if you are talking about *that*."

"Then we'll start with the girls. I was hoping you might be able to help me decide which lesson plans to use and to think of ideas for things to talk about? If you wanted to. I won't take time away from your schoolwork, of course."

"*Oui, bien sûr*," she said with a mixture of pride and embarrassment. She was a funny girl. She was smarter than the rest and she knew it, but if anyone else acknowledged this she was instantly uncomfortable. "Lily," Fati said as we continued on, "you will live here for two years?"

"Well, two years in total."

"*C'est beaucoup!*" She shook her head at the dusty red ground beneath our feet.

"You'll probably be in your first year of university by then. What do you want to study?"

"Science, I think. Physics was my favorite subject last year. But I liked algebra as well. My mother thinks I should study medicine. She thinks I could be an *infirmier* or maybe a *sage femme* and work with women. Sort of like you do."

"It would be very interesting work. You're very smart, Fati. Whatever you decide to do, I'm sure you will be a success," I said.

"What did you study at university?"

"I studied English."

"English? You didn't study medicine?"

"No, but I am more of an educator. I was trained to teach people about health and to help people organize so that they can teach others." It was like this whenever we walked into town together. Each time we learned a little more about each other. It was a slow process, it required patience. Sometimes she offered more than other times, and sometimes so did I. It seemed today we were both in a more convivial mood. Perhaps my offer had earned me more of her confidence. "Do you want to go to the university in Lomé or Kara?"

"Kara," she said without hesitation.

"Why not Lomé? It could be exciting, going off to study in the capital."

"*Oui,*" she agreed with a shrug, but seemed unconvinced of the allure.

"Either would be a good choice. I suppose Kara is closer."

"It is closer—" She hesitated. She was still smiling

absently at the ground. But this was a different sort of smile.

"Aha! Closer to what? Or should I say who?" She grinned, shaking her head. She'd been found out and she knew it. "You have to tell me. Who? A boy?"

"Oui—"

"What boy? A boyfriend? How come I've never met him?"

"Oh, Lily," she giggled. She'd never acted so giddy before. For the first time I recognized some of Adiza in her. "He lives in Sokode, now. He moved there to finish school. You see, he will take the BAC II this year." It obviously made her proud to say it. "Then he will go to university in Kara. So I must pass the BAC I this year. Then, when I finish school next year, if I pass the BAC II, I will go too."

"Of course you'll pass both exams. I'm sure of it. Does he visit here often?"

"It has been a while now, because of school. But his family still lives here. Next time he comes I will introduce you," she said.

"Promise me you will. I'd love to meet him."

The remainder of our walk was quiet but for the rest of the way Fati still smiled that same silly smile. Thinking of the boy whose future she had decided to join with hers.

When we arrived in town, the market had reached its peak. Market day was a bit like shopping at the mall in the run-up to Christmas. There were thick crowds of people and tables upon tables topped with lush displays of fresh produce. The strangest part about it was that each and every table was topped with a display almost identical to the one next to it, replicated fifty times over among the women. How any of them could make a profit competing against their own mirror image I never understood. Fati understood, though. She knew exactly where to find the best prices, the biggest tomatoes or even, if we were lucky, green beans as they came into season. We made the usual rounds, pushing against the crushing crowds of people, all trying to make their way through the narrow, ill-defined paths that led endlessly to new undiscovered corners but always gave out into more of the same.

Eventually we came out from the other side of the market and crossed the main road to the special section set up solely for the sale of yams. This was the spot that signified the end of our marketing. After we greeted Gladys, Fati and I normally parted ways. We spotted Gladys sitting in front of several piles of yams, speaking fervently to the woman sitting next to her who sat before an almost indistinguishable pile.

"Lily!" she called. "Welcome! How do you find the market today?"

"Oh, it's very good. There are many people."

"Yes, come sit." She patted the space next to her on the log. "You are tired. The sun is hot."

"Thank you."

"Would you like some water?" Gladys asked me and without waiting for my reply she yelled for the girl with the round cooler of water bags atop her head to come over. I bought a hundred CFA's worth and gave one each to Fati, her mother and the woman she was speaking with. "Lily, buy some yams. We will make *fufu* tonight."

"Sure," I said. She turned to Fati and ordered her to

inspect the piles, picking out the best-looking yams from each bunch.

"She will pick them," Gladys explained, and I nodded. It was a job best left to Fati, since I was far from a yam connoisseur. When Fati finished, she piled the chosen yams before her mother, who tallied up their worth. I gave Gladys the money and we agreed that she would bring them back with her in one of the cars when the market was finished.

"Lily, *je vais aller*," Fati said, dusting her hands from the dirt that covered the yams.

"*Bien, à ce soir*," I said and Fati waved as she disappeared into the crowded streets with Gladys yelling after her.

"That girl!" She shook her head. "I told her not to be late tonight. She pretends not to hear me. It is difficult now. She thinks she knows everything. She thinks I am the foolish one. She doesn't listen."

"I think we're all like that at that age."

"It is true. I was just like her. I told her, 'Be careful, or you will end up like me. Is that what you want?'"

"She's a smart girl," I said. "She understands what's at stake. And she has plans. That's important." Did Gladys know about the boy? I decided not to mention it.

"It is good if you come for dinner. She will be home early."

"I look forward to it, you make the best *fufu*." It was half past twelve and I was supposed to meet Cynthia at noon. I sent a quick text to let her know I was on my way.

"You are going?" Gladys asked as I gathered my things.

"Yes," I said. "I have to meet my friend here. I forgot the time, I am already late."

"You must go," she said, motioning for me to leave. "You must not keep your friend waiting. See you in the evening!"

The chaotic, festive atmosphere of market day continued along the main street, which was filled with vendors who poured into every corner, overflowing from the central hub of the market itself. I stopped in a boutique and picked up a few sachets of gin, a card for phone credit and a pack of *Concord Verts*. Inside the bar was a lively scene. The downstairs was full, mostly of men, all dressed in their best *complètes* and drinking beer or Sport Actifs inside or at the little iron tables that lined the street, café style, in front of the tiled blue building. When the woman behind the counter saw me, she motioned to the cement steps that led to the rooftop bar. A few of the more intoxicated patrons tried to call for my attention, with shouts of *anasara*. I said hello and did my best to be polite without encouraging their attentions. Upstairs, the terrace was quiet. Cynthia sat alone, surrounded by piles of crinkled-up paperwork and a glass half full of beer. Her auburn hair was tied tightly behind her head and her pink tank top almost matched the color of her bare skin beneath it. I noticed her computer was closed and pushed to the side.

"*Bonne arriv*ée, Lily!" she called out from behind her dark sunglasses.

"Yes, I finally made it," I said, unloading my bags on the table next to her. "It's crazy out there. Do you want anything? I need a drink."

"Oh, you brought gin? Could I steal one please? This beer isn't doing much for me right now." I had picked up some extra gin in anticipation of this.

"Cross your fingers there are some cold tonics left."

"I'm crossing my fingers there are any left at all, warm or cold." I laughed and headed back down to the bar area. The woman was busy rushing from the cooler to the counter, opening bottles and exchanging cash. I ordered two tonics and watched nervously as she dug through the large box refrigerator. While Cynthia might have been well adapted enough to drink warm gin and tonics, I was not yet at the point of finding it an enjoyable experience.

"We are both very lucky today," I said as I set the bottles down, their moisture making rings on the wooden table. "How's it going, then?"

"Don't ask. I just spoke with the school inspector downstairs. He said there's going to be a teachers' strike, nationwide. So, I guess I'm looking at a few weeks of twiddling my thumbs. Also, there's no signal today." She motioned to the laptop and the small USB device that was meant to provide internet service but rarely did as promised.

"You're just a bundle of good news. It's a shame about the strike, though. I was going to meet with the director of the Lycée on Monday about starting a health club."

"I wouldn't count on that."

"What's it about?"

"The strike? What it's always about." I sat back and lit a cigarette. Cynthia was obviously troubled by the news. I couldn't blame her. I was disappointed myself. The club had been my first big idea and I was eager to get it off the ground.

"How long will it last for?"

"Who knows? Days, weeks?" she said, mixing her gin and tonic. I decided not to ask any more questions. "It might be all government employees. Your *dispensaire* could be closed as well."

"Really? But what do people do?"

"The hospital in town will keep a few people on to keep things going."

"What the hell are we supposed to do all week?"

"I'm thinking of escaping to Kara for a few nights. There's a hotel there with a pool. You can pay 1,000 CFA and just lay there all day. There's also this amazing hamburger place and you can buy wine that comes in bottles."

"Wine from bottles? Sounds like paradise," I laughed.

"Have I convinced you to join me yet?"

"It's tempting but I think I'll wait to see what happens."

"I'll tell you what's going to happen: it will be at least a week, maybe two, before anyone goes back to work. And nothing will get solved. In another month, we'll go through it all again." Cynthia had been teaching English here for a little over a year. She had some of the cynicism that comes with experience in this line of work, but most of the time it was defied by her optimistic Midwestern upbringing. She'd come to Africa bearing a box-fresh Bachelor's degree in anthropology and decided to spend a year or two teaching English here while she decided whether or not to continue her education or enter 'the real world', as she put it. She was a few years younger than me but because she'd been here longer she liked to play the part of my older, more experienced counterpart.

"It happens often?"

"It happened last year at the same time. Trust me, it will be at least a week. Probably two."

"If that's the case, I'll see you in Kara."

"I'm sure we wouldn't be the only ones. Plus, I might know a place we can stay for free. There's another American that runs a small NGO in the city. You haven't met him yet but he's part of our little network here. He never minds having people around."

"Yes, well, we'll see. It really isn't working?" I asked, eyeing the laptop.

"You can try it. I gave up after it took forty-five minutes to load my Gmail and another thirty to open anything. I wouldn't even attempt to check Facebook."

"Eh, no, it's fine. Not like I'm expecting anything exciting anyway."

"You know, in Kara, the internet is like—"

"Alright, alright. I'll probably join you if it goes like you say it will." I looked out into the crowded street below us. Everything was still rushing along. Moto horns, children shouting, the laughter and clinking of glasses from the downstairs terrace. Why all the excitement and commotion had abruptly made me feel so incredibly lonely I didn't understand.

"How's it going for you, anyway?" Cynthia asked, her tone softening. She must have sensed my change of mood.

"Oh, it's going. Slowly but surely. It is annoying about the strike, though. I was feeling a bit homesick last night. I find the busier I am, the less time I have to think about it. And I was really looking forward to getting this club going."

"Yeah, I know. It can be frustrating here. The strike won't last forever. But it isn't good to be bored. Come to Kara, Lily, I'm telling you. You'll thank me." She lit another cigarette. "And you know, I still get homesick like that from time to time. It's normal. Especially in the beginning. I think I cried to my mom on the phone every other night for the first month. Lord knows how much money I wasted in Togocel credit. I probably could have taken ten vacations back by now. I told myself, 'If you can just make it a year you can go home after that. Just make it a year.' Now look at me. I'm going into year two and already contemplating a third. You're just getting started. If you do get a bit down, which is bound to happen from time to time, just try to concentrate on all the good you're going to do. And all the people you're going to help. Not to mention all the doors an experience like this opens for us once we're finally back in the land of plenty. That's what I do. It helps. Trust me."

"I trust you."

"Do you want to come back to my place? Drink some wine and make dinner? Watch a movie?"

"Thanks, but I promised Gladys I would eat with them tonight."

"Well, you know, my door's always open. It helps to have friends close by. And you know what else helps?" She held up her empty glass. "Shall we?"

Cynthia had been right. Sunday morning, it wasn't the goats or the pounding of *fufu* or the heat that dragged me out of bed at dawn. It was the persistent tapping of the *infirmier* at my door. He stopped by on his way to church to tell me that our meeting with the school inspector was cancelled and not only would the teachers be striking, but so would all government employees.

"We will open the *dispensaire* for a few hours on Monday but there is no need for you to come in," he said.

"And what about Tuesday?"

"Probably the same."

"But I could still come in, I don't mind. Maybe I would still have a chance to speak with some of the patients?" I said, desperate to find a way to fill the days and empty hours that would now lie ahead of me.

"The *matron* and I will barely have enough time to talk to them."

"Alright. I understand."

He turned to leave but then he hesitated at the screen door.

"This evening," he said after a moment of obvious deliberation, "why don't you come have dinner with my wife and I?"

"Oh, I don't—" He looked at me, his forehead creased in confusion. What could I say? It was nearly impossible to say no; excuses weren't very easy to come by here. "Okay, thank you," I said, accepting his invitation with about as much enthusiasm as he had taken in offering it.

The rest of the morning passed slowly. I took a walk around ten to get some air, before the sun got too hot and everyone retreated inside for *repos*. I stopped by to say hello to Fati and her family but their compound was empty. The main road was busy with villagers dressed in their stylish *complètes* coming back from service at the local Evangelical church. I searched for Gladys among them. Perhaps that was where she had been. But I didn't see her. She might have been a Catholic. The Catholic church was in town. I had been once with the *infirmier* and his wife. His wife had been very pleased to learn I was a Catholic, though I did explain I no longer practiced. Still, she urged me to try it once and thankfully left it alone after that.

Most of the people in the village were not Catholics, though. No, most of the people were Muslims. But regardless of what they called themselves — Muslim, Catholic, Evangelical, Jehovah's Witnesses (Cynthia even claimed to have met a Scientologist once) — most of the people here still practiced the old animistic religion. There were pockets of the south that took their Christianity more seriously. The same with the Muslims in the north. Here, they seemed to have clung a little more steadily to their old beliefs. Perhaps being so out of the way had allowed them to carry on unnoticed, mixing the old with the new. Fati's father was a Muslim but his brother was an animistic priest of sorts and they still went to see him for ceremonies and to make offerings. *Féticheurs* they called them. Or at least that was how the French had translated it. They also called them *charlatans* and the people continued to use the word without irony or any hint of negative connotation.

I walked back toward my compound, passing the local mosque just across the road. When I had first arrived, the call to prayer woke me every morning at the first hints of dawn. Now I seldom heard it at first light; my ears had grown numb to its interruptions. But in the afternoon and evening, when that deep haunting voice bellowed over the speaker, there was an unexpected comfort in it. To be reminded so abruptly throughout the day of the existence of an idea greater than yourself. It helped to keep things in perspective.

At half past six the *infirmier* came to fetch me for dinner. He arrived on his moto and seemed completely unaware of the needlessness of such an act when his house was less than a quarter of a mile down the road from mine. We arrived at the door within seconds. It was a private compound just off the main road, gated like mine but with no cement. We sat down in the living room, saying little. He was one of the few people in the village with electricity and he certainly made good use of it. The small front room was overtaken by a large TV that was hooked up to a satellite cable and picked up channels from Senegal, Côte d'Ivoire, and Nigeria. Underneath the TV sat a large stereo system that looked ten years out of date in its bulk. He fiddled with the numerous remotes in an attempt to turn on the television, stereo and cable, alternating between them, never sure of their exact purpose or what the results might be. His wife was still busy in the kitchen. After a few moments of fumbling around he achieved success with the television and offered me a glass of wine. I readily accepted. It was difficult to relax with him.

"It's bad about the strike."

"*Oui*," he nodded, taking a seat across from me and pouring two more glasses of wine, one for himself and his wife.

"How long do you think it will last?"

"*Je ne sais pas.*" He shook his head. "Maybe a few days, maybe weeks."

"Is it about money or resources?"

"*L'argent,*" he smirked. "But resources too. It's bad here, you see it in the *dispensaire*. Every day how many people come? And it's just the two of us, the *matron* and me, responsible for everything." He threw his hands up in frustration. "We are always running out of medicine, supplies. It's very difficult."

"*Oui.*" I nodded in sympathy.

"*Et chez vous*? It's different there, isn't it. You have big hospitals and lots of equipment." He grinned as he shook his head at the absurdity of it. It was almost accusatory, as if I should apologize for coming from such a place.

"Yes, but they are not run by the government," I said. "It is good for people who have money, but not so good for the people who do not."

His wife appeared with two pots of *fufu,* a large one for the two of them to share and a smaller pot for me. She greeted me as she set the plates down on the coffee table and sat next to her husband.

"*Mangeons,*" she said as she dipped her fingers into the dish of plain water then into the pot of fluffy white *fufu.* "My husband tells me you are going to start a health club for girls?" she asked. His wife spoke French very well. Like her husband, she was obviously more cosmopolitan than her surroundings. Her style was slightly different from that of the other village women. While she wore *pagne,* it imitated a more western style, as did her hair and jewelry.

"Yes, hopefully, when the strike is finished."

"Good. At the Lycée or the CEG?"

"I thought maybe start with the Lycée and then start another at the CEG in the spring. I was going to speak with the inspector about it."

"You should do one club for both," the *infirmier* interjected between mouthfuls of *fufu*. "A lot of the girls in CEG will be as old as the ones in the Lycée."

"It's true. And even for the ones who are not, it is good to start young," his wife confirmed. The *infirmier* poured us all another glass of wine. I took a large gulp. The sauce was hot and spicy, a necessity in order to counter the bland and empty taste of the starchy *fufu*.

"And the women at the *dispensaire*, you must teach them as well," the *infirmier* continued. "Of course, it's not so bad for the older women but for the girls it is a real problem. They don't know anything. And then, when they get pregnant they take things—dangerous things from people who say they are doctors or nurses. Just before you arrived here there was a girl, she was thirteen, fourteen maybe. She died from these drugs. It happens all the time."

"Is it the same in the south?"

"Sometimes, in the smaller villages, but..." He paused to continue eating, his annoyance evident as he tried to find the right words. "The people here. They are very superstitious. The people in the south, well—they trust science more!"

It was difficult to attempt such complex conversations. Everything had to be simplified, cut down to basics. Sometimes it was strangely poetic. Most of the time it was just frustrating. There were things I still wanted to say but for much of it I didn't yet have the vocabulary. For example, was it science they didn't trust, or outsiders like him and me? It was a question for another time, perhaps.

We continued eating and turned our attention to the television. He had put on a Senegalese sitcom about a backwards villager thrust into the big city. Made up of mostly slapstick gags, the program was easy enough to follow. The villager was frightened of telephones and thought cars were exotic animals from the jungles. When we finished, I thanked them for the meal and declined his offer to drive me home. It was dark outside, and I used the flashlight on my little Nokia to illuminate the short path back. As I neared the compound, the voices of Usman and Jean called to me from the darkness. They came scurrying into the compound with me.

"Lily, *photo!*" Usman cried as they followed me inside the house. There were two other boys with them that I had never seen before and they all continued relentlessly, "*Photo, Photo!*" I ushered them inside, so as not to disturb the old women. Adiza and Brigitte appeared, hearing the commotion, followed by Fati, who had no doubt come to oversee the others. Usman was gibbering relentlessly to Adiza, urging her to translate to me.

"He said this boy wants to see your camera. He said when Usman told him you let us take pictures with it, he called him a liar," Adiza explained, giggling, delighted by the drama and the vexation of her younger brother.

"Alright," I said and Usman's eyes lit up in triumph as he savored his victory over the others. My quiet evening slowly descended into chaos as the boys pulled books and magazines from my shelves. Usman and Jean were going out of their way to show off their familiarity with my home to the newcomers. They causally helped themselves to books by Tolstoy and Hemingway and issues of *The Economist*, explaining who knows what to the others who watched, afraid but eager. One of the older boys kept glancing back over to where I sat, frightened I might turn on them at any moment and use my authority to interrupt their fun, as grown-ups tend to do. Instead, I handed the camera to Adiza and the room filled once more with excited cries of "*Photo! Photo!*" Adiza shouted to them and they clamored about the room in search of the right books and random kitchen utensils to pose with. Adiza and Brigitte directed the boys, taking their artistic responsibilities surprisingly seriously. There were heated discussions on who should stand where, with what book, and which spoon. Every time the camera flashed, instantaneously the children dropped their props and rushed over to see the tiny images of themselves captured on the screen. After a while, the older boy, the same one who had been watching me so carefully just moments earlier, was overcome by his excitement and reached inadvertently to grab the camera out of Adiza's hands. Instinctively, she slapped him on the side of his head and shouted at him, silencing the others with the shock of her violence. Fati was quick to intervene, taking the camera from Adiza and ordering her to take the boys home. Fati stayed behind to help me pick up the mess of magazines and books that had been left scattered sadly on the cement floor.

"Lily," she said softly after they had left. "You must not let that boy back into your house."

"Oh, ça *va*," I said. "He's okay. He was just excited."

"No, Lily," she said, almost in a whisper, "You don't know—his grandmother is a sorcerer!" I stopped with a book in hand to examine her face. Was she serious? This same girl whose favorite subject was physics and wanted to go to university to study science. She continued dusting off the couch cushions, as if what she had said was nothing so extraordinary.

"A sorcerer? Really?"

"*C'est vrai.*"

"But how do you know?"

"Everyone knows. She killed his parents and she cooked them into food. That is why he is an orphan. You must not let him in your house. The old woman and Brigitte will talk."

"But is *he* a sorcerer?"

"No," she said. "But it still is not good."

Chapter Three

The restaurant where we were meeting was only a few minutes' drive from Kara's main station. But as my moto driver pulled up out front it became evident that it wasn't actually a restaurant, or not in the way I imagined it would be. It was more a collection of large, circular booths lined up outside, under straw roofs. Loud voices speaking English carried obtrusively across the empty courtyard.

"Lily! *Bonne arriv*ée!" Cynthia shouted when she spotted me. The table was covered in empty beer bottles. "This is Matt," she said, pointing across the table to a twenty-something man with dark hair and even darker eyes, poring over a laptop. Matt looked up from behind the screen, barely registering my arrival. Cynthia scooted in to make room. "You know Anna," Cynthia said.

"Anna? Oh, my God, Anna!" The last time I had seen her was almost four months ago in Lomé, on our last day of training. Her black hair, once long, now an uneven bob; her olive skin now a deep brown. "Sorry, that ride was terrible, I'm all out of sorts."

"Yeah, anything longer than five minutes in a bush

taxi will do that to you. I was so excited when Cynthia told me you were coming!"

"Well, there wasn't much use in hanging around the village all week. Should I go in and order? I need a drink..."

"That's the Lily I remember from training!" Anna cried. Apparently, I had a bit of catching up to do. "You ring a bell, see there on the side of the booth. Someone will come within the hour."

"It isn't that bad," Cynthia said. "But if you want food, be prepared to wait."

"The internet is fucked," Matt said, slamming his laptop closed.

"Aw, poor Matt, he's been having a rough time since we got in. The ATM at Echobank ate his debit card and they wouldn't let him take money out of his account without his passport," Anna explained. "And that's after we traveled over three hours by bush taxi to get to the bank."

"It's bullshit. I had my government-issued *photo* ID and everything." Matt closed his eyes and shook his head. "Sometimes this place..."

"Try again tomorrow, maybe someone else will let it slide," Cynthia said.

"Otherwise we'll have to occupy Echobank!" Anna shouted.

"Yes, we'll camp outside until our demands are met and I have what's rightfully mine!" Matt slammed his fist on the table.

"Inside might be better, they have air conditioning," Cynthia said.

"I don't know why anyone would want to spend more time in Echobank than absolutely necessary," I said.

"Oh, you don't know! You're going to love this. It's a shame the internet is down, or I'd show you," Anna said.

"'Know what?"

"Jesus! Have you been living in some remote African village for the last few months or something?" Matt said dryly and Anna waved at him to be quiet.

"There are these massive protests going on in New York, apparently for weeks now," Anna said.

"Really? Over what?"

"The Wall Street bailouts, I think it started as, at least. When the internet comes back you'll see. They're calling it Occupy Wall Street. They've been going on for weeks now. I don't think there's ever been anything like it before. I'm impressed really, I didn't think we Americans had it in us."

Anna and I had bonded during the grueling first few months of training. She'd caught me secretly reading Emma Goldman during a particularly boring lecture in French on the government infrastructure. She insisted on buying me a beer after class and we spent the rest of the afternoon discussing theories of collectivist anarchism, with her dropping names like Bakunin and Kropotkin. Our fate as friends was sealed.

"If the internet comes back," Matt said.

"Or when we go back to John's place," Anna said.

"You're sure it's alright if I stay there with you guys?" I asked Cynthia.

"Of course, I told him you were coming. He's got a nice place and there's plenty of room for you," Cynthia said.

My decision to join her had been somewhat spontaneous and I had left most of the details to Cynthia to work out. After the strike had continued into mid-week, Fati and her family left to go work their plot of land outside the village. My choice was either to escape the idleness and join Cynthia in Kara, or risk losing my sanity.

"Where is John, anyway?" Matt asked.

"He's busy working, unlike the rest of us," Anna said.

"We've already eaten but you should order something if you're hungry—it does take a while," Cynthia advised when the waitress arrived with a menu.

I ordered a beer. "How's the pizza?"

"When you haven't had pizza for months it's divine," Anna said.

"There he is!" Matt called as a tawny-looking man in a button-up shirt made of *pagne* approached the table.

"*Bon arriv*ée!" Anna and Cynthia shouted in unison.

"What took you so long?" Matt asked as he and Anna made room for John on the other side of the booth.

"Meeting ran late, or started late. I can't remember which any more," John said, checking the time on his phone. "Jesus, it's two already? It's been a long morning."

"Beer will help," Anna offered. "We've had it pretty rough today as well."

"Looks like it," John said, motioning toward the table strewn with bottles.

"Yes, and we still have a pretty strenuous afternoon of lounging by the pool ahead of us to get through."

"I'm not sure how you'll manage."

"Where there's a will…"

"I suppose I missed lunch then?" John asked, grabbing

a menu from the table. "Or are we skipping the solids today?"

"We ate already but Lily's just ordered," Cynthia said.

"Ah Lily, yes, sorry for being so rude. It's nice to finally meet you. These two were very happy you would be joining us," he said. "I've heard a lot about you."

"Only good things, I'm sure," I said.

"Speaking of pool," Matt said, "what do you guys say about heading off soon? I need a *repos*."

"Are you coming to the pool?" Cynthia asked, turning to John. My arrival had been ill-timed.

"No, I think I might just go back and rest," John said. "You guys go ahead, though. I can drop Lily off on the way, after we eat."

"I feel bad taking off after you've only just gotten here," Cynthia said, looking at me.

"Oh no, it's fine," I lied. I desperately wanted her to stay but not as much as I hated the idea of being an inconvenience.

"I don't bite," John said, perhaps sensing my discomfort.

"Are you sure?" Cynthia asked.

"Don't worry. You said it could take a while," I assured her.

"Alright, fine," she said. When the waitress appeared again, John and I ordered while the three of them quickly paid up. I ordered another drink.

"So, you're just west of here then?" John said after we were left alone.

"Yeah, it's a little village about an hour or so west off the *Rue National*."

"I've been out that way some for work. It's a beautiful area."

"Yes, I'm very lucky." I took a sip from my drink. "What is it you do, then? Cynthia said you work with an NGO here?"

"You could call it that. We have a small office here in Kara. Mainly, it's me and one other guy. We do some basic infrastructure work. When we have the money, that is. Mostly we run trainings throughout the year, hygiene and sanitation. That kind of thing."

"How long have you been working here?" I continued, asking the obligatory questions of a 'getting to know you' routine.

"About three years. How long have you been here now?"

"About six months in total, including training."

"I started out in an organization like yours."

"Really?"

"Yes, but in Morocco. How long is your assignment?"

"Two years."

"You think you'll stick it out?"

"That is the plan," I said, slightly offended. Was it written on my face, the difficulty? The doubts? I thought I did a pretty good job of hiding it.

"It's nothing personal. You'd probably be surprised at how many people don't. Two years is a long time. It's difficult work. But it does get easier."

"So they say."

"Really it all depends on your expectations. A lot of people expect to do too much. They're easily disappointed. They get frustrated."

"Right, well, mine are quite low so hopefully that shouldn't be a problem," I said, and John laughed. "So, where are you from, anyway?"

"I'm from Ohio originally."

"Ah, a fellow Midwesterner."

"Well it's been a while since I've been back. What were you doing before you came here?"

"I was working for a newspaper in Detroit."

"And what brought you here?" he asked.

"Oh, you know, a change of scene," I said.

"It's quite a change."

"Yeah well, I thought I'd have more to write about here than I would hanging around there, waiting for things to happen, but…"

"But?"

"These protests in New York, you know about them?"

"Yes, I've heard."

"I've been waiting so long for something like that to happen. Now that it has, I'm all the way over here."

"I wouldn't worry too much. I doubt they'll last very long."

"I wouldn't be so sure."

"I would."

"Really?" I asked. "I mean, don't you think, with everything going on in the world, especially since the bailouts, people are getting more and more tired of things? I can't help but feel things are coming to a head."

"Well," he grimaced. "You know what they say: every generation thinks they're on the cusp of some great revolution. Some epoch-altering movement. It's the vanity of youth, I guess."

"Maybe they think it because we always are. Maybe that's what's moving us forward. Maybe that's progress."

"A fan of Hegel, then?" he asked. I was irritated now, both by his dismissive tone and my ignorance of Hegel.

"I'm not that familiar with him, actually."

"Yes, well, he has a theory similar to what you're saying. You might find it interesting. Keep an eye out, there's all sorts of books that float around between us all. I'm sure he's out there somewhere." He sighed, leaning back in his seat. "You get a lot of time to read in this line of work, that's for sure."

I said nothing. He obviously enjoyed the authority of his experiences. I was finding it somewhat suffocating. Still, he was attractive, in spite of his arrogance. A little rough around the edges. Stubble on his chin and burnt red skin. I guessed him to be slightly older. A little more than thirty, maybe.

"I'm sorry," John said, realizing the silence had gone on an uncomfortably long time. "I'm just thinking about work. I had a meeting this morning, and I got some bad news. It's kind of spoiled my mood."

"It's alright. What was the bad news about?"

"A project I've been planning for some time now. I just found out we won't have the funding. Well, not all of it at least. Not enough. It happens, though. Like I said about adjusting your expectations."

"What was the project?"

"We were looking to build some water pumps in some of the smaller villages in the region. Most of them aren't far off from where you are. A lot of the villages out there are pretty remote. Many of them still don't have a source of potable water for miles, if you can believe that. As a health worker, you could certainly relate to the problems that causes."

"How much were you short?"

"Too much."

"Could you still do a few at least?"

"Maybe," he said as he fiddled with the cap of his beer on the table. "It's just that the more parts we buy, the cheaper it is. I'll have to look at it all again when I get back and see." He took another big gulp from his beer.

The waitress appeared again with John's order.

"Go ahead," I said after he had sat a minute without touching the plate piled high with French fries and a gourmet burger.

"Would you like some?" he asked. "What did you order? There's really no telling how long it might be."

"Pizza. No, I'm fine, I've waited this long." He sat still, not touching his food. I laughed at his manners. "Alright, alright, give me some fries, then."

The pool wasn't far. I told John he didn't have to take me all the way there but he insisted. When we reached the street he pointed me toward a large gated building. Inside the lobby there was a sign above the front desk listing prices for entry. I paid the 1,000 CFA and went out to the courtyard. Cynthia and the rest of them were easy to spot. They were the only ones there. The pool was exactly what you might expect from a mid-range hotel anywhere in the States. It was large and surrounded by plastic lounge chairs and the water was crisp and clear.

"How was the pizza?" Cynthia yelled, taking a break between laps.

"Divine," I called back and pulled up a lounge chair in the empty space next to Anna.

"This is the life," she said from behind her imitation Ray-Bans. She was flipping through an issue of *The New Yorker* that must have been at least six months out of date. She set the magazine down and handed me some sunscreen. "So tell me everything. What sort of miracles have you performed so far? How many lives have you shaped? Changed for the better?"

"Where to begin? So far I've been spending most of my time at the *dispensaire*. I'm excited to be working with the women there but the only problem is they don't speak much French. The *matron* speaks the local language but the *infirmier* doesn't. So, she's constantly running back and forth to help him. She doesn't have much time to help me on top of everything else. And no one likes the *infirmier*. Really, I can't blame them, he is a bit of a snob."

"I had the same problem with the director of the hospital near me. You want to talk about snob. I didn't realize until Matt came to visit me that mainly it just annoyed him that I was a woman."

"Yeah, I've gotten that vibe too. What happened when Matt came to visit?"

"Oh God, you should have seen this guy! Falling all over Matt like it was the second coming of Christ. He assumed Matt was my boss. I swear, every day my life feels more and more like a third world version of *Mad Men*. And then going to Matt's village, that was a real trip. The way everyone's so respectful to him. They actually listen to him! It's infuriating. Have they asked you to build anything yet?"

"No. Why? Has anyone asked you?"

"Oh lord, I get about a request a day for something. A school, latrines. There was somebody that used to work for us in village a few miles away, and they built a clinic, so it's pretty much assumed I'll do something equally magnificent. Sort of like when your neighbor buys a new car or something. Keeping up with the Joneses. I can't seem to explain to them they have two schools nearby, and a clinic. Even if I were to get the money to build them a clinic—which, don't get me wrong, they could definitely use another one—there's no way the government would send anyone to work there. And latrines are just too political." I laughed at the idea of political toilets.

"Thankfully, I haven't come up against that one yet. We've got it all as well, so to speak." It was true. While we could apply for funding for various infrastructure projects, when it came to schools and clinics, it was up to the government to staff them. The country was riddled with the empty remains of western vanity projects. "Well, anyway, All in all I'm pretty happy with my post. I am looking forward to starting a health club at the school. The *infirmier* has been pretty adamant about my working with young girls to try to prevent unwanted pregnancies. At least I have him on my side in that regard. I know not all of the local health workers are as ... progressive in their views on that sort of thing."

"Well, that's good at least. I just want this strike to be over. But even then, I'm not sure I'll be able to do much. I guess we just have to be patient. Everything takes time."

"Yeah. But I think once we get some of our own

projects off the ground we'll start to feel more useful," I said.

"Or at least we'll have less time to think about how useless we feel," Anna said, picking up her magazine.

On the way back to John's we stopped at a shop that sold wine in bottles, just as Cynthia had promised. John's place was on a street on the outskirts of the city, lined with other large houses, all close to one another but separately gated in, providing a sense of seclusion. Inside, the floors and porch were clad in tiles, instead of the usual drab cement. Cynthia showed me to her room, where she'd placed an extra cot for me. While she and Matt were busy in the kitchen, I opened a bottle of wine and went out on the porch to have a cigarette.

"Enjoy the pool?" John was standing in the doorway. He'd exchanged his *pagne* and khakis for a gray t-shirt and basketball shorts. He looked much more relaxed than he had earlier.

"Yes, I did indeed. Nice place you've got here."

"Thanks." He sat down in the empty chair across from me. "So, I had an idea this afternoon after we had lunch. You know how I said I was short for my project? I think I found a way to get some of the money."

"That's great."

"Yeah, well, it isn't certain yet."

"How will you get it?"

"That's up to you, really."

"Me?"

"I've been thinking. You know how I said most of the villages are around your area?" He leaned forward, pressing his hands together as he spoke. "So, technically, the work falls under your jurisdiction. And water sanitation is very directly linked to population health."

"True."

"You also have access to some grants designed for these kinds of projects that I don't."

"I see."

"But you wouldn't be involved purely for funding purposes," he added quickly. "I could use someone to help me manage the project. It's basically just me and Issa so we could use all the help we can get."

"Can I think about it?"

"Of course. If you stick around tomorrow, I can go over things with you in more detail. But it really is a very worthy cause."

"I've no doubt. Let's talk tomorrow," I said, smashing my cigarette into the cement.

"Great. Sounds like a plan."

When I awoke the next morning, I had that momentary lapse of memory that normally follows the first night in a new place. Cynthia was still curled up in *pagne* on the cot across from mine. Voices were coming from the main room so I walked out into the kitchen and found Anna and John sitting at the table. The humid morning air mixed with the smell of fresh coffee.

"Good morning!" Anna said, her voice bright and fresh. "You disappeared early."

"I was tired. I guess I haven't had that much excitement in a while." After dinner, the travel and wine had all caught up with me and I'd gone to bed while the rest of them had carried on for hours into the night.

"Coffee?" John asked, nodding in the direction of the beaten old French press on the counter.

"Are you sticking around today or heading back?" I asked Anna as I poured a cup.

"Sticking around. I'll go back tomorrow. As long as John doesn't mind," she said, looking at him. "I vaguely remember it being decided last night that we would all stay another night, but I don't remember if you agreed."

"I don't think I had the chance to," John said.

"Right, well, it's been decided anyway. You'll stay too, Lily?"

"She has to," John said. "We have a meeting scheduled for this afternoon."

"What? Are you doing work?" Anna looked at me in exaggerated shock. "I thought we were all on strike—you know, solidarity with the workers and all that."

"Don't worry," said John, "I won't take too much of her time away from your day at the pool, or is it just the bar today?"

"I can't say, it's too early to make those kinds of decisions."

"I have to go into the office for a bit this morning, but I thought I could come back around two and go over more of the details with you?" John said, addressing me. "If you're still interested, of course."

"I'm still interested, don't worry. Two is fine."

"I guess I should be off. Don't work too hard today." John gave Anna a pat on the back.

"You're a traitor to the cause!" Anna shouted, waving her fist at him as he waved goodbye.

While the three of them headed back to the pool for the afternoon, I stayed in and for the first time in months I was able to shower without having to use a bucket. The water was freezing but the heat made it so that it didn't really matter. Cynthia left her laptop and USB key so that I could browse the internet. I spent most of the afternoon catching up on what was happening in New York. But as I looked over the images of the protesters who filled Zuccotti Park, they lost something with the distance between us. I couldn't help but get the feeling that John was right and it would all be over soon.

When the front door opened again I was surprised to see John back so soon. I'd forgotten how quickly the hours could disappear into a click hole.

"I picked up some street food and a couple beers if you're hungry," John said as he kicked off his sandals, his hands full of black and green sachets of food.

"What is it?"

"Couscous. And some skewers of... goat meat? I think it is, at least." While John went to change out of his *pagne* and khakis, I inspected the food. Possible goat meat sounded less than appetizing. I put a few scoops of greasy red couscous onto a plate.

"Shall we sit outside?" I asked when he reappeared in a plain t-shirt and jeans. He dumped the remnants of the sachets onto a plate and followed me out onto the porch.

"So, we've already been working on this project for a long time now. We spent the last year identifying these sites. We've got a little over sixty percent of the funds raised. You would apply for the rest. We've already got a basic budget worked out but the next step would be to conduct site visits with my colleague, Issa, and possibly one of the mechanics we're working with for a final assessment."

"What sort of timeframe would we be looking at?"

"Well, we're ready to go. We could start the visits as soon as possible. Your grant application would be due by the end of the year if we wanted to qualify for the next round of funding. Once the money's in, we order the parts." He licked the greasy goat meat juices from his fingers. "I think the whole thing could be done this time next year. If not sooner."

"And what would our chances be, do you think, of getting the grant money?"

"How good are you at writing proposals?" he asked. "We need to really tug at their heartstrings, you know. 'Water is life' and all that. There's a fair amount of funding you've got available to you. But we'll still be competing against other projects and we'll probably be up against schools. Everyone wants to build schools. They don't realize that half of them sit empty once they're built."

"How many sites would we visit?"

"Ten at most."

"And how many pumps can we build?"

"Hopefully at least five, maybe seven. Once we do the assessment of the sites we'll work out the final budget." I sat for a moment, thinking it over. What else could I apply for funding for? Like I'd told Anna earlier, we had everything already.

"Okay. I'm in."

"Are you sure?"

"Yes, I'm sure."

"Alright then," he said, slapping his palms to his thighs. "Welcome aboard!" He seemed pleased but not terribly surprised by how easy it had been to convince me. "I'll have to arrange it with Issa, but I thought we could all sit down together and he can fill you in on his side of things and we can work out a plan for the visits. Hopefully we can manage that over the next week or so. It's best to do it before Harmattan. The roads are worse then, because of the dust."

"Makes sense."

"It's a good project, you know. And it shouldn't take too much of your time away from your other work, either," he said. "Let me go find some papers I brought back from the office with me, surveys that we used to help identify the sites. It's very interesting. Also we have a preliminary budget drawn up which I can show you…" His voice trailed off as he disappeared into the house. We spent the rest of the afternoon discussing numbers and logistics. When the rest of them arrived back at the house, it was almost dusk

"Jesus, are you guys still going?" Matt asked as they entered the gate. "You're really making the rest of us look bad with all this work garbage."

"We'll stop now, I promise," I said, closing my notebook.

"They're the ones that should feel guilty, Matt," Anna said. "They've betrayed the revolution, abandoned the workers! *Our* consciences can rest easy. I never trusted John, but I expected more from you, Lily."

"I'm sure the workers felt your support from the pool," John said.

"You've replenished the supplies then?" I asked. Cynthia's arms were full of grocery bags in the shape of wine bottles.

"Of course," Anna said, sitting down next to me. Once again I needed to catch up to their slightly more lubricated state. Tomorrow I would be back in village, but I didn't want to think of that now. There was a pleasant haze beginning to settle around us. The night was humid and the darkness hung thick, and everything was softened by a feeling of camaraderie. There's a commonality among compatriots that you never notice until you're somewhere else and it's gone and then reappears unexpectedly without warning. A shared foundation, a subconscious mythology that connects us in ways we can either embrace or deny but exists nonetheless. I found it there sitting among them and unexpectedly, I welcomed it. After a little while the rest of them decided to go inside. I hung back to smoke a cigarette.

"Too many cooks in the kitchen." Matt was swaying drunkenly in the doorway. "Can I have one?" I handed him a cigarette. "So," he said, sitting down on the bare tiled floor and leaning against the stone railing, lighting the cigarette. "I'm trying to guess something, but I'm not sure."

"What might that be?"

"I'm trying to figure out which one you are." He looked at me, his eyes slightly narrowed.

"Okay, I'll bite."

"Well, I have a theory about the people that come

here. Some of them really do believe in what they do. They really, honestly think they're making a difference. Now, I'm not judging them for it—maybe they are, maybe they aren't. That's not the point."

"And the others?"

"They're the ones who are escaping something. For them the work comes second."

"I see. So, which am I?"

"I'd say you're escaping something, but I haven't gotten to the third type yet."

"And they are?"

"The third type is just a combination of the two. They believe in the work but they're also escaping something. They're the worst kind really...." he said, shaking his head.

"You think I don't care about the work?"

"Oh, you can care. But you're skeptical of it."

"Which type are you?"

"I think I started out as the first type. The believer. For as long as I can remember I wanted to be a teacher. Everyone would say what a noble profession it was. What important work it all was. I believed it, too."

"But you don't any more?"

"No," he said, taking a hit from his cigarette. I waited for him to elaborate but he only stared off into the darkness. "So, was I right about you then?"

"No. I'm not a believer, and it's true, I'm skeptical. But I don't think I'm escaping anything either."

"Why are you here, then?"

"I guess I wanted the opposite of an escape. I wanted to face myself. I wanted to see the world, to challenge what I thought it was."

"How's that working out for you?" he said. I smiled. "Alright, so you've found a hole in my theory, but I'm drunk so forgive me. Everything seems much simpler when you're drunk."

"Yes, it's much easier to find the answers but the problem is, will they still sound as true tomorrow?"

"Sometimes. I still think my theory holds up in most cases. I just need to add your category to the list."

"Which is?"

"The searcher," he said confidently.

"Oh, that's quite a cliché, isn't it?"

"Isn't that what you are?"

"Perhaps I started out that way."

"So, you've found it?"

"No."

"But you still think you might?"

I was quiet.

"I didn't think so," he said, flicking his cigarette.

"And why don't you believe any more?"

"That's not the question."

"What is the question?"

"The question, my dear Lily, is why on earth did I believe in the first place? It's really cute to see, you know? People like you, when they first arrive. All full of hope and wisdom. Like Rome before the fall. Give it time, my dear. Give it time." He was drunk. Beyond drunk. Chances were he didn't know what he was saying. Even if he did he'd never remember it tomorrow. The rest of them carried on happily inside, their laughter breaking through the night in sharp contrast to the dark turn our conversation was taking.

"I need more wine," I said.

"Now you're escaping!" Matt called to me as I opened the door.

Inside the others were crowded around Cynthia's laptop waiting for a video to load. I poured some wine and sat down at the table. The buffering on the video was crawling and none of what they were saying was making any sense to me. I had missed the joke. I wanted to be as drunk as Matt was. I wanted the answers to come to me easily. I didn't care if they still sounded true in the morning. I sat watching them, trying to place them into Matt's categories. Cynthia was a believer. Anna was escaping, or maybe she was searching like me. John was a believer, but I got the sense he was escaping something as well. Matt said that was the worst kind. Matt had been a believer but now he wasn't. What was he now? And what was I, then, if I wasn't searching? He was right after all. And I was right that it was a cliché. So, what then? What would I do if I wasn't so sure any more that I would find what I was looking for?

Chapter Four

Detroit
March 14, 2011

I had told Sonia not to come until seven but that had been a mistake. I'd thought I needed some time alone. Time to reflect. It turned out I was wrong. I hadn't needed time. All I'd really needed was a drink.

"You want another one?" The old barmaid stood there with one eye covered by a patch, her voice stern and without patience.

"Sure, why not."

She refilled the empty glass with the cheap, metallic liquid they tried to pass for wine. I didn't mind it. I didn't come here for the wine. There was something about the ambiance that had struck me when I first stumbled upon the neon sign late one evening during my first year of university. Perhaps it was the tired stained-glass lamps and dark wooden paneling. It was old, it had a European feel to it. The kind of place you might stumble upon down the backstreets of Paris, or maybe somewhere in Spain. Though I'd never been to either. Behind the bar, above the unhappy rows of half-filled liquor bottles, there was an old photograph showing a horse-drawn carriage by the same neon pink sign that still hung out front today. Perhaps I enjoyed its ghosts.

On the weekends, the bar was loud and full of students, and artists and wannabe artists, but during the day it was usually empty, except for workmen who came in for a beer and a burger at lunch and the local drunks who camped out all day, chatting up the one-eyed barmaid. A couple of afternoons each week I came in with my books and notebooks and sat in the corner with a glass of wine and wrote for a few hours. No one bothered me, the barmaid never gave me the slightest hint of recognition, aside from remembering my drink order once in a while. I preferred it that way. No small talk, straight to work. If I could work, of course. If the words were there, or not so much the words but the confidence to write them down.

If I made a list of all the places and things I would miss the most, this place would be near the top. Funny the way life works. For so many years I'd desperately wanted an excuse to move on from Detroit, and now that I had one, I was getting all sentimental about it. It was natural to feel a certain sense of loyalty to the past. I always had trouble with the past. I was too idealistic about it and it always made me a little unsure of the present. I had to try to brush it aside, for now. Sure, I would miss things, but that was life.

"Hey!" I swirled around on my bar stool to see Sonia, dressed in black and gray with her signature red lipstick and black, painted eyes. "Alright Lil?" she asked, pulling up the stool next to mine. "What's going on? Can I get a drink?" she called to the woman. I took the letter from my bag and slid it across the bar counter.

"What's that?" she asked.

"It's a letter."

"Well, no shit."

"Read it."

"Congratulations Ms. Elbourne, we are delighted to inform you…" She looked back up at me. "What is this?"

"It's a position I applied for."

"It says something about West Africa? What the hell, Lily? Why didn't you tell me about this?"

"I didn't think I would get it, to be honest. The entire application process took over a year. I had to do a physical and two rounds of interviews."

She took her time to read the whole thing. "Are you seriously considering this?" Her dark eyes were wide with doubt.

"Why not?"

"What do you know about doing aid work, anyway?"

"I'd get three months of training."

"It seems kind of sudden, Lil."

"Well it's not really. Like I said, I applied over a year ago."

"But you didn't tell anyone you were applying, for a whole year?" She set her drink down grimly on the sticky wooden counter. For years Sonia and I had moved about in similar circles but never spoken. Mainly because I had been afraid of her. There was an underlying violence in even her most subtle movements. The way she reached for her drink. The way she opened a car door. It made you afraid that at any moment those waves of instability might irrevocably break the surface calm. I was her closest friend and yet, as much as she claimed to love me, it still gave me a sinking feeling that somewhere in the back of her mind she would be equally pleased at my destruction. Initially these were the qualities that drew me to her. We knew each other's flaws and we accepted them. Rarely had I found someone as accepting of them as she was. She'd forgive me. Once she recovered from the shock of it.

"Look, I need to get out of here. I need to do something. I'm going crazy."

"I don't know, Lil."

"What don't you know?"

"I thought you were trying to finish your collection? I thought that's what you were going to do. I don't see the connection."

"I will finish it. But I'm stuck. I've been stuck for months now. And you know, it makes sense. How can I be expected to write about life if I've never been anywhere? Seen anything outside this stupid city. When I'm stuck behind a desk writing shitty copy almost every day."

"But Africa?"

"Why not? At least it's something different. I want an adventure! And think of the good I could do, you know? Instead of always bitching about how messed up the world is. Why not try to make it better? You know what I would be doing there? I would be working with women, teaching them to take control of their health, empowering them to—"

"Does anyone else know?"

"Not yet."

"Well, I don't envy you there." She shook her head as her red lips formed an unsympathetic grin. "This place is dead, Lil. Why don't we slam our drinks and head over to the Stick."

I agreed. I was done here. I paid my tab and we left the bar. She wanted to drive so I left my car parked on the side street across from the bar. I was sure not to leave anything that looked remotely valuable in view. I'd lost enough windows in this town to have learned that lesson the hard way. We drove the two blocks to the Magic Stick. In any other city you would have been able to walk those two blocks, especially on such a mild evening. Not here, not in Detroit. The air was beginning to warm up and spring would soon give way to summer. But I wouldn't be here for that. She lit a joint and offered it to me as we swerved down Woodward. I took a small puff and declined any more. I wanted to be out of my head tonight, not back in it.

Sonia was right: the Magic Stick was crowded and loud and it felt more like the kind of place to begin the type of evening we were looking for. The patio was full, so we took the last set of seats at the bar inside. The music was blaring, and people were wandering up and down the stairs as some band was starting to set up for a show later. Everything was awash in neon hues and the weed made it all blend together in a dangerous harmony, allowing me to observe the chaotic scene as if it was playing out just for me.

The bartender was busy with the man in the fedora seated next to Sonia and it took a while for her to notice us. It was hard to tell if he was annoying her or if she enjoyed his attentions. I ordered a vodka soda and Sonia ordered the same. Having broken away from conversing with the bartender, the man had begun noticing Sonia. She had a presence that made you notice her, not because she was more beautiful than the next, though she was obviously attractive. There was something different about her that struck you immediately and made you react without knowing why, and maybe because you didn't know you were drawn to it.

"How was work?" I asked once our drinks arrived.

"Work was work. Same old crap." She was working as a shop assistant in an upscale boutique in Birmingham, a wealthy suburb just outside the city. She liked the discount and she did well on commission; she could artfully flatter her way into any sale she wanted to if she was in the right mood. But the clientele wasn't easy, mainly appallingly rich and 'arrogant assholes', as she put it. She'd worked there for years, though she insisted it was only temporary. She was trying to find something more permanent, but the sort of work she was looking for, that changed from day to day, even hour to hour sometimes. "You know, two years is a long time," she said.

"It isn't that long really, in the grand scheme of things."

"Maybe. But, I don't know … it can be. I just want you to be sure you know what you're doing?"

"Of course I know what I'm doing." In fact I had no idea what I was doing. That was half the fun of it. "Look, if I hate it and I think it was all a terrible mistake, I can always come back."

"What about your grandmother? You're all she has."

"That's not at all true," I said sharply.

"You know what I mean, though."

"She'll be alright. She's got enough people around her. I'm sure I'll be able to call. Maybe even come back and visit once."

"Won't be easy, though. And you know, it could be dangerous over there," she said. I rolled my eyes. She was unsure about it so she was trying to make me unsure as well.

While Sonia was too distracted to notice, I kept catching the eye of the man in the fedora next to her. He was obviously trying to get the attention of either one of us. He was handsome enough, but his eyes had a weathered look to them. He tried to hide it while he bantered with the bartender or gave a faint smile when he caught my eye. I smiled back, taking pity on those inconsolable eyes.

"I guess you've made your mind up, then. But what am I supposed to do for two years without you?" she asked sadly.

"Aw, you'll be alright," I sighed. "After a week or so you probably won't even miss me."

"Not possible." She shook her head. "I'll be right back. Order me another when she comes around." As Sonia headed for the bathroom, I was suddenly very aware of the space that had shrunk between me and the stranger. I struggled not to glance over at him, having lost my excuse, my buffer. I was left awkwardly trying to meet eyes with the bartender to order another round while avoiding his. Finally, she saw me.

"Two vodka sodas," I said. "But could you do one with a lemon and one with a lime, please?"

The stranger took his chance. "Are you the lemon or the lime?" he asked with a coy grin.

"Oh lord." I rolled my eyes. "Please don't," I said, but I couldn't help a smirk.

"Well, it was either that or something equally awful," he said, laughing.

"You've been thinking about it for some time, then?"

"Yes—you haven't made it easy, though. I almost lost hope. I nearly resorted to 'Do you come here often?'"

"It might have been better."

"Dammit, yes." He shook his head in exaggerated disappointment in himself. "Classics, stick to the classics. So, do you come here often?" he asked, in a faux-serious tone.

"Yes, I'm a regular here. Every day I come to drown my sorrows and the sorrows of the world in vodka sodas until I'm blissfully ignorant of all of its injustice."

"Funny that I haven't seen you, then. I do the same, except with beer. And I must confess, selfishly, I've only been concentrating on my own sorrows."

Sonia appeared between us and flashed me a mischievous look of approval.

"Who's your new friend, Lil?" she asked. "I'm Sonia."

"Sonia, I'm Jack, it's a pleasure to meet you, and Lillian?" he said.

"Lily," I replied.

"I see. You hadn't even gotten to the names yet. Excuse me for interrupting."

"That's alright," Jack said. "I was only busy horrifying your friend with awful pick-up lines. You've saved me."

"I'm sure she wasn't horrified. She always plays hard to get," Sonia said, doing my flirting for me.

"Does she? So, I shouldn't take it too personally, then?" Jack said, looking at me as he spoke.

"No, she appreciates the effort, even if she doesn't show it." Sonia continued to tease, and I blushed.

"What are you ladies up to this evening?"

"You're looking at it," Sonia said. "What about you? Know of anything exciting going on tonight?"

"I wish I did. I actually should be getting back to work," Jack said.

"At nine o'clock on a Friday night?" Sonia asked, taking over the conversation.

"Yeah. I'm on a deadline, unfortunately. I'm working on a commission right now. Painting. My studio is a few blocks away. I just needed to get out for a while and I found myself here. I'm glad I came, though," he said smiling at me. It was a dangerous smile.

"You're an artist? You know, Lily is a poet."

"I wouldn't go that far," I said quickly, embarrassed by such a bold statement.

"A poet?" Jack asked, ignoring my protest. "I should have guessed." He shook his head at his glass.

"It's more of a hobby."

"It always is at first." His tone suggested he understood something of my struggles. "I know you said you're a regular here, and while I could be a romantic and just hope we meet again some night, I think it would be better to play it safe and maybe exchange phone numbers, just in case the fates are unkind."

I hesitated.

"I'll give him your number, Lil, if you won't," Sonia interjected.

"Alright," I said and he handed me his phone to type in the numbers.

"So you know whether to answer or ignore it," he said, pressing send when I handed the phone back to him. "Well, ladies, enjoy your evening. It's been a pleasure." He tipped his hat and was gone, into the crowd.

"He was cute, Lil!" Sonia exclaimed after he'd left. "And he's an artist. Right up your alley."

"Please," I laughed. "Everyone in this fucking town is an 'artist'. I'll believe it when I see it. Besides, I'm not exactly looking to start a relationship right now."

"Who said anything about a relationship?" she laughed. "Just a little fun before you go. You've got nothing to lose."

"Yeah, we'll see."

"He's going to call you."

"Maybe."

"So what do you want to do, then? We could head back to my place. See what Paul and those guys are up to?"

"I should really be heading back."

"Are you going to tell her tonight?"

"I think so."

"How do you think she'll take it?"

"I don't know."

Somewhere around one in the morning, I turned the key to the large oak door of my grandmother's house, not worried about waking anyone. The faint sound of voices carried into the foyer from the living room television. Inside, the foyer was bright. My grandmother was an eccentric in many ways. The odd hours she kept, reversing her days and nights, sleeping when the sun rose.

The large old house itself reflected her unconventionality. Objects that should have been used as ashtrays and tissue boxes sat on golden tables, overflowing with orange and red silk flowers. A white miniature Christmas tree with bright golden lights was in place all year round beside the old stone fireplace. Opposite the tree hung an old wooden cane carved with animals. A gift from somewhere in the Middle East. The walls were adorned with strange golden trinkets made up of surprising combinations of things. Violins and harps, the astrology signs of her children, old Victorian silhouettes of strangers, and mirrors large and small filled each room. If you took the time to examine the pieces individually they could seem odd or curious, but somehow it all wove an intricate pattern of black and gold and you were lost in the splendor of it all and didn't mind so much the details of what made it so alluring. Every one of her five children, and most of her dozen grandchildren, had a key to the house and could be anticipated unannounced at any hour, expected to come and go as they pleased. Day and night the ground floor was kept lit as if to signal to her collection of stragglers there was always sanctuary to be found here.

"Who's in my house?" her familiar voice called from the living room.

"It's me, I'm back," I said, making my way to greet her, as she sat perched on the end of the long black sofa.

"Hi honey," she said smiling. "Were you out with Sonia? There's wine in the kitchen, if you want."

"Would you like anything?" I asked and she swished a small glass on the table next to her with her golden fingernails.

"Sure, why don't you freshen me up." With our drinks settled, I took my usual place across from her. "So what did you girls do tonight?"

"Oh, we just went for a drink downtown," I said. She looked so happy, so unsuspecting. "Did you get your hair done today?" I asked, dragging it out even longer.

"Yes, do you like it?" She patted the salt-and-pepper bouffant, feeling for the newness of the style with her golden fingertips.

"It's very nice," I said. It looked almost the same to me. A littler sharper around the edges. She looked like Liz Taylor. She dressed like Liz Taylor. She smoked and drank like Liz Taylor. I wanted more than anything to be like her when I was older.

"She always does it too short but it's fine. It grows fast. So it was just the two of you then? You're back early."

"Yeah," I said. I drained my wineglass and got up to refill it. I could never hide anything from her. But she was waiting for me as she always did. Confident I'd spill it all out, whatever it was, when the time came. There was really no use. "I got some news today," I called from the kitchen.

"News? What kind of news?"

"I got a job offer."

"Really?" From the tone of her voice she was obviously pleased. "Where? I didn't know you were looking? At another paper?"

"No," I said, sitting back down across from her. "It's something slightly different. I think I need a change."

"Well, congratulations, honey! Tell me all about it."

"It's actually in Africa." She looked at me and I could

see her eyes were wide but more so with amusement than disbelief.

"I'm sorry, honey." She took a cigarette out and lit it. "But did you say Africa? Like as in Africa, Africa?"

"Yeah…"

"How did that happen?" She leaned in. She was almost excited for me. What had I been so worried about?

"It's a program I applied for, a while ago now. I would teach people how to be healthy. It sounds like a lot of the work would focus on women and girls, teaching them things about sexual health, prenatal and post-natal care, that kind of thing. And I would go through training first. Then I would go somewhere, to a little village, I think."

"Would you have electricity? Running water?"

"Some people do and some people don't. It depends on where you go."

"But you don't know where you'll be yet?"

"I know the country but that's all."

"Where is it?"

"Togo. It's a tiny sliver of a place, between Ghana and Benin in West Africa. It's a peaceful place, I've been reading up on it. They speak French there."

"They teach you French, then?"

"Apparently."

"How long will you go for?"

"It's a two-year assignment."

"Two years?" I nodded. She sat quietly for a moment, contemplating in minutes and months the distance that would soon lie between us.

"It isn't that long," I said quickly. "When you think of it, it's a drop in the bucket really."

"You know, your grandfather and I always used to say that you were different. He was so proud of you," she said, her eyes glazing over, for it was still difficult for her to speak of him. "I think he would have liked to travel more. Though he did travel some during the war. He was lucky, he was sent to Germany instead of Korea. So, he did get to see some of Europe at least. He was only gone for a year but I'll tell you, to me it felt like forever. You know, that was my dad's one sticking point when it came to us getting married. He said, 'Wait until he comes back from the war. Then you can get married.' He was right. I got it later. But then? I didn't want to listen to him. I was so sure. I knew it, he was the one. But you always are at that age. Your grandfather had a theory about all that. He hated when people called it 'puppy love'. He'd say, 'No one takes you seriously when you're young. But that's when you feel things the strongest.'"

"Because life hasn't made you doubt yourself so much, I guess. You're less afraid."

"Maybe that's it. Well, whatever it was, we were very lucky to have all those years together." She wiped a small tear from her eye. "I'm sorry, honey. I don't mean to go on. I just miss him so much sometimes."

"I know. I do too."

It had been two years since he'd died but sometimes it felt like only days. To me at least. I couldn't imagine what it felt like for her. We had all been quite a trio. The three of us had spent so many nights staying up all hours, a glass of red, a Jack on the rocks with a splash of water and a vodka tonic. I would listen for hours to their stories about the lives they had lived before anyone of us knew them.

The stories about the daughter of a Lebanese butcher and a Polish runaway who fell for the son of a stuffy old German businessman. They had caused quite a stir for their day but it couldn't stop them. They were very lucky people because they had been happy in ways that many people don't allow themselves to be. Perhaps because it took a sort of blind faith and a rejection of reason that were becoming more and more unfashionable in modern times. They had really loved each other. It was something they couldn't hide. His death had taken her by surprise in many ways because she had expected to go first. Everyone had expected her to go first. She smoked too much and never quit, even when her heart got bad and the doctors said she wouldn't make it more than five years if she kept on the way she was going. That was almost fifteen years ago now. She hadn't changed a thing, of course. She smoked a little less—but only a little.

It was really something to be said for the power of the mind. For always believing, hoping for the best in life and ignoring anything that contradicted that hope. That was what got my grandmother through it when my grandfather died. That and a resolute sort of certainty that they would indeed meet again in another time and place. I believed it too, though I didn't necessarily believe in that sort of thing. She made you, somehow. I had always considered her somewhat of a mystic and looked to her for answers and advice, which she never gave lightly and only when she knew I was asking for it. I didn't know why I had doubted her reaction so.

"Two years, eh? I'll have to figure out what I'm going to do with myself," she laughed. I sighed, feeling the return of the guilt from earlier. "Don't worry honey, when you get to be my age, you sure do realize, time goes by faster than you think it will," she said. "And, of course, if you don't like it there's no reason you can't come back sooner," she added. "But I'm sure you'll be fine. Things always work out the way they are supposed to."

I wanted to believe her. She held an infinite trust in the universe, a trust that I tried to imitate. It wasn't always as easy for me, though, for while she had known its magic for a lifetime, it still had much to prove to me. But tonight I would believe her. Because I felt it in my bones. The excitement. The relief. I believed her because it finally felt as if my life was about to begin. And because she was rarely ever wrong.

Chapter Five

Togo
October 31, 2011

"If your boyfriend buys you an expensive gift, you should show your gratitude by having sex with him.'"
Fati read the words from the pink-covered *Life Skills* workbook as I sat on the floor making posters in scraggly written French for my talk at the *dispensaire* the next day.

"*Vrai ou faux?*" I asked, looking up at her, and she laughed.

"*C'est faux,* Lily," she said, shaking her head. The strike had ended shortly after my visit to Kara and I was able to meet with the school inspector. He was very enthusiastic about the idea of a club. He arranged for me to work with a science teacher from the Lycée. We'd agreed that the club would commence the following week and that girls from both the CEG and the Lycée would be invited to participate. I had given Fati the book of lesson plans to look through to find inspiration. We'd already decided on the first day's activity and she had become distracted by an exercise in a chapter she found near the back of the book, ambitiously entitled "What is Love?". She moved on to the next statement.

"'If someone you love says they will find someone else to have sex with if you won't have sex with them, they do not really love you.' *Oh, c'est vrai.* But you know," she continued, "There are many boys that tell the girls that, and there are many girls that believe it."

"Yes, it was like that when I went to school too," I said as I concentrated on correctly copying down all the information that was to accompany my talk in a carefully executed display on the crisp, white sheets of paper. One wrong accent mark, one incorrect spelling and I'd have to start the whole thing over again. It was tedious and time-consuming work. How I had taken for granted the days of copying and pasting information onto PowerPoint slides.

"We have to do this activity, Lily," she said and I nodded as she carried on reading. "'If you love someone and truly care about them, you should show them by having sex with them.' *C'est vrai*," she said. I stopped and looked up from my poster board.

"Really, do you believe that?"

"*Oui.* If you love them and they love you, why not?" she asked.

"Well ..." I sat for a moment. Fati's eyes were on me, daring me to question their conviction. There was an official line I was meant to give here. I was sure the correct answer in the booklet was 'false'. But both of us knew that life was never as simple as that; such things couldn't actually be reduced to a simple true or false answer. "It is one way to show someone you care," I said carefully. "But there are many other ways that have ... less risk. And you should never feel that you have to," I added quickly. "If someone said, 'You don't love me if you won't have sex with me,' would you believe that?"

"*Non,*" she said and a half-smile crossed her face. I recognized that look. I had given it many times in my life to others I was certain were not as enlightened as I. It was strange to be on its receiving end.

"But," she continued, "if you really love someone you will want to have sex with them."

"True," I conceded. "But just because you want to, doesn't mean you should. What if you get pregnant? Or there are diseases to worry about. Besides, if you are very young, how can you be sure that you really *are* in love?" I asked.

"You just know," she said, with eyes like she held a secret I couldn't possibly understand. Perhaps she did. Had I ever been in love? No. I had carefully and purposefully avoided it for these past twenty-six years. Maybe once, when I was about Fati's age, I had almost been convinced. Luckily, I was able to talk myself out of it.

"Are you in love?" I asked, seriously, and she laughed, embarrassed at first. But then, with a defiant sort of satisfaction, she confirmed it with a confident nod. Everything had been leading up to this. Was she really? It was evident from the pride with which she made her confession that she believed it, and that was all that really mattered. We'd passed the point of no return.

"Do you know how to use a condom?" I asked. She hesitated then shook her head. I got up and went into my room and returned with the wooden phallus that had been provided to me by my work, along with a few condoms. I set the items on the table and handed her the condom. She held it a moment, and then looked to me.

"First you must check the date to make sure that it hasn't expired," I said, as I showed her where it was to be found on the small, white plastic wrapper. "Now, you have to open it and make sure not to damage the condom when you tear the packet." I handed it to her to try. She opened it and then examined the condom to identify which way was the right way around to unroll it. She was more familiar with this than she was letting on. "You want to put it on?" She picked up the wooden phallus from the table and pinched the end of the condom and unrolled carefully. "Very good," I said. "You do know then?"

"Oh, Lily," she said. It was obvious she was embarrassed by her experience.

"Where did you learn?"

"There were people that came to the school last year from Kara. They work with people that have AIDS. They came to talk to us about how to prevent it and they showed us," she said.

"It's important to use condoms," I said. "There are other ways that stop you from getting pregnant, but they don't prevent HIV or other diseases you can get."

"*Oui*," she said, looking down at the ground.

"If you ever need any condoms or if you have any questions about anything, you can always come to me."

"*Merci*," she said, and I searched her face to see if she believed me, but our talk was interrupted when my phone rang from the bedroom. "*Je vais aller*, Lily," Fati said, using the interruption as a means of excusing herself as I got up to get my phone. Before I could protest she was gone.

"Hello?"

"Hello, Lily," said a familiar voice.

"Oh, hello, John."

"How are things out there?"

"Good, moving along now that the strike has finished."

"That's good. Listen, I've spoken with Issa and it looks like we can't come out any sooner than two weeks from Friday. Is that okay for you?"

"That should be fine," I said.

"Great. Also, I thought we could begin the site visits that weekend too. I figured if we came out that Friday, I could maybe stay with you and we could do them all over the weekend. It would be easier, more efficient I think, than going back and forth from Kara."

"Sure," I said. A funny feeling rising in my chest as I said the words.

"Perfect, I look forward to seeing you again," he said. I hesitated, unwilling to return the compliment.

"Yes, see you soon then," I said.

"Goodnight, Lily."

It was something in the way he said my name that gave me an anxious yet excited feeling. I sat for a moment after we spoke. Perhaps I was imagining things. It was easy to do here, with so little to distract you.

The day of the club, I arrived at the school early. The students had yet to be released from the final hour of classes and the courtyard was quiet. I was nervous but I was trying to relax because it would be very dangerous if my nervousness was obvious to the students. There was a very rigid order of authority here and it could damage my credibility if they saw me sweat. Monsieur Robert, the science teacher I was to work with, had not been able to meet me before the club, so I wasn't able to discuss what I had prepared for the day with him. This lack of coordination only added to my anxieties. I took a deep breath as I approached the door of the inspector's office.

"*Bonsoir!*" he called to me as I peeked my head in to see if he was at his desk.

"*Bonsoir,*" I said, shaking his hand.

"Come, I will show you your room. Monsieur Robert will be there shortly, they are just finishing up the last classes," he said as we walked along the corridor. "We made another announcement this morning. I think many girls will come. Do you need anything else?" We entered the large empty classroom.

"*Non, merci.*"

"*Bon.* Monsieur Robert knows where to find you. I'll leave you to set up," he said, and I was left alone. I unpacked my materials. The cement room was stifling despite the countless little windows that covered each wall from top to bottom. The sweat was dripping from my face and arms as I hung the flip chart over the blank chalkboard at the front of the room. It was a large room with rows and rows of desks. We would be lucky to fill more than three or four rows. Monsieur Robert had yet to arrive when the sound of the bell rang out and the rising wave of voices engulfed the empty courtyard. I stood outside the door so they knew where to find me. A group of girls in light brown uniforms walked toward me. They looked incredibly young. No more than ten or eleven at the most. Maybe it was wrong to have combined the two groups into one. Maybe the age difference would make things too difficult. The girls greeted me hesitantly as they entered the classroom, muttering a barely audible *bonjour* with a slight bow as they selected a group of desks near one another.

"*Bonne arriv*ée," I said. Soon they were followed by an older group of girls. They wore white button-up shirts with light brown skirts to signify they were from the Lycée. They greeted me with more confidence and took seats closer to the back. Slowly the room began to fill. It was almost twenty after three. What if Monsieur Robert didn't show? I had no desire to find out how I would do alone with a room full of eighty adolescent girls and my funny French accent. I glanced over my workbook, not really reading the words but trying to mask my nerves.

"*Bonjour* Lily!"

"*Bonjour!*" I said, relieved as Fati, Brigitte and Adiza entered together. A young man carrying a briefcase followed behind them. He smiled as he held his hand out to introduce himself.

"*Bonjour!*" he said in a strong voice that assured me of his clout. "*Je suis Monsieur Robert.*"

"*Bonjour,*" I said, my voice breathless with relief as I shook his hand.

"Wow!" he said, looking around. "*C'est bon!*"

"*Oui.*"

I showed him the posters and explained the lesson I had prepared. It was a fairly standard exercise I'd learned in training where the girls were asked to list what things they needed to do and practice in order to achieve the future they desired. We made each suggestion like a plank on a bridge that would eventually get them to their goals. Monsieur Robert nodded as I explained.

"Very good," he said. "But first we must do an icebreaker."

"Of course," I said. Luckily I had anticipated this. The room was now full of voices.

"You are ready?" he asked, looking at me. He walked out into the front of the room.

"*Attention!*" he called out authoritatively. "*Attention!*" Slowly the voices faded. He turned to me to take the lead and I looked out at the room of curious, eager eyes all on me.

"Welcome to the first meeting of our Girls' Health Club! My name is Lily. Before we start we're going to do a little icebreaker, so you must stand up," I said, motioning for them to stand. The girls looked around at one another, waiting for someone else to stand first.

"You heard Lily," Monsieur Robert jumped in. "Stand up!" At his insistence, everyone was on their feet.

"Okay," I said, "Who can tell me who Barack Obama is?"

"*Il est le président de chez vous*," one of the voices of the older girls called out from the back.

"*Très bon!*" I said. "So, when he wanted to be president, during his campaign, he said something very important and I want us all to say it together, okay?" My words were met with curious but quiet gawks.

"*Vous comprenez?*" Monsieur Robert repeated, "During the campaign, President Obama had a saying and Lily is going to teach us it." He looked at me. "You will go first?" I nodded.

"Okay." I gave three loud claps then shouted "*Oui!*" raising my right fist; then three more claps; "*Nous!*"

raising my left fist; then three more loud claps; "*Oui, Nous Pouvons!*" I shouted, raising both fists one by one into the air. Monsieur Robert clapped loudly in approval.

"*Très bien! Très bien!*" he said. "Okay, now everybody, *Oui Nous Pouvons!*" He turned to me to start. I gave three loud claps and the girls mimicked my motions, the chorus of their voices calling out the words. Everybody cheered.

"And in English, how do you say it?"

"'Yes, we can,'" I said.

"Okay, one more time in English. Yes, we can! Can you say it in English?" he asked the room and they called back. "Very good!"

I waited for a moment for the room to settle and recited my well-rehearsed speech on where I came from and what I came here for. I stopped here and there to give Monsieur Robert a chance to summarize and correct my French or rephrase things in a way the girls would be more familiar with. Many of them had various levels of the language themselves and so we were all struggling in our own ways with communication. Still, it appeared their attention was ours to lose.

First, we asked the girls what they wanted for their future. Most of their answers dealt with finishing school and being healthy. When we asked the girls for examples of what might get in the way of them achieving these things, they shouted out the dangers that threatened the happy picture we had painted of what a contented life might hold for them. They listed diseases like HIV or AIDS, not finishing school, becoming pregnant, drugs, malaria—there seemed to be many obstacles. One by one we dealt with each threat and asked the girls what they could do to keep from falling prey to life's many misfortunes. It was all going extremely well, up until we decided to tackle the problem of HIV. I asked the girls how we could prevent HIV or AIDS and dozens of hands shot up.

"*Abstinence!*" the first girl to be called upon shouted. Monsieur Robert and I nodded.

"*Condoms!*" the next girl called out happily.

"Those are not for you!" Monsieur Robert yelled harshly before I could speak. The room became serious and silent as all the previous conviviality was sucked out without a trace. "For you it is abstinence. That's all you need to worry about." The young girl was mortified with shame.

"But—" I interjected. I hadn't a plan before I spoke. I didn't want to contradict him in front of the girls. It would be viewed as terribly disrespectful on my part. But I also didn't want to give the girls anything less than they deserved in terms of information. "Abstinence is best when you are young but, when you are older, condoms are a good method for prevention." I looked to see his reaction, and he gave a grudging nod, still stone-faced. We carried on awkwardly as I explained each of the other methods of protection, being sure to emphasize they applied to future circumstances. Slowly, I won them back and they began to enascertain again, more cautiously now. We ended with Monsieur Robert insisting that we do the Obama cheer once more. I was hoping to have a moment to speak to him at the end about what had happened, but he rushed off and I didn't get the chance. Outside, Fati was waiting for me.

"*C'est bon,*" she said.

"Thank you for helping me," I said. She shook her head, too shy to accept my gratitude. "What did you think of Monsieur Robert?" I asked as we walked.

"Oh, *il est très bon,*" she said without hesitation.

That Friday, at the weekly baby-weighing session, I told the *infirmier* about Monsieur Robert's reaction to the girl's answer.

"I don't know how to explain to him that the whole point of the club is to talk about these things: contraceptive methods, confidence-building," I said as I sat across from him at his desk.

"I'm not surprised." I waited for him to say it, *Les gens du nord*, but he only sat with his eyes narrowed. "Give me his name, I will speak to him."

"I'm happy to speak with him myself—"

"It will be better coming from me."

"I could go with you?"

"It might make him uncomfortable. Defensive. Don't worry, I will talk to him. It should be fine after that. You won't have any more issues."

"Alright, fine. There was something else …" I began, but then, I couldn't quite figure out what it was I wanted to say.

"*Oui?*" The *infirmier* sat across from me, never losing his impatient frown.

"Well, it was funny because a lot of the stuff we covered, they sort of seemed to know it all already. How to prevent HIV, how to use a condom…"

"Yes but do they understand the risks? Sure, maybe

they know how to use a condom but do they understand why they need to?"

"I guess, in theory."

"You have to make them see what is at stake."

"Right, well, we're just getting started anyway. You're right. It just surprised me. How much most of the girls already knew. Thank you for speaking to Monsieur Robert for me."

"*Pas de problème.*"

That evening Gladys came by for her usual evening greeting alone with the boys. She said that Fati would be along shortly for her usual study hour but she never came. I was washing up after dinner and getting ready to turn in for the evening when I heard a tapping. In the bright glow of the porch light, two figures waited beyond the screen door. It was Fati and, next to her, a tall, handsome young man.

"*Bonsoir*," I said, ushering them in. The young man hesitated but Fati assured him it was alright.

"*Bonsoir*, Lily," she said, smiling. She seemed nervous, too, but she was trying hard to act as though this was just another normal visit. "I want to present to you my friend, Kpante."

"*Bonsoir*," said the young man, giving a polite bow of the head.

"*Bonsoir*, Kpante," I said.

"He came from Sokode for the weekend," Fati explained. "His father is ill. He is in the hospital in town."

"*Courage*," I said.

"*Merci*," Kpante said. "He will be alright, but my

mother was worried. She wanted me to come home to see him."

"Sit down, please," I said and they both took a seat on the couch and I sat across from them. They both seemed unsure of what should happen next. Finally, Kpante spoke.

"Fatima has told me much about you. She said you have become her good friend."

"We have become very good friends," I said. "I would be lost without Fati. She has helped me more than she could possibly know."

"Oh, Lily," Fati said, growing more self-conscious.

"You come from the United States?" he said. "Which part?"

"Michigan," I said.

"Aha," he said, nodding. "It is in the north?"

"Yes, the middle of the north."

"It gets very cold there?"

"Yes, in the winter. Soon it will snow. Maybe it already has."

"I would like to see that. I would like to go to the United States," he said, his eyes growing distant. "Someday Fati and I, we will come visit you there."

"I would like that, very much," I said. "Fati told me you both want to study together in Kara?"

"Yes, next year I will go. Then, when she passes the BAC, she will come too," he said, his proud eyes on Fati as he spoke. Fati smiled. She was proud too, though it embarrassed her, to have it all in the open. It was obvious he adored her. Of course, this was the boy she had chosen. She was a smart girl. I shouldn't have doubted her.

"It is a good plan," I said nodding.

"And you like Togo?"

"Yes," I said. "Very much."

"It is very different *comme chez vous*?"

"Yes, in some ways."

"Bon," Fati said rising. "We must go, it is late. *Bonne nuit*, Lily."

"*Bon, au revoir*," Kpante said as he shook my hand again.

"*Au revoir*," I said and they were gone.

So, that was love. I looked over at the empty space they had only just deserted. On their departure, they'd taken with them a bit of warmth, a bit of light. How young they were. How easy to dismiss. But they had something, the two of them. They had a dreamy look in their eyes when they talked of places that were distant and things they would do and see together. Even in the correct set of circumstances, with fortune in your favor, it was still difficult at times to see. To dream. Hopefully life would be kind to them. Hopefully it would let them see.

Chapter Six

The arrival of my fourth month in village brought with it hints of Harmattan, the dry season. The lush greenery of rainy season slowly faded, almost unnoticed at first, until everything became a mess of browns and reds and the sky became tinted orange with dust as the Saharan winds carried its reminders of the far-off desert to our doorsteps. Along with them came the slow realization that time was passing. Sand through the hourglass. The letters that came often in the beginning, full of reminders, had become scarce. Probably because, for the most part, they had gone unanswered.

When the weekend of the site visits finally came, John arrived early. I was still aiding in the weekly baby-weighing session at the *dispensaire*. Luckily for him, the village was small enough for him to find me with a simple phrase, "*Où est la blanche?*"

I was sitting at the table, marking the last of the record books, when he appeared. It took a moment for my tired brain to register its familiarity with this obviously out of place white man.

"Oh, hello!" I said, with a bit too much enthusiasm. "Did you try to call? I must have missed it."

"I did try to call, but don't worry. It wasn't hard to find you," he said, wiping the Harmattan dust from his face.

A few of the women who were left waiting for the final vaccinations were watching, and smiling as they whispered playfully to one another.

"Lily, *c'est ton mari*?" one of the women teased. I shook my head and felt my cheeks grow hot. I was more embarrassed by the fact that their teasing had caused me any embarrassment at all. Thankfully, just then, the *matron* emerged from the consultation room and her excitement over the arrival of this new *anasara* took the attention away from my humiliation.

"Lily! Who is this?" she asked.

"This is my friend John, he lives in Kara," I explained. "We're working together on the project I was telling you about." She was followed by the *infirmier*. He, too, was intrigued by John's arrival, though he tried not to show it. He greeted John in French, reaching out to shake his hand with a sense of respect and formality that surprised me, as I was never quite privy to such a display from him. I had also mentioned the project to him earlier that week, but he'd taken little interest. Now, he was asking all sorts of questions, nodding along with serious consideration as John spoke. I disappeared in their exchange as he addressed only John with his inquiries.

We left the clinic and decided to get a drink because there wasn't much else to do and a moderately chilled beverage in the midday heat was always a good idea. The boutique down the main road usually had a reliable supply of cold beer and a small area of tables outside that were shaded by a few trees. A young woman and a small boy were always there, napping outside or behind the counter until a customer appeared to wake them and demand service. The girl was maybe twenty and very pretty, but also very slow, as though she was always in the midst of a daydream that she could never be fully awoken from. At first I assumed she was simply struck by my presence as an *anasara*, but I soon discovered her blank stare and complete inability to count change or total items correctly were not solely enjoyed by me. That afternoon it was quiet and there was no one in sight aside from the boy, who was lying on the bench outside the door. We took a seat at one of the tables and John rang the rusted metal bell on the table to get the child's attention. Slowly, he rose, rubbing his eye awake, and walked over.

"What's cold?" John asked.

"Fanta, Coca-Cola, Flag …"

"*Deux* Flag," John ordered before he could finish. He turned to me. "Is that alright?" I nodded, and the boy slowly made his way inside the boutique. "Issa should be here soon. He's just gone to pick up a friend who's also one of our mechanics for the project, Naapoo. He lives just a village away from here, not far," he said just as the young woman appeared from inside with our drinks. The boy had resumed his place on the bench.

"Lily, *tu bois*?" she asked, cracking open the bottles.

"*Oui*," I said, and she giggled, yelling something back to the boy. She stood for a moment after she had placed the drinks on the table, just staring at us, smiling a juvenile sort of smile, but she was too old to get away with such games. It made me a little uneasy. While it was mostly men that drank here, I had seen a woman or two drinking a beer from time to time. It wasn't unheard of and didn't warrant such attention. "*Merci*," I said harshly, and she laughed again and went to sit by the boy on the bench.

"So," John continued, ignoring the girl. "Once Issa gets here, he can explain to you our approach for the next few days. You see, one of the things he's suggested for these visits is that we try to assess whether or not the villages are motivated enough to keep up on the maintenance that might be required once the pump is built."

"Motivated? That sounds kind of condescending. Why wouldn't they be motivated to have clean water?"

"Well, with enough time, the pumps can break or need repairs. And if the villages don't have the money to replace a part, they just sit there, for years sometimes. Eventually, they rust and need even more parts and it gets even more expensive. What Issa is going to do for each village is to train them in proper upkeep and try to get them to set up a village fund so that they can have some money set aside for when something goes wrong."

"I see. So, the site visits are like an interview process as well?" John nodded. "I get the logic but it still feels a bit condescending, don't you think?"

"I know what you're saying," he said, but his dismissive tone said otherwise. "It's for the best in the long run when you think about it. For the villagers themselves, especially. We're empowering them to take a more autonomous role in their future."

"Wow, you have been in this line of work for a long time, haven't you?" I teased but instantly I regretted it because his cheeks flushed a bright red. Before he could defend himself, his cellphone buzzed on the wooden table. He swiftly answered. Giving directions in French, he got up to peer around the wooden fencing that encompassed the bar and hid us from the main road. There was the roar of a moto pulling up on the other side of the fence. Seconds later, John reappeared, talking excitedly to a man I assumed was Issa. Another man trailed silently behind them.

"May I present to you Lily," John said.

"Lily!" Issa said, stretching his hand out to me. "*C'est bon! C'est bon!*" They both took a seat and Issa called out to the girl who was still sitting on the bench, observing our interactions. She had made no effort to ask if the newly arrived patrons wanted a beverage. "*Ma sœur, encore deux Flag s'il vous plaît!*" he commanded, and she lazily made her way into the boutique. "Jean has explained most of the project to you already?" He asked, turning to me, eager to begin.

"'Yes," I said.

"Good. Now we must decide how many sites we will visit over how many days. It is difficult. Some of the roads are not so good and they'll be getting worse this time of year. But most of the places Naapoo and I know well," he explained.

The girl returned with the beer and resumed her place opposite us on the bench. She sat expressionless, with her face planted in the palm of her hand, as if watching a TV program that was not particularly interesting. This was not sitting well with Issa. He continued to speak, but all the while he was glancing, intermittently, with annoyance in her direction. Most of what Issa was saying I had already gathered from John, but I listened patiently as his excitement grew with each detail, as it does when one is discussing important plans that have been plans for too long and are finally about to become realities.

I guessed Issa to be a little older than John. Gray hair crept around his ears, but his eyes were filled with a youthful hunger. Originally from northern Benin, he moved to Kara to study at the university there because it was cheaper than any of the universities back home. He studied history and when he finished his studies he decided to stay in Togo. He began teaching, being sent to various places across the north of the country. But then he was recruited by someone from the Red Cross to help run one of their youth programs in the Dapaong. He was introduced into the world of international aid work. Seeing it as a way to have even more of an impact than in the classroom, he had spent the last ten years of his life working for various charities and Non-Governmental Organizations across the country. He'd been working for John's NGO long before John arrived. Aside from a short stint back in Benin, most of his work had been in Togo. Having spent years at university studying its history, he didn't really recognize his continent's trivial colonial divisions. And while he'd been in his current line of work for a long time, his years in the field hadn't diminished his spirit or tired his enthusiasm. There was a sense of urgency in his desire to do good work for these people. We sat and listened, entranced, as he explained his vision for the project.

Issa looked over again at the girl and young boy. They were still entranced by us and I could not quite discern if this embarrassed him, made him angry, or both. It was very bad manners on their part. Meeting Issa's gaze, I shot them a disapproving glance and shook my head, but the girl only laughed, and to Issa this was unacceptable. He leaned in and said something to John in a quiet tone so that I couldn't quite make out what it was.

"*Comme tu veux,*" John shrugged, and Issa yelled something to Naapoo across the table. "He thinks we should go into town to work," John translated, his eyes falling on those other eyes behind me, the eyes of the girl and boy that had never left us. "He thinks it might be better there." We gathered our things and paid for our drinks, and when Issa called the girl over for the money, he gave her a short lecture in the local language for her rude behavior. As he spoke she retained an empty sort of smile. She didn't seem the least bit embarrassed though she mildly tried to give that impression. We headed to the roadside where the motos were parked.

"You go with Issa," John said. "Naapoo's moto is … It's just safer to go with Issa," he said, searching for the right word.

"Are you sure?" I hesitated.

"It's fine. I'm not risking my life or anything," he assured me and we were soon all on our way down the dusty road into town.

We arrived at Petit Baobab, the place I normally met Cynthia. We resettled ourselves at one of the many empty tables on the upstairs terrace and the usual barmaid greeted us all, already familiar with Issa and Naapoo. We ordered more beer and it felt as if a weight had been lifted somehow. There was a breeze coming across the balcony, sweeping past the mountain, whose plush green peak was slowly turning a dusty red.

"It is better here," Issa said, clapping his hands together. "Sometimes the people, especially in the smaller villages, they don't know how to behave." He shook his head to indicate his disapproval.

"Yes, well, that woman is ... Most people in the village are not like her," I said, feeling defensive, but Issa sensed this and he nodded, trying to assure me not to take offense.

"Of course," he said. "It is like that everywhere sometimes. I am sure even *chez vous*. If I went to a bar somewhere, dressed in *pagne*, speaking French, people would stare at me like she did," he said, placing his hand on his cheek and trying to mimic the girl's wide eyes and vacant smile. Everyone laughed.

"Depends on where you were in the U.S.," John said. "But aren't you used to women staring at you like that anyway, wherever you go?" Issa and Naapoo clapped in delight at this. I guessed, from their response, Issa had something of a reputation. He was handsome, it was true, and he had the sort of personality to make him appear even more attractive. A dynamism that could be dangerous if one wasn't careful.

"*Oh, c'est vrai Jean, toi aussi,*" Issa chuckled, returning the compliment.

"Yes, when you come visit me someday in the U.S. we will have a contest," John said, pleased with himself.

"*Non,*" Issa said with sudden, exaggerated seriousness. "You will not see me in the U.S."

"You don't want to visit ever?" I asked. Most people

here were far more zealous about the idea.

"No. For me, I prefer it here. Maybe I would like to see more of Africa someday. But the U.S., Europe ..." He made a face that needed no further explanation. "My brother, he moved to France. He tells me every time I speak with him, 'Why don't you come here? It is better. The schools are better. The roads are better. Everything is better!' But why must people always be chasing what is better? Here is my home. Here, I am with my people. Why not do what I can to make Togo better? Or Benin? Or Ghana?"

"You are a good man, Issa." John slapped him on the back. "But I am a little offended—wouldn't you even consider a trip to the States to visit an old friend someday?"

"Perhaps someday, for you Jean, I will go," said Issa, loosening his stance. "But for now *les gens de Togo* need me. We have work to do. Has Jean told you about my idea for the visits?" he asked, turning to me.

"Yes, the 'interviews,'" I said, but before I could say anything more, John butted in.

"Lily doesn't like the idea," he said. He meant it as a way of continuing his teasing of us all, but I flushed bright red. I had said all of this to him in confidence; it wasn't for him to speak for me.

"No, it isn't that. I just find it a little ..." I turned to John, "How do you say condescending?"

"She thinks it's mean to assume people wouldn't be motivated to have clean water," John explained. "To ask them to prove it."

"Mean?" Issa looked genuinely upset at the accusation. "Mean, no, no," he protested. "You see ..." he sighed, looking for the right words to explain himself. "People here, they get very used to having Americans, Germans, French, all coming in to build schools and wells and hospitals. They get lazy, complacent. And when the wells break, they just wait for the Americans and the French and the Germans or anyone to come fix it. It isn't good. They must learn to take responsibility."

"I see. But if the money isn't there, how can they take responsibility?"

"That's why we ask them to save, to think of the future," Issa explained.

"I understand, I do," I said. I wanted to ask what happens if there's a bad harvest and no one can save that year, or another tragedy occurs that interferes with raising funds. But I didn't. It wasn't the right time to get into all that. He reminded me of the *infirmier* in a sense. His diagnosis and prescribed solutions seemed to simplify things and place blame where I failed to find it. But he wasn't like the *infirmier* exactly, because he still believed he could change people, that he could make a difference. Well," I said, not wanting to sound naïve. "I just want to be sure we help those that need it most, motivation or not."

"We will," John assured me, and Issa nodded.

"Of course we will," Issa said.

"It's more of a formality. And it could very well be what makes the difference between winning that grant money or not. Sustainability and all that. Everything must be justified. Even a human's right to clean drinking water. You made fun of me earlier for using the lingo, but it's a game and you haven't been here that long. You're just learning the rules. Unfortunately you have to play by them."

"See, that is why I like working with Jean," Issa said, giving John a slap on the back in his turn. "He understands that side of things very well. Me, I'm not so good with all that. I'm better when it comes to working directly with the people. So I leave John to play their games. And usually he wins. Together, so far, we have accomplished many good things. We make a very good team, John and I. I think with Lily, now we will accomplish even more!"

"I hope so," I said.

When we finished at the bar, Naapoo invited us to have dinner with him at his house. When we arrived, his wife had already begun to prepare the *fufu*. She was a small, quiet woman and she greeted us kindly in the local language and then left to bring out the dishes of food. I supposed she spoke little or no French as she said nothing after her greeting. She did not eat with us, either: we sat on wooden chairs in the courtyard of Naapoo's compound and she placed the dishes on a small wooden table before us, then disappeared again into the house. We ate in silence, dipping our right hands in *fufu* and sauce, and when we finished Naapoo's wife reappeared with bowls of water to wash with. The sun had almost disappeared now, and they offered to drive us back to my village before we met again at its rise. They dropped us off just outside the cement gate that encircled my compound.

"We'll see you here tomorrow at six!" Issa shouted to us as they turned their motos to go and we waved and nodded in agreement as we entered the gate.

"Will they really be here at six?" I asked.

"Knowing them, it may be earlier," John said.

"Wonderful," I said. John stopped as we reached the middle of my empty compound. He was staring up at the mountain, as the last little bits of twilight were gently fading behind it, and it reared up from behind the collection of houses scattered at its foot.

"You have a beautiful view," he said. I saw it again for a moment, as I had seen it for the first time, through new eyes.

"Yes," I said. "I'm very lucky." I pointed to the shower and toilet outside the entrance and then I showed him the spare room with the cot. He dropped off his dusty backpack and I offered him a glass of wine. He sat down, quietly glancing around and taking in my little set of rooms.

"Ah, lots of Russians!" he said, eyeing my bookshelf.

"You've read some of them?"

"Does that surprise you?" It did, but before I could question him any more there was a knock on my screen.

"Lily!" Fati's voice came from the porch and I beckoned her to enter. She had her notebook in hand and had obviously come to study but stopped when she realized I wasn't alone. Swiftly her demeanor changed and became more formal. She gave a quick bow and muttered, "*Bonsoir.*"

"Fati, this is John. He's the person I'm working with on the pump project I was telling you about." She relaxed some as the reason for his unexpected presence became clear. "We are going to begin our visits to the pump sites tomorrow morning."

"*Ah bon,*" she said, nodding. "*Bon arrivée,* Monsieur

Jean," she said, still smiling. "Tomorrow you will begin?"

"*Oui.*"

"*À quelle heure?*" I had forgotten about the market.

"Early—six in the morning until late into the evening," I said. "I won't be able to walk with you to the market tomorrow."

"*Aye, c'est beaucoup,*" she said. "Lily, I will go. *Bonne nuit.* You must rest for tomorrow. You must sleep," she said, looking from me to John with a smirk. I ignored her insinuations.

"*Bonne nuit*, Fati," I said as she left.

"Who was that?" John asked.

"That was Fati," I said. "She comes over in the evening to study sometimes. She's very smart, she's almost graduated," I bragged. "She's pretty much my best friend here. Well, pretty much my only friend here," I laughed.

"It's funny, to be back in a place like this," he said, sipping his wine. "I visit the smaller villages for work, but it isn't the same, living in Kara. It reminds me of my time in Morocco."

"Were you in a small village?"

"Yes," he said, his eyes lighting up with the memories. "I lived in a sort of compound as well, with a family. It was … Well, I miss them very much sometimes. In some ways they were more of a family than anyone I left back home."

"Have you gone back there since you left?"

"No. I really should. It's been far too long. You know how it is, though; things always seem to come up. New work opportunities, projects. But, in all the other places I've lived in, it was never like that again. I never belonged to them as much as I belonged to that place."

"I can imagine. It will be very difficult to leave here one day."

"Yes," he said, growing silent. "Well, I suppose your friend was right. It's getting late and we have a long day ahead of us."

"Yes, I suppose so."

"Well, *bonne nuit*, Lily."

"*Bonne nuit*," I said as we retreated to our rooms.

Chapter Seven

A full day spent riding on the back of a moto is exhausting in ways that were, until then, quite unfamiliar to me. The nervous, agitated feeling of being so open and exposed in such a fast and unpredictable vehicle is the least of it. Before you even realize it, your nerves are numbed by the jerks and the bumps of sand and the ducking under branches until every twitch and tensing of the muscles becomes instinctive. It is the sun and the heat that get the most tiring, as midday approaches and you feel the ache in your back start to rise to your shoulders and you would give anything for a normal wooden chair to sit on for an hour or two, just to realign your spine enough to continue on to the next village.

We left at six in the morning, as promised. I rode with Issa. The first village was about an hour and a half west of mine and much of the road there was not really a road at all. It was more of a dirt footpath, so full of dips and bends that I was afraid that at any moment Issa might lose control and we would go tumbling off the moto to our deaths or some horrific, disfiguring accident. But I underestimated him and we arrived safely at each destination.

I had never been so far west before. Being over sixty kilometers from the *Rue Nationale*, I considered my village to be a fairly remote place. Still, the villages we visited that day were different. When we arrived at a site, crowds would gradually gather. First came the children, unafraid in their curiosity, until the adults followed and their presence demanded timidity. The differences were first evident in the children. They were thinner, their clothes were more tattered, and the dirt that caked them was thicker. The first village we went to was more than ten kilometers from a potable water source.

Issa spoke to one of the men who came forward from the crowd to shake his hand. The man obviously understood our reason for being in such an unlikely place. He then went off to fetch whoever it was that had arranged for us to come. Finally, a group of men made their way to the front of the crowd. One by one they greeted Issa with formal familiarity and bowed slightly as he introduced us as part of his team. I stuck my hand out to shake their hands and they smiled at us with gracious but serious smiles. Then one of the men began to speak. He spoke anxiously, his voice full of intensity as Issa translated for us.

"He said they have no water for drinking or washing in," Issa said, though the man spoke faster than he could relay. "He said that the children are too sick to go to school because their stomachs constantly hurt, and they are always sick. He said that the nearest pump is too far away for the women to carry enough water to cook and bathe with every day. There is a river a few kilometers away, but the water is not suitable to drink. They drink it because they have to."

The man spoke with anger. With the same disgust and disbelief I was to hear in so many voices that day. There was a level of desperation in his eyes I hadn't encountered until that moment. How could people be expected to live like this? That was what he was saying. How is this still possible?

We listened and nodded and struggled to find the appropriate way to express ourselves. John was the first to speak.

"Il est à cause de cela que nous sommes ici," he said. It is because of this we are here. The man nodded. He led us to the site where the pump would be placed, and the crowd trailed behind, now registering why we were there, and the excitement grew as a bit of hope mounted in them. Issa and Naapoo exchanged a few words then he spoke again to the villager.

"Do you have a group of people that would be responsible for the maintenance of the pump? Could you begin to raise small amounts of money, so that the pump could be fixed if it broke?"

The man nodded eagerly to every question. Issa reviewed the conditions with the group that now identified themselves as the elders and, therefore, the spokesmen of the village.

"These are my colleagues. We have to visit other villages because there are not enough funds for everyone and, based on how much you are in need compared to the other villages, we will decide if we can help. You understand?"

The man nodded again.

"Okay. We will call you after we have visited all of the villages."

The man verified his number on the tattered application and Issa made sure he could read the numbers. Slowly a group of elders made their way to us to shake our hands and to thank us. They offered us food and water, but Issa explained that we had many other places to visit and we had to be on our way.

It was a scenario that repeated itself in each village: the speeches, the commitments. The moments of confusion that ensued with each arrival and the time it took to collect the appropriate audience to greet us. So-and-so had to fetch so-and-so, and then he had to gather the others so that the hierarchy of the elders was not offended. Sometimes they would bring wooden stools for us to sit on, and sometimes they offered us water we had to pretend to drink because we couldn't offend them, although we knew it wasn't safe. Sometimes the women pushed thin and malnourished children forward for us to see. In one village, a woman made her way to the front of the crowd to present us with her foot which was infected with Guinea Worm, a disease supposedly eradicated from the country years ago. Other villages were different: the desperation had passed over them and had left only doubt and disbelief in our promises that things could change. There wasn't one village we visited that didn't need our help.

When we returned to my compound that evening, it was after eight o'clock. Everyone had already gone inside

The Ardent Witness

and the compound was still and silent. I warmed some water on the stove for us to bathe with and we took turns showering, scrubbing the dust from our exhausted bodies. When I returned from my shower I found John again at my bookshelf, examining my collection.

"I've helped myself to a glass of wine," he said, "I hope you don't mind."

"Not at all," I said, "I'll just be a second. Pour me one as well." I went in to change and then joined him again in the living room.

"This sure isn't very light reading. Have you read *Notes from the Underground*?" he asked, flipping through the old, yellowed pages filled with the words of Dostoevsky.

"Yes, a while ago though. I wanted to reread it. But you know it's not always good to reread things. Sometimes it ruins it."

"Sometimes it does," he said, putting the book back on the shelf. "It is a good one, though. Of course, my favorite would have to be *The Brothers Karamazov*."

"Really?"

"Again, I've surprised you," he laughed.

"Yes, I'm sorry. I don't know why."

"You've read it then?"

"Oh, of course. It was my introduction to him."

"Well, now, that surprises me. Most people start off with *Crime and Punishment*."

"Yes, I read it much later, but I found it less inspiring."

"I suppose if you start out with *The Brothers Karamazov*... How does it go again? 'If God doesn't exist then everything is permissible.' Really makes sense, doesn't it, after a day like today."

I laughed. It was a sad sort of laugh. The kind of laugh that comes out when you've not hope enough to cry or grow angry, because anger means you still think there's something on the other side of it.

"So, there is no God then," I said, shaking my head. "You know, sometimes it makes me really think about reincarnation."

"You're kidding?"

"How else can you explain it? Why should I be so lucky? Fate? Chance? It can't be so simple."

"You really believe that?" he said with an appalled look. I laughed.

"Oh, I don't know. I suppose it just helps me to ease the guilt, the idea that I somehow worked my way up to it." I poured us each another glass of wine. "You know, if I think of all the things I was unprepared for when I came here, the guilt I feel would be at the top of the list."

"What do you feel so guilty for?" Did he not feel it, too?

"Why was I so lucky? Just to be born where I was born? What did I do to deserve it? How can you reconcile yourself to that if there is no reason for it? How can I go back now, knowing that my life is so undeserved?"

"But at least you realize that and you feel an obligation to fix it. Not many people do. That must count for something, the fact that you feel a responsibility to do something about it, to help people less fortunate."

"Oh, you really think your two or three years here are some grand gesture?" John looked at me a moment. I could see he was surprised by my bitterness. I was surprised by it as well. I hadn't meant to sound so accusing. I took a deep breath. I was tired. I shook my head. "I'm sorry. I just can't figure it out and sometimes, like you said, after a day like today … I find it very difficult."

"Look, you can't keep beating yourself up about it. It'll drive you mad. If you really need to, assign some meaning to it, call it God, whatever you want, but you have to move on. Don't let it consume you," he said, taking a sip of his wine. "You have to think about the people today, all the people we'll help with our project. That's what's important, not wondering if it all 'means anything'. So what if it doesn't? Would you not do it then?"

"Of course not," I said indignantly. "But I suppose we won't unravel it all tonight, will we? It's getting late."

"Yeah, I guess you're right. Better rest up for another big day. Goodnight Lily," he said as he took the last gulp of his wine. I went outside to brush my teeth and when I came back he had disappeared into the spare room. I turned off the lights and retreated to my room. I lay down in bed exhausted. What was it I had been trying to say, anyway? It all started with Dostoyevsky. Then the guilt. Assign some meaning to it and move on. How could he look at things so simply? Men. Men look at life like that. But that was an easy way out. Perhaps I did make too much of it. The world is chaos and we're all just trying to do our best. Or at least most of us are. There is no meaning. God does not exist. Everything is permissible. If you can still do your best in the face of all that, it must be worth something. Whether it means anything or not. It had to be worth something.

The next day we started again at six. The strategy was the same as the previous days, to begin at the villages that were the furthest west and then slowly work our way back in. This time, however, the roads seemed even more treacherous. John and Naapoo were struggling to keep up with Issa and me. Naapoo's old moto was unable to handle the dusty terrain with the same ease as Issa's. After the first few visits, something went wrong with Naapoo's moto and we were forced to leave him on the side of the road while we searched for a mechanic in the nearest village. John and I squeezed onto the back of Issa's moto, and when we arrived at the next town he dropped us off at a little boutique with some tables and chairs outside and he rode with the mechanic back to Naapoo to assess the damage. John and I sat, exhausted, in the heat. The boutique sold little more than biscuits, batteries, cigarettes and shots of *sodobe*. The exhaustion was making me feel famished, but we had no food and we weren't meant to stop for lunch for another hour or so. The prospect of that happening on time was beginning to look grim. "We were very lucky yesterday. This was bound to happen with the shape Naapoo's moto is in," John said. "Well, it's about noon. *Eh, mon frère, il y a des boissons froides*?" he called to the small boy in the boutique, who looked no more than ten. The child nodded eagerly and named the usual beers. John ordered two Flags then grinned at me ironically. "Maybe they have a generator?"

When the boy returned with the tray of beers, we each reached to feel the temperature. They were warm. Hot, almost. "*J'ai dit des boissons froides*," John teased him, but the child just stood there with a blank look on his face.

"Oh, I don't care," I said, signaling for him to open the bottles. I'd never liked the taste of beer, but I was developing a new appreciation for it. We looked out at the tiny cluster of huts that decorated the small portion of road. It was barely a village. What did they do to pass the hours of each day?

"I've been thinking about our conversation last night," John said. "All morning, actually. You know, not many people think about these things. Most people, really. It's one of the more refreshing aspects of this line of work. Meeting people that are more like-minded."

"Do you really think people don't think about these things? I think they do but they don't know how to act on it. It's too overwhelming."

"I think you give people too much credit," he said.

"Maybe you don't give them enough," I teased him.

"Look, if you came from a small town like I do, you might think differently."

"I come from the suburbs. It's close enough," I said. "People are people, it doesn't really matter where you are."

"Perhaps you've seen too much of the world and not enough of your own country," he laughed.

"Is it really as bad as all that?"

"Yes, it really is. It's a cliché of small-town America. I couldn't wait to leave. Where I come from, Africa is an abstract idea: jungles, and war, poverty and AIDS. You think you should feel guilty? Talk to those people for a few minutes. You'll feel like a saint. I couldn't wait to leave."

"So you went to Morocco?"

"I went away to college before that, at Penn State. God, it was glorious," he smiled, closing his eyes in exaggerated delight at the memory of his escape.

"What did you study?"

"Poli Sci."

"Poli Sci at Penn State. I bet that was interesting."

"It was. Of course, my father wasn't too keen on funding a degree that was—how did he put it? 'Economically unreliable.' He thought I should study something more career-oriented like business or engineering. He's still stuck in the days where you could get a Bachelor's in business and be set for life. He's worked for Goodyear for almost twenty years now. I didn't want that life anyway, but even if I did, good luck finding it. Still, it was rough after I graduated. I spent a year doing odd jobs, mostly construction work. I was trying to save up enough to move to New York or D.C. But then, somehow, I got to looking into doing some development work abroad. I spent three years in Morocco. Then I did some work in Benin for a couple years. Then I wound up here."

"How long will you stay in Togo?"

"As long as I have a job."

"Don't you miss it back home?"

"Sure, I miss some things. I miss my family. But, generally, I like it here. Sometimes I prefer it even."

"Really?"

"Is that so hard to imagine?"

"Well, I mean, I do like it here," I admitted. "And I know that someday there will be many things about this place that I'll miss, for sure. I just don't know if I could see myself ever preferring it."

"You miss Detroit then?"

"I do. To be honest, a lot more than I thought I would. I miss going to shows and galleries and readings. It's so quiet in village. Too quiet. It drives me mad sometimes."

"So, you were one of those types then?"

"What type is that?" I asked skeptically.

"A hipster, city girl," he said teasing.

"I guess. I wasn't as bad as most of them, though," I said, laughing, just as John's phone buzzed on the table.

"*Oui, Allô?*" John answered. Issa's voice shouted from the other end. I hoped it was good news. I tried to ascertain by John's expression whether or not we would be continuing, but he gave little away, muttering only a '*oui*' or 'aha' here and there.

"So?" I asked when he finished.

"It looks like they've fixed it, for now at least. They're on their way here. We've lost an hour or so. Hopefully we can make up for it." He called the young boy over to pay for the beers and by the time he had returned with the change, Issa and Naapoo had pulled up near the road. Once again we were on our way.

The rest of the afternoon went smoothly. We didn't have any more technical problems and were able to complete most of our visits, albeit more hastily than we had the previous day. We would have to make up the others somehow. We decided to stop for some food and a well-deserved beer upon returning to town. I found some *soja* while the rest of them bought some meat from a man grilling kabobs just outside of the bar. When everyone had their little plastic bags of food we settled at a table upstairs, aching and starving.

"*Bon travail tout le monde!*" Issa raised his beer to us as we collapsed into the little plastic chairs on the terrace of the bar. "Good work, very good work." His enthusiasm and energy were admirable. The rest of us were not as able to convey our excitement due to an overwhelming sense of exhaustion.

"Will we be able to fit in tomorrow the ones we missed today?" John asked, I didn't want to think about tomorrow. Issa turned to Naapoo and they discussed the matter for a moment before turning to us.

"Well, it's not good," Issa said. "Naapoo's moto needs a part. We were lucky this afternoon, but I will have to take him to Sokode tomorrow to try to find it. I think by Monday or Tuesday we can finish." He looked to us for confirmation of the new plan.

"I'm pretty flexible. It depends on Lily, really," John said, turning to me.

"I give talks at the *dispensaire* on Mondays and Tuesdays. Wednesdays, I run my club in the afternoon. Could we do the same again? We could begin Friday afternoon?"

"It is not good to wait so long," Issa said, frowning. "See, the roads are already getting bad. Harmattan is here."

"Well, maybe I could skip the talks, I guess…"

"No, no," Issa shook his head. His eyes narrowed as he spoke to Naapoo in the local language, explaining the difficulty. "Jean and I, we can go by ourselves on Monday and Tuesday, if Lily doesn't mind? If we wait any longer the roads will be too bad. But I don't want you to feel like we don't need you—you're very important to this project. It's just that time is not on our side."

"Thank you," I said. "I understand. You should go ahead then." I realized there was another way in which he differed from the *infirmier*. He treated me as though I was an equal in this game.

"Then it's fine with me as well," John agreed.

"*Bon*! It is settled!" Issa said.

"We'll have to write the grant applications after that," John said.

"How long do you think that will that take?" I asked.

"Not long, if you can get a decent enough internet connection for a few days. I've been meaning to ask you, you aren't heading back to the States for the holidays, are you?"

"No, no plans for that anytime soon."

"Well, the school year should wrap up by mid-December, and everything slows down after that. I thought maybe we could head down to Lomé to work on things the week before Christmas?"

"Wow, it's almost Christmas, is it?" I laughed. "It feels like years since I was in Lomé."

"It will be worth it, trust me. You'll see when you have a decent Wi-Fi connection. Also, I thought it might be a good excuse to meet with your department head. You could try to butter him up before we hand everything in. I know Jeremy pretty will and he really appreciates that sort of thing," John said.

"I'm not really the buttering up kind, but if you think it would help I could try to set something up." We finished the rest of our drinks too tired to make much conversation. John decided to head back to Kara for the evening since we wouldn't be able to continue our visits. Naapoo offered to drive me back, but Cynthia had sent me a message to ask if she could meet me for a drink—I had missed our normal post-market cocktail hour—so I declined and stayed on alone as I waited for Cynthia's arrival.

There was no one else seated upstairs and I felt the loss of my compatriots' presence more severely in the silence. It was nearly the end of November. Thanksgiving would be next Thursday. I had known this but I had been able to detach from it. I had been able to not think about it because the heat and the dust were so far removed from a Midwestern autumn that it had allowed me to think that, perhaps, life was not continuing as it had been somewhere else, before I left it there. It was an endless summer that would continue for two years or so, and then when I returned someday, the seasons would pick up again and we would have things like Thanksgiving dinner and Christmas at my grandmother's house and snowy white evenings and Christmas songs on the radio as we drove past the twinkling lights displayed on big happy houses and restaurants and shopping malls, and there would be that excitement in the air that came to me still. The remnants of a happy childhood. But now I had almost forgotten all that. I had been away a while, now. I should call home, write a few letters, emails, something at least.

"Sorry it took me so long," Cynthia said, apologizing as she appeared at the top of the stairs. She set two cold beers on the table. "I ran into a teacher I work with on the way in. I couldn't get away. I think he was hitting on me, but I couldn't tell."

"You know Thanksgiving is next Thursday?"

"Shit, you're right. I've been so busy catching up with my lessons since the strike I completely forgot."

"Christmas is a month away. It's a hundred degrees outside. Just doesn't feel right."

"Last year I tried to get everyone together for Thanksgiving, but it's tough, because we still have classes that week. But hey, you should come over! We'll make dinner, drink a few boxes of wine. I go in late on Fridays anyway."

"Sure."

"Christmas is different. Someone will have a party or something. I'll find out and let you know."

Chapter Eight

Detroit
April 1, 2011

My last day in the office was quiet. Someone brought a cake into the break room, wishing me good luck. My workload had lightened over the course of the last two weeks and so I filed in the final drafts of my last few stories, and when that was finished I decided maintaining the pretense of having things to do was no longer necessary. It was a slow day, anyway, and outside the sun was bright, rousing me to escape the stuffy office interior. If I snuck out early, while most of the others were out in the field, I would be able to avoid the fuss of awkward goodbyes. There was only one goodbye I didn't want to avoid.

Raymond didn't have the common ego that most people developed in this line of work over the course of a successful career. Journalists, generally, are terribly obnoxious people. Even the ones that know a thing or two can't help but see themselves as oracles, privy to some higher understanding of how the world works and benevolently inclined to educate the masses. The worst of them are sufficiently clever and just easy enough to talk to that they get lucky with a scoop once in a while. My editor Raymond was neither of those things. I would be hard pushed to find someone else who would take the time to help me develop my craft as a journalist. Should I have desired to do so, that is. I packed up the last of my things and knocked on Raymond's door.

"Come in," he yelled. I opened the door and hesitated a moment in the doorway. He continued his work, not looking up to see whoever it was that had entered his office.

"Well, I guess I'm off," I said.

"Off to Togo then?" he laughed, as he looked up from his pile of papers.

"Not quite yet," I smiled. "I just wanted to say thank you for everything. I really enjoyed my time here."

"We enjoyed having you. You know," he said, pausing with his palms pressed together, "I don't say this lightly: you could really succeed in this field, in a few years' time. I do hope you stick with it. It isn't something I see every day."

"Thank you."

"Good luck! Keep in touch," Raymond yelled as I nodded and quietly closed the door and left the office for the last time.

So, that's it then. I was free. Outside, the sun and the fresh spring air were a welcome relief. I wanted to hold on to this moment, I wanted to mark it somehow, to make note of the occasion; it represented something. A new beginning. But something more than that. I decided to head toward midtown for a glass of wine at my usual spot. Maybe Sonia would be around to help me celebrate.

Inside, the dark and dimly lit interior of the bar was in stark contrast to the sunny afternoon that played out just beyond the old wooden window frame. A few stray strands of sunlight reflected off the stained-glass ceiling lamps and the smell of cigarette smoke and stale beer hung in the air. I ordered my wine and retreated to my usual spot in the back, next to the jukebox whose selection never changed.

My mind kept going back over Raymond's words as I left. It had meant something to me, his acknowledgment of my talents. But what he had really been trying to say was something else. You're throwing away a great opportunity. You're on a track here and this track is a good one. A stable track. Why wasn't that good enough? Why wasn't I satisfied with that? Maybe he was right. Maybe I would regret it. Right now it didn't feel like it.

I sent Sonia a text but she didn't answer. It was almost six o'clock now. I'd give it an hour and wait to see if anything came up. The idea of simply going home seemed anticlimactic. I pulled my book from my bag and tried to concentrate on the words, but my mind was too agitated by excitement to concentrate. I tried to write, but again my nerves were not in the right temperament. I had broken free of something. I didn't know what it was exactly. It had something to do with that track that Raymond had alluded to. I had jumped the rails myself. There was an idea I was turning around in my head. It might have been a terrible idea, but then again, maybe it didn't matter so much. It had been a little over two weeks since the night of the show. He had called once and I'd never returned it. I was sure he had forgotten me by now. Still, here I was, only blocks from where we first met. I stared at the little mobile device that held such sway in the course of events, temptation and curiosity creeping at my fingertips. I flipped it open and found his name in my contact list and quickly pressed the button to call. Instantly, I regretted it and a wave of relief came over me when there was no answer and it went to voicemail. It was time to call it a day. Some things just aren't meant to be. I finished my wine and gathered my books.

Suddenly, my phone buzzed violently on the table. Please let it be Sonia. But the name Jack flashed brightly across the little blue screen. How silly it would be to have just phoned him and not to answer. I'd made my bed.

"Hello?" I said, my voice sounding strange and distant.

"Is that the poet?" the voice on the other line chuckled in exaggerated disbelief. "After all this time?"

"The poet," I repeated and laughed. "Yes, I suppose it is."

"Well, how are you? I thought you'd forgotten me by now," he said in a teasing voice. It gave me courage.

"I was wondering, I know it's a bit out of the blue, but I'm downtown now and I thought maybe you'd like to meet me for a drink?"

"I'd love to, I thought you'd never ask. Give me twenty minutes. I'll come and meet you."

I went back to the bar and ordered another glass of wine. There was no reason to be nervous; I had nothing to lose if it went badly. We'd have a drink. If it went well, I'd suggest another drink or dinner or something. If not, I'd make my excuses and say goodnight. Just then my phone buzzed again. This time it was Sonia.

"Hello," I answered.

"Hey Lil, what's going on? How was the last day?"

"It was alright. What are you up to?"

"I just got off work. Do you want to swing by?"

"Maybe later. I'm actually meeting that painter for a drink."

"Painter?"

"Yes. From the Magic Stick. The other night?"

"Oh yeah! Well done, Lil, you finally called him back. Let me know how it goes. Text me if you need an excuse to leave," she offered, half joking.

"Thanks, I'll call you in a bit," I said. Just as I hung up with Sonia, Jack walked in. He looked around for a moment without seeing me in the back, missing me in the darkness. He seemed taller than I remembered him. I gave a slight wave to catch his attention and as soon as his eyes found me I remembered their strange sadness and the impression they had made on me the night of our first meeting.

"You're hiding in the shadows back here," he said. "I'm going to grab a drink, do you want anything?" He glanced at my newly filled wineglass.

"No, I'm fine for now, thanks." He returned quickly with a beer in hand. I cleared the table of my books as he took a seat across from me.

"So, you've finally found the time to meet," he said. "I was beginning to lose hope."

"Well, I'm glad you didn't," I said for lack of a better reply. I took a large sip of wine and tried to find a way to cut through the inevitable awkwardness of first encounters.

"Were you working on your paintings?"

"Yes, I was," he said enthusiastically. "They're almost finished, though. In fact, I guess they are. I think I've just been pretending they need more work. Sometimes it's hard to be finished. It means you have to start again with something else," he laughed.

"It was a commission, you said before? Who's it for?"

"Oh, some swanky little restaurant that's opening soon. They wanted a Detroit theme. Old Detroit. They didn't give me much time, but I think the work ended up alright."

"So, do you normally do commissions like that?"

"Well, presently, I take what I can get. As long as it interests me, that is."

"Did you study it formally? Painting, art, all that, I mean?"

"For a while." He hesitated. He looked at me for a moment in silence and I found his eyes in mine, those sad, green eyes. He smiled and shook his head at his beer glass as he had the first evening we met. He had become aware of my little game of deflections. "But I feel like I've been talking since I sat down. What about you? Tell me about your poetry. I see you're reading Keats." He glanced down at one of the books I had shoved aside to make room for him. "So, into the Romantics, are you?"

"Yes." I would have to give a bit now before I could gain any more. "I mean, in terms of artistic movements, I guess you could say I'm a Romantic. The modern stuff isn't really for me."

"Really? I think it's one of my favorite periods of paintings as well, though I don't know as much about the literature," he said. "The modern stuff isn't really for me either. So, aside from reading Keats and writing poetry in crummy little dive bars, what do you do with yourself? Or haven't you much time for anything else?"

I laughed nervously. The stakes seemed to be rising.

"I wish that was all I had time for. I sort of compromised my artistic integrity a bit and got a day job writing for the newspaper. I think the profession of poet may be the only one less financially viable than that of a painter, so I had to do a bit of selling out, but only a bit." I smiled as I said the words, trying to make light of my tragedy.

"Have you managed to publish anything, poetry-wise I mean?"

"Oh sure, I've tried," I laughed. "But not yet. I know, I know. Persistence is key. It can take years and all that. The thing is, those are very dangerous years. A lot of compromises can be made. Many people wind up very far away from where they started. When you're young, everyone thinks they've got it. They're going to be something. They've got the spark. But then, as you get older, the conversations start to change. It's not so much about living anymore as it is about surviving. Compromises and adjustments are made. You take a job to pay off your student loans, then you get comfortable. You stay in it because maybe you get married. You have kids. You take out a mortascertain. Before you know it, you're forty-five. And the spark? All those things you were going to do? The things you were waiting to create? It's too late. You've missed your chance. Even worse, you think it was silly to have felt that way to begin with. Sure, everybody feels that way when they're young. They're meant for some great life. They're capable of creating something beautiful. It's holding on to that that's difficult. Believing it as everyone else around you starts to settle. To want less and less."

"And which way do you think it will go for you, then?" he asked. His eyes seemed to be searching mine for something—what exactly it was, I didn't know. Reassurance perhaps. How silly I must have sounded. The wine made it all more easily said. But something made me think—hope—that I had found someone who might understand. There was a tragedy in his eyes that I recognized and somehow it urged me to continue.

"It depends on what day it is," I laughed. "I believe in my poetry. I believe I can write something important. It's just that, well, to be honest with you, I've been stuck. I think it's because I know I'm lacking something. But I don't think it's something you can learn directly, like you would learn from a course or a book. It's an understanding of sorts. Of life, of the world, of everything. And I'm not sure that I'll find it here, either." This time I stopped myself before revealing too much. "But you must do alright? To have people pay you to paint?"

"That isn't always the case. In fact, most of the time it's the other way around: I paint and then try to find people to pay me," he said. "I need to start working on my own things again now, try to get a show here, or something. I'm just a little stuck on inspiration. I think that's why I didn't want to be done with these. I'm avoiding the blank canvas that looms in the near future." He smiled gently. There was a kindness in his melancholy eyes that had escaped me before in my skepticism. "You're different than I expected," he said, and I made an exaggerated grimace. "Not in a bad way. No. Definitely not in a bad way. Let's have another drink." He went to the bar and returned with another round.

"You know, what you were saying, though …" he said, as he resumed his place across from me. He was choosing his words carefully. "It's an easy trap to fall into, creatively. Doubting yourself. I don't think you're lacking anything. I think you know everything you need to know already. You just need to trust yourself, that you know it. But sometimes that's the hardest part."

"Yes, maybe," I said, thinking it over. Perhaps he was right in some ways and I was right in others. "I'm not so sure it's all that simple."

"It never is," he smiled. "So how would you find it then? This thing that you're missing?"

I paused. This was the perfect place for me to show my hand. To say, well, in just a few short weeks I'm taking off. But something stopped me.

"Oh, I don't know. Sometimes I think I'll never know for sure. At least it keeps things interesting," I said.

"That's one way to look at it."

"How about you? How will you find your inspiration? How will you conquer the next blank canvas?"

"Something will come along. It always does if you're open to it. You know, I would really love to read some of your poetry," he said, glancing down at my little pile of notebooks. "Maybe it would help me to get the wheels turning."

"Unfortunately, I don't have any finished pieces with me."

"Next time, then."

"I would like to see your paintings as well," I said. I was genuinely curious. I liked the way he spoke about his work. He wasn't too eager to explain himself, the way a lot of people are when given the chance. Perhaps he really was an artist.

"Well, they're only a few blocks away," he said. "If you're interested." He smiled again and we sat for a moment in silent suspicion of one another's intentions. "We could go and just take a quick look then maybe grab a bite to eat," he pressed on. Oh, what did it matter in the end. Like Sonia said, why not have a little fun before I go. Better to regret the things you do.

"Alright." We finished what was left of our drinks and gathered our things. "My car is parked around the corner," I said, as we stepped outside.

"It really isn't far. It's safe to walk it but it's up to you."

"That's fine." In the absence of the sun the air had become much cooler. We walked quickly down the deserted streets, absent of passing cars and lined with dark, abandoned old houses, lost in the silence of their forgotten purpose.

"Have you lived in the city long?" I asked.

"Yes, I just moved back a few months ago. I grew up here. I've moved around, but I always wind up back here. What about you?"

"I'm in St. Clair now." I left out the bit about my grandmother. "Where did you move back from?"

"I was in Chicago for a while. Here we are," he said as we reached the front of a battered brownstone house. "I'm renting the top loft for now. I got a deal while the landlord's fixing up the bottom rooms. I think he's hoping to rent them out to students, eventually."

We climbed the creaky wooden staircase up three flights. Inside, the loft was dark but a large window cast the room in a faint mixture of moonlight and street light. The room appeared to be divided into a living area and a work space. In the corner sat two large canvases. The infamous paintings. While Jack fiddled with the lamp, I walked over to them. The first was a scene I recognized immediately. It was a painting of the old downtown shopping district. The mammoth Hudson's department store loomed behind the old storefronts of Kerner's and Crowly's. It was a mythic sight to those of us that never knew those days of Detroit in all its glory. It came alive through the intricate details of the old cars out front and the shoppers on the sidewalks.

The second painting was of a group of musicians in an old underground jazz club, from the 1920s. While the paintings were very different, they seemed to hold, in essence, the same abstraction. It wasn't merely a scene that one saw in passing, it was a moment. Two moments captured both by their realist qualities but also laced with the aching mist of moments past. The rosy glow of happy memories, and like so many memories, they took on an idealized form. It wasn't so much what had happened as how it was remembered. It was a striking blend of melancholy and pure joy captured in little strokes of paint.

"They're very beautiful," I said, once he had illuminated them in the cold white lights. "You're very talented."

"Thank you," he said, standing beside me, studying his work.

I tried to think of something else to say to sound

intelligent and thoughtful, the kind of thing that knowledgeable people say when they look at paintings. The truth was I didn't know much about paintings. But I did know that these were beautiful and that I felt it in a way that was different and true. It was the same feeling you get when you hear it in a piece of music or stumble upon it in the pages of a book. It was a genuine understanding of the human condition, one that can take many forms, and while many attempt such feats, rarely do they fully accomplish such ambitious endeavors. He seemed to be one of the few capable of it.

"It must be hard to part with them," I said. "To wonder what people will think. Will they truly appreciate what you've done?"

"Oh, I can't worry about all that," he said with a laugh. "Once we've parted ways it's done, and I have no control over what happens then. Chances are no one will pay much attention to them. They'll just be background noise."

"They should be in a gallery."

"That's pretty flattering," he said, looking at me and not the paintings. I wondered so many things about him. I wanted to know him better and a tinge of grief crept over me that I wouldn't have much of a chance to. "Well, would you like to grab some food or something then?" he asked.

"Yes, we could," I said, but then I had other ideas. "To be honest, though, I'm not terribly hungry but…"

"We could grab a bottle of wine from the store and come back here if you'd like? Unless you need to be going."

"Sounds alright to me," I said, and we headed back out into the night.

"So, where did you study, then?" I asked as we found ourselves once again on the abandoned pavements.

"I studied here in Detroit for a few years but then I took a semester off to travel and work and I never got around to actually finishing school. I think it turned out for the best in the end," he said as we walked. We reached the shop and I picked out a cheap bottle of red wine and paid the man behind the plated glass.

"I owe you a round, I like to keep things even," I said, brushing Jack off when he tried to pay.

"If that's the case, now that you've seen my work, I think you'll have to share yours," he teased, opening the door for me as we left the shop. "You know, I didn't believe you earlier when you said you didn't have any of your poems with you. You must at least have them memorized."

"Alright, alright." I shook my head, laughing. "We'll see how shy I am after another glass of wine."

"Did you study writing, then?" he asked as we once again made our way up the dark and creaky staircase into the loft.

"In a sense. I studied English. I tried a few creative writing classes, but they really were awful," I said, looking around as he rummaged about in the makeshift kitchen for glasses. He filled two coffee mugs instead and handed me one.

"I know exactly what you mean," he said, smiling at the coffee mugs. "Sorry, it's all I've got. I moved back about a month ago and then I got this commission and I haven't had much time for anything else."

"Why did you leave Chicago?"

"Oh, it's a long story. Or a short one." He stared into his coffee mug. I waited for him to say more but he was quiet.

"Music?" I asked, eying the iPod and speaker stand on the corner of his work desk.

"Be my guest. But don't think I've forgotten. You owe me a poem. One at least," he teased.

"Yes, yes of course."

I reached in my bag and handed him a thin black Moleskine. "Those in the front are mostly finished," I said, and I walked over to the desk to search for some music. He had many predictable choices to choose from, so I put on a Beatles album to fill the silence as he stood, wine in one hand and my notebook in the other, intently studying my work. I pretended to browse his musical tastes as I waited for him to finish. He took his time with it, turning the pages slowly. We were already two tracks into *Let It Be* and he'd yet to speak. I couldn't take it any longer.

"Well?" I asked, laughing.

"They're very good. You should really do something with these," he said, looking up at me, finally. I tried to read his expression, his voice. Would he have told me otherwise?

"Thank you," I said. "Some of those I've sent off but, well, nothing yet."

"What about a reading? An open mic night?" he went on, flipping back through the pages.

"Yes, it's a good idea." We stood for a moment in silence and I glanced back over to the paintings again. There was a scarcity of chairs and the only place to sit was either the bed or the floor. I walked over to the bed and sat down on the corner of the crisp white cover. "I'm very jealous of you in a way," I said. "You're very fortunate to live like this."

"You might be the only person to say so," he said, standing across from me. He hesitated, perhaps deciding how this would go. Perhaps he didn't want to seem too eager. If only he knew there was no test. I wasn't playing coy. I had made up my mind ages ago. I liked him very much. True, I hadn't had the time to really get to know him, but there were other ways I still could.

"I would be happy in a place like this, alone with my notebooks, devoted to my art." I said the last part in a purposely pretentious tone. Jack grimaced. I had embarrassed him.

"You know, it's not all that romantic. Today I got paid for my work and tomorrow I might be a waiter in the same restaurant where my pictures hang, or the pictures of someone else like me."

"Yes, but it takes courage to live like that. Courage not many people have. I think you're very brave."

"What you call courage someone else might say was madness. Or, even worse, stupidity."

"No, no. It's like what I was trying to say earlier. About compromises, about winding up very far from where you started. I always imagined that my life would be a great adventure. That I would do things, see things. That I wouldn't be like the rest of them and buy into the whole need to settle down somewhere. To give up on my dreams for the need to be practical. To have all of my passions sucked out of me in a pointlessly grueling nine-to-five office job that I can't stand. Counting down the hours.

Wasting away. I'm terribly afraid of winding up that way."

"I don't think you have to worry about that," he said, sitting down next to me on the bed.

"No?" I asked.

"No," he repeated, smiling. "You are very different than I expected."

"So are you. But not in a bad way."

"No," he laughed, placing his lips on mine. "In a very good way."

Chapter Nine

Togo
December 15, 2011

"Shall I help you with those?" Gladys asked, pointing to a pair of basins filled with water and a few dirty dishes I had just been preparing to wash. She'd stopped by for her usual morning greeting but today she was lingering awkwardly after we'd made our usual exchange. There was something more she wanted to discuss, but she was struggling for a way to begin.

"No, no," I said. "Would you like some coffee?" She stood, still hesitating, then her focus shifted to something behind me.

"What is this?" she asked, and I turned to see what it was that had grabbed her attention.

"Wine?" I asked, smiling, seeing the box alone on the shelf. She knew exactly what it was. "Would you like some?" I had to remember there were no rules here about socially acceptable drinking hours. Many days began at the local *tchuk* stand, with a calabash of the sweet and sour beer-like brew. She nodded sheepishly, satisfied, and I poured us both a glass. She finished hers in just a few large gulps.

"I want to talk to you about Fati," she said, as if the small amount of liquid in that cup had given her courage. Her tone and eyes grew serious. I guided her over to the small wooden table in the center of my makeshift kitchen area and we sat down. "She is pregnant."

"Fati?" I said. Though I had heard her correctly the first time.

She nodded.

"Are you sure?"

"That's why I have come to you. I thought maybe you can help us. You know she is a very smart girl and school for her is almost finished."

"Are you sure?" I repeated. "Has she seen a doctor?"

"No, but she has not bled for two months."

"She should go to the *dispensaire* and take a pregnancy test." I was still unwilling to accept it as fact just yet. Gladys was quiet. I sat for a moment, unsure of what to say. Gladys raised her empty glass. I poured us both more wine.

"You see," she continued, again after a large gulp. "There is a nurse …" She paused and looked up at me, as if to see whether or not I knew where this was going. I waited for her to say it. She went on, carefully. "He has medicine she can take but it is very expensive. Ten thousand CFA. I have four I can give her, but that is all I have. Her father, he cannot know. If you can give her the money she will help you, she will clean and do laundry to pay it back."

"This man, this nurse, is he from the village?" I asked.

"No. He is from another village near here. It is not far. He has helped many girls, he is a nurse, you see." She repeated the last line almost as if to convince herself.

"But, Gladys, surely you understand these medicines can be very dangerous—" I shook my head. "Look, I want to help, I do. I understand you want her to finish school, and if there was a safe way to go about it I'd help you, no matter the cost—but this? You know I can't help you put Fati's life in danger."

Gladys was quiet. She stared hollowly into her wine glass.

"I'm sorry," I said, softening my tone. "But even if she does have a baby, she can still finish school. We can both help her—"

"Her father will not agree to pay the fees."

"Then I'll pay her fees."

"He wouldn't allow it. He would insist she stay home and care for the baby."

"What about the father? His family? Maybe they could help?"

"Oh, Lily." She shook her head. Finally a smile crept across her tired face. But it was a sad smile. Full of anguish. Full of pain. "We are not in America."

"Let me find out what I can from my colleagues," I said. "Just don't do anything yet. Maybe there is a safer way."

"Yes," she sighed. "Find out what you can. I must go." She got up from her chair with a trace of defeat, and perhaps even resentment.

"I will, soon. I promise," I said as we said our goodbyes. I wondered if she was angry with me or Fati, or perhaps it was life in general. A cruel joke had been played on her.

After she left, I called Cynthia and arranged to meet

her that afternoon in town for drinks. Maybe a student had come to her in the past, too. Maybe she knew who this 'nurse' might be. I got there first, so I ordered a beer from the bar and chose one of the empty tables upstairs to wait. When Cynthia arrived, I quickly told her all I knew.

"I don't know what to do," I said in frustration.

"Yeah, that's tough," she said. "The biggest problem is you don't know how far along she is, and that makes it hard to know if she could safely induce an abortion, even if the medication is legitimate."

"I know. But are there other ways? Have you ever heard of anyone being safely assisted by any doctors or nurses around here?"

"Well, I have heard rumors that a *sage femme* in Kara would authorize the procedure, but it was for older, married women who already had a lot of kids and, of course, had money. I doubt she would do it for a teenage girl. If the rumors were even true."

"Do you know what medication she is talking about?" I asked.

"No, I don't really know what they use here."

"The problem is, even if it's a legitimate drug, usually they recommend only using them within the first nine weeks or so. Gladys thinks she's around two months."

"Well then, chances are she's at least three," Cynthia said.

"But maybe Fati is sure," I said.

"Maybe. But in my experience concepts of time vary substantially here. It just isn't as important to keep track of. I don't know why. But I do know, from what I've seen, one man's two months is another man's two years," she said. I knew she was right, or at least she had a valid point. We sat for a moment without speaking.

"What do I tell her?" I asked, feeling defeated.

"Her mother sounds reasonable. Maybe she could help her? She could finish school and her mother could take care of the baby?"

"Maybe. She said the father wouldn't go along with it. But she could have just been upset," I said.

"I know you want to help her. I would too. But you have to think, Lily. If something went wrong, you wouldn't be able to forgive yourself," Cynthia said, her eyes on me echoing the harshness of her words. Don't even think about it. I sighed.

"I wish there was another way." We finished our drinks and I made an excuse to leave. I wanted to be home in case Fati should stop by. But Fati never appeared that night, nor was there any sign of Gladys and the children.

The next morning, I went to the *dispensaire* for the final session before the break. When everyone left for *repos* I decided to try to speak to the *infirmier* in as vague a way as possible about Fati's situation. He sat with a smug grin on his face as I recounted my story of a young girl in trouble wanting to take some strange medicine from some 'nurse' in a neighboring village.

"This happens all the time," he said, shaking his head. "I told you, that's why we must talk to them. Teach them how not to get pregnant."

"Yes," I said, feeling slightly attacked. "But this girl, what should I tell her friend to tell her?"

"It's dangerous!" he exclaimed. "She could die if she

takes it. Or get very sick. And it may not even work."

"Maybe if I can get her friend to let me talk to her, or possibly you could talk to her and tell her it is dangerous?" I asked.

"Yes." He shrugged his shoulders. "You can bring her here and I will say the same thing. I doubt she will listen, though," he said simply.

"Alright," I said, ignoring his last statement. "I'll talk to her friend and see what I can do."

Back home, I sat on my bed, unsure of whether or not to begin packing. I was supposed to leave with John for Lomé the next day. I couldn't leave before speaking to Fati. But what could I tell her? What would I say? It sucks, but what can you do? Your whole future just down the drain. It wasn't fair. It couldn't be that way. Not for Fati. Perhaps in Lomé, I could speak to my program director. Maybe he knew of someone. I would pay for it all. I'd take her to Lomé. It wasn't an issue of money, but I couldn't have her in danger.

I heard a faint tapping at my door. There was Fati, her head bowed, like someone who had been caught for a crime they'd been certain they could get away with.

"Bonjour Fati, comment ça va?" I opened the door and motioned for her to sit down.

"Ça va," she said. I searched her face for more, but she only looked tired and perhaps a bit unsure. She was waiting for me to speak of it.

"I saw your mother yesterday," I said gently. "She told me everything. And about the medicine, but I've just spoken to the *infirmier*." She looked up at me, mortified. "No, no, I never mentioned you. I said it was a girl from town. He doesn't know, I promise." I paused, and she seemed satisfied with my assurances. There was a flicker of hope in her eyes as she looked up at me, anxiously awaiting my words. "Oh, Fati, I understand, I do," I broke down. "In my country it would be legal, and you could do it all safely and it would be fine. But here it isn't. It isn't right, I know but it's just how it is. If you take this stuff, this 'medicine,' you could die, and it isn't worth that, however bad you think it could be."

She looked up at me and smiled as if I were being hysterical, and this time she tried to reassure me.

"Oh, Lily," she said. "I have to finish school. I want to go to university. If I have a baby, I can't."

"But your mother, she can help you?" She said nothing. "Does Kpante know?" She shook her head no. "Look, I know you have your plans but if something happens to you, you won't go anywhere," I said, my voice growing harsh. "Maybe you should talk to the *infirmier* here if you don't believe me? He wouldn't tell anyone," I offered, hoping maybe he could convince her.

"No, Lily," she said in the same knowing tone everyone seemed to be using with me lately. "He is not from here," she said as if that were reason enough.

"'Oh Fati," I sighed. I was pushing up against a wall I could not budge from any side. "I want to help you, but I can't give you the money. I can't, knowing it could harm you. Please, I have to leave for Lomé tomorrow but promise me you won't do anything. I have an idea, I'll try to speak to some people there. Maybe I can find a safer way." While I really did hope what I was telling her was true, I also wanted to have some assurance that she wouldn't act on anything while I was away.

"I understand," she said sadly. "*Bonne nuit*, Lily." She left quietly into the darkness. If she was angry with me, she showed no sign of it.

The next morning, I left early to take a moto to Sokode where I was to meet John. We decided to travel together from there by bush taxi, a journey that could range anywhere from five to eight hours. As the moto driver pulled into the section of the station with cars departing for Lomé, I spotted a pale, blond figure on a bench near the ticket office, shelling peanuts.

"*Bonne arrivée*," John said, smiling, as I walked toward him. "I've got us both tickets already. I've also scored us the front seat." He nodded in the direction of the van that would be ours.

"How is it looking?" I said, trying to estimate how long we had to wait before our departure.

"I would say it's a little more than half full." He offered me some peanuts. I declined. "You should eat something if you haven't. Or get some bread to take. It's going to be a long day."

"There isn't a Starbucks nearby, is there?"

"I believe you might be able to find a gourmet cup of Nescafé somewhere around here if you look hard enough," he said, smiling.

"I don't believe in Nescafé. It's sacrilege, in my book."

"Beggars can't be choosers," he said, shaking his head at my snobbery. "So, I was thinking that when we get to Lomé we could stay at Galion."

"That's where we stayed when we first arrived."

"Yeah, it's a popular one. They have good Wi-Fi and the restaurant isn't so bad, either."

"How much do rooms cost?"

"Well, it would be about six thousand CFA a night for the cheap ones. Eleven if you want to go half on an air-conditioned one?"

"They have air conditioning?"

"In theory."

"Well, it's Christmas, after all," I said. I was also trying to ignore the part of me that was curious to see if the air conditioner was the only selling point.

"I like your reasoning," John laughed.

"I'm going to have a walk around to look for some bread, or something. Do you want anything?"

"No, thanks," he said. I left my bag next to his on the front seat of the van and went to have a wander around.

The amount of time it would take for the last passenger to manifest was indeterminable. It could be minutes or it could be hours. Still, no matter how long it took, the car would not depart for its destination until there were four passengers to fill the back seat and at least two in the front. Cars and motos pulled in and out of the dirt parking lot and new waves of passengers arrived. They carried with them lugascertain made up mostly of oversized plastic shopping bags, sacks of yams, sometimes even livestock, mainly chickens, tied at the feet. As soon as they entered the station, the men chased after them, shouting the names of cities and towns. Some I recognized, many I had never heard of. Swiftly, they descended upon them and scooped everything up to be loaded high onto the roofs of cars and vans. Their efforts seemed to defy gravity and most certainly safety precautions. All around there were women selling bread and other small goods piled high in baskets they balanced with seemingly little effort atop their heads. I bought a few small rolls a hundred CFA's worth of water bags, and wandered back to where John sat.

"Any news?" I asked.

"I asked the chauffeur and he said we're waiting on two more spots. Shouldn't be too long."

"I don't know if I'll ever really get over the absurdity that a vehicle meant for fifteen people at most can't depart until there are at least thirty to fill it." John only shrugged. He seemed to be well adapted to the Togolese concept of time.

At about half past ten, the driver gave the signal that the quota had been met and boarded the van. I was squashed in the front seat with John, which was, admittedly, better than being squashed in any of the rows further back. It was an intimate sort of way to travel, knee to knee, shoulder to shoulder. What were the rest of them thinking? The car full of blank and patient faces. What had led to such complacency? Allowing the *syndicates*, the men running the stations, to pack them inhumanely into stuffy, dangerous, inadequate vehicles to traverse broken roads, piled on top of one another in submissive discomfort. No one but me seemed to notice. Resignedly, I plugged my ears with headphones to drown out the terrible pop music the driver had begun to blare as we left the station. John did the same and he quickly dozed off beside me, his head resting awkwardly against the window. I couldn't sleep, not just from the discomfort but because my mind kept going back to Fati. There wasn't much else to distract myself with. The scenery was a repetitive blur of roadside town after roadside town. The thousand or so songs on my iPod had become equally monotonous. Eleven thousand CFA for a hotel room. Only slightly more than Fati needed. It was about the equivalent of thirty dollars. But it wasn't about the money, If I could know that it would be safe, I would pay, whatever the cost.

We arrived in Lomé just before dusk and caught a taxi from the station to the hotel. As we pulled up to the colonial-styled building, the glow of the electric lights made it look more glamorous than it was in reality. There were a few people having dinner in the restaurant and a band had just begun to set up on the patio. We found the owner behind the bar and it didn't appear that availability would be a problem, from the cupboard full of keys that hung behind him. He led us to the annexed building behind the main hotel where the larger, air-conditioned rooms were located. Inside, there was a double bed and a cot to one side, and a large bathroom. The owner showed us how to turn on the air conditioner and a loud noise accompanied by a weak burst of cold air filled the room. When he left I stood for a moment, staring at the cot and the bed, unsure on which to place my bags.

"You can have the bed," John offered.

"Are you sure?"

"Do you want to get some food from the restaurant? I'm starving."

"I do, but I think I'd like to rinse off first. You can go ahead if you want. I can meet you down there. I won't be long."

"Good idea. I'm going to take a walk and look for some water. When you're done I can have a turn."

He left the room and I was happy to have my privacy. Perhaps it was a mistake to have shared a room, even if it did save some money. It wasn't that much, after all. I hated to admit it to myself, but there was another reason I had gone along with it. It was a strange thing, the energy between us. Sometimes I felt an almost primitive attraction to him. It made me uneasy and a bit too combative. All the more infuriating was that he obviously flirted with me, but he seemed incapable of acting on it. Oh well. I undressed and jumped into the cold shower. Either it would happen or it wouldn't. But I wouldn't give him the satisfaction of letting me be the one to make the first move.

The air conditioner was running full blast, but it seemed little more than a glorified fan. John still hadn't returned so I went out to the patio to order a drink.

Outside, the place was getting busier. I took a seat at an empty table opposite the band and I ordered a glass of wine. When I'd first arrived, Hotel Galion had been just another addition to the long list of comforts that I was choosing to forgo. Now, looking at it through eyes used to the monotony of village life, it had gained a veiled and quirky allure. The clientele that evening were an interesting mix. There was an older French gentleman sitting opposite a young Togolese woman at the table across from me and another group of French or possibly Lebanese men inside, near the bar. Weary German backpackers sat behind me, uttering things in their unintelligible tongue. There was an excitement about the place I hadn't felt in a long time. The atmosphere was somehow romantic in the sense that it made me realize I had wound up somewhere very far away from where I had started. I was stranded here now, among the outcasts and the vagabonds that make up an exiled community. I belonged to nowhere, nowhere belonged to me. It was both a liberating and terribly tragic feeling. The band started up. The faint and familiar chords of "Wild World" drifted out into the night air.

Chapter Ten

I hadn't set foot near the compound since I'd finished training. The guarded white building stood out sharply along the sandy, brown streets. There was a security guard outside and I presented my ID and signed in on the sheet of paper. Once inside, I struggled for a moment to remember which way to go. There was a small set of conference rooms, in which our training had been held, and another smaller set of rooms that served as a medical unit. The guard, realizing my confusion, pointed me past the conference rooms toward a corridor that led to the offices. The offices were a strange West African imitation of what an office should look like. There was a waiting area with a few empty plastic chairs and a table with magazines that must have been months, if not years, out of date. Next to the door that led to my boss Jeremy's office was a desk where a secretary might sit, but there never was a secretary. The empty seat only accentuated the absence of one. The only thing that made it feel like an office was the blasting air conditioner that retained the ability to make me freeze in one-hundred-degree heat. I walked past the empty desk and gave a reluctant knock on the door.

"Come in," Jeremy called from inside. "Welcome, Lily. Sorry, I hadn't realized the time," he said from behind his desk, motioning for me to have a seat. He was dressed in khakis and a brightly colored button-up shirt made of *pagne*. It was the development workers' uniform, but somehow it always seemed strange on white non-natives. John had worn the same when we'd met that afternoon in Kara. It was as though they were trying too hard at a style that they couldn't quite pull off. But it was never really down to anything specific, just the overall effect. Jeremy sat there, smiling, and I smiled back uncomfortably as I took a seat across from him. He couldn't have been more than thirty-five and so I could almost forgive his over-friendly countenance, but I always found it mistrustful in figures of authority. "So, I understand you're applying for the development grant this round?" he said.

"Yes," I said, happy to get straight to the point. "It's an ambitious project, but I've partnered up with an NGO in Kara. They're going to provide some of the funding. They're a very experienced team. I'm lucky to work with them."

"Yes, I know John well. He does good work in the north," Jeremy said. "I'm not sure who else will be applying. I know someone in the central region was possibly working on a school, but I haven't heard anything concrete. I haven't received any applications yet. They usually come in pretty close to the deadline. But I think it's safe to say, you have a pretty good shot at getting the money."

"Well, that's good to hear. I hope so," I said, unsure of where else to take the conversation. I was never one to brown-nose. We were giving water to people who needed it. I wasn't sure how else to sell that if it didn't sell itself enough already.

"There is one small concern I have, though," he said, pausing, and I waited for him to elaborate. "Is John still working with Issa—Apeko, is it? Are they still the two running everything?"

"Issa Apeloko, yes," I said.

"Well, he's worked with our organization in the past and I know, overall, he's helped a lot of people but there were some rumors a few years ago about a project he was involved with." He paused again. It seemed a bit more for effect than from a desire to choose his words with delicacy.

"Rumors?" I tried to make my tone mask my increasing impatience.

"Yes, it was before John's time. I'd only been here a month or so myself, actually. But the guy John replaced, he'd been working on some project with one of our guys in the north. Latrines, I think it was? The project was a success—everything was built and it all worked—but afterwards, our guy began to suspect that Issa might have inflated some of the costs. I guess once everything was finished he wound up with a nice new bike or something like that."

"What are you saying? You think he was skimming money off the top for himself?"

"Like I said, there were rumors, nothing concrete, but I just wonder..." He sighed to give the impression that he was unsettled by his own words. I couldn't help but think he enjoyed the gossip more than he was troubled by it. "All I ask is that you and John confirm the cost of everything with the suppliers yourselves. If you haven't already, I mean?"

"Yes, well, we're going to work out the budget while we're down here. I think it was John who got the quotes for most of the parts. I don't know if Issa was involved," I lied. Issa had done most of the liaising with the suppliers.

"Do me a favor and just be sure, would you? I trust John, and you of course, to use sound judgment."

"Yes, I'll make sure before everything is submitted."

"How is everything else going for you, then?"

"It's going well," I said. "There was something else I wanted to ask you."

"Sure," he said. I was having trouble recovering from the previous bombshell, but Jeremy continued smiling, as if we had been discussing the weather. I took a deep breath.

"I started a health club for girls and one of the girls, well, she's come to me recently. She's pregnant and she's only about seventeen, she'll graduate next year, she's so bright—" His eyes began to dim and it was evident I was losing his interest. "But anyway, I know her family quite well and her mother came to me when she found out, you see. She wants her to finish school. She asked me if I could help her to find a way to have an abortion. I told her everything we were told to say, that it's illegal and dangerous, but I'm afraid she may not listen and I don't know if you know if … if there's anything else I could tell her?" He looked at me carefully. I tried to judge whether or not I had assumed too much by asking. He folded his arms and leaned back in his chair.

"I see," he said. "That's a tough one, but you did the right thing."

"I know, it's just …'

"I know it's hard, but like you told her, it *is* illegal here and you can't—we can't as an organization—be advocating anything that would be against the law. And it is very dangerous." I nodded. It was foolish, I realized, to have placed any hope in this man.

"Well, thank you. I appreciate you taking the time to meet with me," I said, eager to get out as soon as I could.

"My pleasure, like I said. It sounds like you're doing great work out there. Just double-check those numbers and I think you'll be approved, no problem."

Once I got back to the hotel, I went out to the patio and ordered a drink. There was nothing to be done about Fati. I had already known this, but the final defeat stung a bit. And now Issa. I held little regard for Jeremy. Why even entertain the idea that these rumors meant anything? Maybe Issa had been in trouble? Otherwise, how could he do something like that after all his talk about the work? His ideals? How to tell John? At best, he might laugh at the implications, but at worst … Oh, why couldn't anything be simple? I took a large gulp of wine. This place, this place was getting to me. Its contradictions, its absurdities. Nothing was clear-cut, nothing was easy. What was I supposed to do about it all?

I flagged the waitress down and ordered another glass of wine just as John came in through the gates. He waved when he saw me and walked over.

"Hey, why aren't you busy writing?" he said, his voice

light and teasing. He took a seat across from me. "How did it go, then?"

"Well …" I paused as the waitress approached to take John's order. "Jeremy had some concerns about Issa."

"Concerns?" His eyes narrowed.

"He said that Issa had been involved in another project with our organization a few years earlier and there were rumors that he had been inflating some of the costs to make a profit."

"You can't be serious?"

"That's what Jeremy said."

"It's bullshit."

"Look, I know that Issa's your friend—"

"What? You actually believe him?" he asked, raising his voice slightly. It was clear this wouldn't go the easy way.

"Maybe he was in trouble? Did he ever mention any of this to you? Or a time when he might have been struggling? A problem in his family back home? Anyway, it's not that I believe Jeremy, I'm just telling you what he told me."

"But you know Issa. He would never do that. Even if he was in trouble. Think of how much this project means to him."

"But if he was desperate?"

"Does Jeremy have any proof?"

"No, he said it was only rumors. But listen—" I tried to calm him to down. We just needed to decide on how to handle things together, so we'd get the grant approved. "Jeremy didn't make a big deal about it. He just wanted assurance that we were the ones to arrange things directly with suppliers. All he wants is for us to verify everything before we submit it."

"Verify everything? What? In case he's scamming us too? Jesus, Lily. So, you do believe him then?"

"No!" I said, but that wasn't entirely true. "I don't know. I don't want to believe him. Look, you know Issa better than anyone—"

"And I know he would never do something like that."

"Then there's no harm in verifying everything," I said. John glared at me. His anger had now been displaced from Jeremy onto me. I hadn't planned on challenging him directly but there was something in his certainty that provoked me.

"I can't believe after everything he's done for this project, for us, that you would believe this bullshit. That you would question him."

"I'm not saying I believe it. Jesus Christ, calm down!"

"You do, though," he said. "You don't need to say it." He shook his head and got up to leave. "I'm just going to take a walk, I need to clear my head." He put a few thousand CFA on the table for the beer.

I sat for a moment wondering what had just happened. I should have just left it alone. The restaurant was quiet tonight and the sun was just beginning to set behind the white plaster facade of the hotel. Jeremy was an ass. Everything he'd said about helping Fati. He didn't care. Rumors. But somehow I still couldn't share in John's unfailing belief in Issa. Why couldn't John even entertain the idea? Poverty didn't make people saints. Quite the opposite in fact. When I'd first met Issa at the bar that afternoon, I had been charmed by him. Seeing only those burning eyes and the excitement with which he spoke of the work. But looking back now, there had been something else there, too. It was dangerous. It was bitter. And why not? This place was making me bitter and I'd lived here less than a year. Imagine a whole lifetime. If Jeremy was right, no doubt Issa had his reasons. Everyone always had their reasons. All that mattered now was the project. The people who needed us to get that grant approved. I had to make amends. I had to tell John I'd already assured Jeremy he'd done the budget himself. Tell John he was right about Issa, no need to doubt him and no need to verify anything.

After a little while John walked back through the gates. He looked to see that I was still there and gave a faint, unsure smile. He hung his head and walked over.

"Look, I'm sorry," he said, sitting down. "I shouldn't have been so mad. You don't know Issa like I do."

"Jeremy is an idiot, I shouldn't have listened to him at all," I said.

"No, it's fine. I shouldn't have overreacted. But I just know he wouldn't do something like that." He was obviously still a little shaken by the whole thing.

"Look, I told Jeremy that it was you that had compiled the budget, anyway. He won't know. You trust Issa so I trust him. Let's just forget it all," I said. "You know, to be honest, I wouldn't have even gone to see Jeremy to begin with, but there had been something else I'd needed to ask him about. Of course, he was completely useless."

"What was it?"

"Do you remember my neighbor? The girl that popped by when you were over?"

"Yes, your friend."

"Well, she's pregnant. I know her mother quite well and she came to me before I left to meet you. She asked if there was any way for me to help her."

"Help her?" he asked, and then he understood. "I see. Shit, I'm sorry. That is a tough one."

"I don't know what to do—everyone I talk to says the same thing. It's dangerous, it's illegal. I suppose that's it then."

"You said the mother doesn't want her to have it. What about the girl?"

"She doesn't want to either. She's so smart, John. It would be such a shame. I met the boy too. He seemed like a nice kid. They have all these plans together."

"Yeah." He sighed, giving it some thought. I hoped, by some miracle, he might have another alternative. "It's tough because, at the end of the day, it is illegal, and you don't want to get into any trouble."

"She says she can get 'medicine' from a nurse—"

"I wouldn't bet that he's a nurse."

"I guess there's nothing to be done."

"You know, maybe it isn't so bad. Sure, a lot of girls drop out, but there are exceptions. You could help her, make sure she has a chance. Encourage her and her mother to help her finish."

"I feel like I already let her down."

"What? How?"

"Oh, my stupid club and my stupid talks on family planning. I knew she had a boyfriend. I showed her how to use condoms. I should have insisted she get the shot. Why didn't I? Because we're in Africa and she'll get HIV?

What were the chances of *that* really? It was a horribly racist double standard."

"Look, Lily, you really need to stop carrying the world on your shoulders. She's a dumb teenager. It could happen to anyone. It does. The best thing you can do for her now is to be there for her. Help her figure out a way to make it work so that she still has a chance."

"I suppose if anyone could defy the odds it would be Fati," I said, trying to convince myself.

The next day we resumed our work. Our goal was to finish everything that evening and submit the application. Cynthia had called, saying everyone was heading to Matt's village to celebrate Christmas. Matt lived about an hour and a half northwest of me, so John and I decided to head back north the next morning. John would go directly on to Matt's, but I decided to stay the night in my village and continue on the following day. I wanted to have a chance to speak to Fati again and tell her everything I had discovered, so as to make sure she got any other ideas out of her head. I spent the last day of our work going over everything I'd written for the proposal and John was busy going over the budget one last time before we submitted everything.

It was late into the afternoon and I was sitting on the veranda upstairs when John came up to join me.

"I'm about finished, if you want to look this over while I have another look at the budget. Then we just need to hit send," I said, smiling as he sat down beside me.

"Sure," he said, and we exchanged laptops. He seemed less enthusiastic about it than I had expected, but perhaps he was just tired. It had been a long few days. We sat quietly reviewing one another's work.

"Looks good," he said, closing the laptop.

"I think we're all set! Should we send it then?"

"I'm just waiting for Issa to call me back. I need to ask him a quick question and go over it with him one last time. After dinner, maybe?"

"Okay, and speaking of dinner, I'm starving. Let's have one last celebratory meal at this wonderful place." John agreed, and we went downstairs to order some drinks. As we sat waiting, John was quiet. Something was off with him. I waited for John to bring it up, but he only sat sulking until I couldn't take it anymore.

"Is everything alright?" I asked, after we got our second round of drinks.

"I had to make some calls when I was going over everything with the budget," he said. It was obvious he didn't want to tell me but was slowly realizing he would have to. "You see, there was one part that Issa had down as two different prices. Not a big difference, but I thought I would call and double-check with the supplier." I nodded. "I asked him for a few other prices and, well... See, there are a few discrepancies. They aren't huge, but... I want to ask Issa about it, but he's in Benin visiting family and I can't get through. I thought he was coming back tonight."

"How big are the discrepancies?" I asked.

"Not big. All in all, they can't amount to more than the equivalent of a hundred dollars or so. Not enough to impact the scale of the project or anything like that, but—"

"Maybe the prices went down?"

"Yes, I asked that. They haven't."

"So, you think maybe—"

"I don't know what to think. I just wish I could get a hold of him."

"Perhaps he's in trouble?"

"Maybe. But why wouldn't he come to me? He *knows* he could come to me. I'd help him. He wouldn't have to do something like this."

"Well, we don't know anything for sure and if it isn't that much…"

"Yeah, but if Jeremy finds out, if he decides to double-check the prices, we'd all look bad. You, me and Issa."

"What do we do, then?"

"I think we should wait. Let me see if I can get a hold of him. We have a few days before the deadline. If I could just talk to him …"

"Will he be back before then?"

"I hope so."

"And if not?"

John sighed heavily.

"I don't know, we have to think. We could look for other grants. Maybe fundraise more."

"It would take ages. That's the whole reason you came to me in the first place!" I protested.

"I know. Let's just hope we can work it out over the next few days."

"And what about internet? What if we can't get a good enough connection to send the application? That's half the reason we're here!"

"Look, what can we do?"

"It just seems so stupid. I say to hell with it. Let's just

send it," I argued. John looked at me, smiling.

"It would be very bad for you if Jeremy found out that we knew."

"I don't care!" I said, though I realized how childish I sounded.

"Give it a few days and let's see what we find out," he said calmly. "And thank you."

"For what?"

"For not saying 'I told you so' about Issa. I didn't know how you would react, honestly. I was afraid you might want to forget the whole thing."

"Look, John, I never doubted that, even if it was true, Issa had his reasons. And I never intended for it to stop us from helping all those people. We don't know anything yet, anyway. I'm sure there's an explanation," I said gently. He looked at me and I could see in his eyes, there was something different in the way he looked back at me now.

"Well, I'm going back to the room," he said when we finished. "If we make it to the station by six we can get the early car."

"I'm going to stay here for a while. I need to check some emails," I said.

"Alright. Goodnight Lily," he said wearily.

I ordered another drink and sat for a moment. Fuck it. What were the chances Jeremy would check anything? He was an ass anyway, and it wasn't much money. I opened my laptop.

Jeremy,

Submitting final proposal now, everything we talked about checked out.

I logged on to the website and submitted the application. I took a deep breath. It was done now. I was tired of feeling powerless in the face of it all. The rules. The bureaucracy. Fate itself even. John was being overly cautious. I finished my drink and went back to the room. John was asleep. I would tell him tomorrow.

We arrived at the station at six the next morning. Luckily, we didn't have to wait very long. By seven we were on the road back up north. This time, I was able to sleep a little on the way back. John dozed beside me for most of the way. We were both exhausted. I decided I would wait until I got to Matt's to tell him what I had done. It would be better that way. We were both too tired and emotional to keep dragging it up. We traveled together as far as my village and then John continued alone, heading west of Kabou to Matt's village. I stopped to get some *soja* in town for dinner and bread for the old women on my compound and made it home just before dark.

The old women in the compound greeted me, smiling, as I entered. Brigitte was also there, preparing *fufu*.

"*Bon arriv*ée Lily," she said as the women urged her to relay a message for me. "They want to know, what did you bring them?"

I gave each of the women the loaf of bread I had just bought in town, as it was the custom to bring gifts when one traveled. I wondered if they would be able to tell that it didn't come from Lomé. If they could, they showed no sign of it. They thanked me happily, and I said goodnight and went inside. It didn't take long for news of my arrival to reach Fati and Gladys. I had barely set down my things when Gladys came tapping at the screen.

"Lily! Welcome home!" she said in her thick Ghanaian English. Fati was with her.

"*Bonne arrivée*," she said as she entered. I noticed that they did not bring the boys with them. I presented Gladys with a pineapple I had bought at the station in Lomé. Pineapples were scarce in the north.

"Thank you," Gladys said, giving a slight bow as she accepted the gift. I waited a moment, unsure if I should speak first about what they had come here to discuss. I invited them to sit down and they both took a seat at my little wooden table, but neither of them spoke. I would begin. I wished I had better news for them.

"How are you?" I asked, first addressing Fati in French.

"*Bien*," she said.

"I'm sorry," I said in English to Gladys. "I have been asking people, people I work with, people in Lomé, if they know of any way we could safely do what it is you asked me about. But they said it is not possible. They don't know of a way, because it is illegal, and they would be in trouble with your government if they helped people." Fati understood; I could see the light fade from her eyes.

"But the medicine? She can take the medicine," Gladys said.

"I asked them about that as well. The problem is, even if it is actual, legitimate pills you have to know exactly how long she has been pregnant. If it is more than two months, it could be dangerous."

"*Oui*," Fati jumped in in French. "But I know a girl who was four months pregnant, and she took something and she was fine. It worked for her," she said excitedly.

"But there is no way to know if there will be complications or not," I said in frustration. "You could die!" I was almost shouting. I wanted to scare her, I wanted them both to understand. "Girls die every day from this sort of things. Some might be okay, but many are not. It isn't worth your life, Fati!" I looked at Gladys and she remained silent, looking at the ground. "I want to help. I don't think it's wrong. In my country it's legal and safe," I explained. "But here, it is just too dangerous."

"Thank you, for trying to help us," Gladys said finally. There was a sad resignation in her.

"But she can still finish the school year," I said. "Talk to Kpante. Perhaps, together, we can all find a way for Fati to finish school next year. After the new year, when the *infirmier* is back, we will go to the *dispensaire* together, to the prenatal clinic." They looked at me, both still lost in their own disappointment. It would take time. But I would not give up and neither would they. They weren't the type. "But please, promise me, you will not do anything dangerous?"

"No, you are right. She will not take the medicine, it is too dangerous," Gladys nodded and Fati only looked at the ground. "We must go. You are tired. You must rest."

"I'm sorry," I repeated, quietly.

"Goodnight, Lily," Gladys said, and they were gone.

Chapter Eleven

It was Christmas Eve, but it didn't feel like it in the blinding heat. It didn't feel like anything anymore. I'd completely lost my sentimentality over seasons. I arrived in Matt's village around three. My moto driver, Mubarak, had made the journey with Cynthia before and knew the way. Matt's village reminded me of some of the places we had seen on our pump visits, a small scattering of mud huts and thatched roofs along a dusty dirt road. It was apparent from the lack of power lines there was no electricity. When we rounded the corner outside Matt's compound, a few small children in tattered clothes emerged to carry my bags and helmet.

Inside the compound, a cement courtyard was littered with mangy dogs lying in what little shade they could find. There was a woman and two young girls washing laundry and they smiled at me when I entered, but did not speak. There were some chairs set up outside, covered in issues of *The Economist* and *National Geographic*. I had to be in the right place, but the others were obviously off somewhere. I glanced around helplessly as the children shouted. Soon, a tall, thin, middle-aged man in a button-up *pagne* shirt appeared from the darkness of one of the rooms. Smiling brightly, he came toward me.

"*Bonne arrivée!*" he said, reaching his hand out to shake mine. "You are a friend of Matthieu's? I am Peter, he lives here with my family. Welcome!"

"Hello," I said. "I'm Lily."

"Matthieu said you would be arriving soon. My uncle lives just two villages away from you! Maybe you know him?"

"Maybe," I said waiting for him to elaborate, but he said no more.

"Your friends are at the boutique. This child will take you. Please, you can put the rest of the things inside there," he said pointing to the set of rooms I assumed to be Matt's. I thanked Peter and set my backpack on the cot inside the door. The rooms were dark, with little light coming through the tiny windows. There was one room with a cot and a kitchen, and another separated by a curtain, just big enough for a bed. Where was everyone going to sleep? I went back out to where the child waited and followed him outside the compound.

As we neared the boutique, the sound of American voices grew louder. Once we rounded the corner there sat Cynthia, Matt, Anna and John around a wooden table, shaded by the awning of the boutique. The table was covered with beer bottles, empty bottles of Sport Actif, tonic water and a half-full bottle of gin. Cynthia was the first to spot me.

"*Bonne arrivée!*" she cried, and the rest of them echoed her greeting. There were two Togolese men next to Matt that I didn't recognize. One of them got up to fetch me an extra chair.

"This is my neighbor, Jacques," Matt introduced us, and I shook hands with Jacques. "This is Martin, he teaches with me at the school."

"Someone get this girl a drink," Anna said, ringing the bell to get the attention of whomever was inside. A young man came out, seemingly overwhelmed by the presence of so many foreigners. I waved him over and asked for a beer.

"They have a generator, but … Well, it might be cold," Matt explained.

"As usual it looks like I have some catching up to do," I said. John smiled at me when our eyes met, the sort of smile that signified a connection apart from the others. I still had to tell him what I had done. I wondered if he had spoken to Issa yet.

"So, tell me again, what happens once you have the chicken?" Anna said, picking up a conversation that had begun before my arrival.

"We offer the chicken to the fetish. It's sacrificed and then, depending on how much it flaps around once its throat has been slit, we see if things will go our way or not," Matt said.

"Do we want it to flap?"

"Yes," Matt said.

"And then they'll scar you?"

"Yes."

"Why again?"

"It's for protection," he nodded.

"Wait, what's going on?" I asked.

"Matt is going to be scarred tonight," Anna said. "And maybe Cynthia. We'll see how many more shots of gin she has. Apparently, it's for protection, but to me it seems a bit counter-intuitive."

"Jacques is a *féticheur*," Matt explained. "He'll perform the ceremony for us. He's been offering to do it for me for a while and he thought it would be good to do it today because it's a holy day for us, in our culture. Good luck, you see." I nodded.

"Can we all attend the ceremony?"

"I believe so." He turned and asked Jacques, who nodded enthusiastically.

"How does one become a *féticheur*?" Anna asked, as if she was enquiring how one might go about becoming a doctor or a teacher.

"It runs in the family, I believe," Matt said, looking to Jacques for confirmation.

"*Oui*," Jacques said. "When I was very young, my uncle, he was a *féticheur* and he recognized the spirit in me. It is passed down through each generation, but you do not know who it will be. You must wait to see."

"And did you study it, then?" Anna asked.

"*Oui*, with my uncle. When it was time, I went to the forest to choose my fetish, or, to have my fetish choose me," he said smiling.

"And how does it choose you, then?"

"It is difficult to explain," Jacques said, sitting back, reflecting seriously. "It is like an energy. You are drawn to it from within you." Fati had an uncle who was a *féticheur* but I had never met him. Never actually seen a holy man in the flesh before. I studied Jacques's face to see if I could find a hint of what made him so different. There was something in his eyes now, as he spoke. Of course, it would be in the eyes. His eyes were of a different sort. I'd seen them once or twice before in others. That sad, strange melancholy. The effect stayed with you, the essence of the person stayed with you long after you had known them. It was sometimes difficult to know exactly what it was that made them stand out in your memory, but still you remembered them. Suddenly, I was aware of the weight of another pair of eyes on me, and I glanced over to John who was watching me watching Jacques. I blushed. He was smirking, shaking his head at me, as if he could read my thoughts and was laughing at me because he knew how badly I wanted to believe in the old mystic.

"We should go, then?" Matt asked.

"Whenever you wish," Jacques said. We followed Jacques and Martin along a small path that ran through some woods, leading to a compound. It was separate from the others, in a clearing. Peter was there, waiting to join us for the ceremony. Inside, Jacques introduced us to his wife. There were a few children running about who came to greet us with curiosity. They were familiar with Matt, but the rest of us seemed too much for them and they kept a safe, but happy, distance.

Jacques showed us inside one of the clay rooms. It was dark and musty, with a distinct smell hanging in the thick, humid air. It smelled of earth or sweat. A tiny sliver of light came through the small door, just enough so that we could see the walls, adorned with strange objects. Ropes, feathers and pictures were placed like a shrine surrounding a large rock covered in paint. The fetish.

We sat in a circle and Jacques took his place beside the fetish. He spoke to it in Kotokoli and he offered it some gin, pouring a small amount over the rock. Then he passed around a cup for all of us to drink from. Its unpleasant, astringent taste was only amplified by the heat as it burned our throats. But we drank it anyway and then again as Jacques passed the cup around a second time. While we drank, he prepared the charcoal, which was then distributed to us on a small slab of rock. Peter showed us that we were meant to taste it, putting a small amount in his mouth and encouraging us to follow him and do the same. I had never tasted charcoal before but if I had been asked to imagine its taste I think it would have been something like that: dull and bitter.

Jacques called out into the courtyard and one of the children appeared outside the door with the chicken. Jacques held the chicken over the fetish, said a few incoherent words and then, with a swift flick of the knife, a bright splash of red spurted from its neck. I understood then that the fetish was not covered in paint. Jacques threw the chicken to the ground as he, Martin and Peter yelled and clapped, trying to make sure the chicken fought violently against its fate. It flapped wildly, spurting blood, and the bright red liquid covered the bare skin of my feet. That was it, the smell that had been so overpowering at first. It was blood. Old dried blood.

Finally, the poor animal settled into its uneasy death. Jacques looked happily up at Matt. The fetish had accepted his offering. John was looking over at me from across the room. This time he looked away when my eyes caught his. Jacques motioned for us to step outside to complete the ceremony. I gasped as we emerged, welcoming the fresh evening air outside the stuffy dark hut. Jacques called Matt forward and Matt, understanding the signal, retrieved the small packet of freshly bought razor blades from his pocket. Jacques examined the pack, choosing one, then, holding Matt's wrist, he made three quick slits on the outside, rubbing the crushed-up charcoal into each fresh cut. He repeated the motion on the other wrist then again on the inside of Matt's forearm. When he was finished, Peter and Martin came forward and gave Matt a pat on the back.

Back at Matt's, there were chairs set up all around the middle of the compound. John had claimed the seat next to mine. I poured some wine and passed the cups around. The young girls passed out plates of rice topped with tomato sauce the same shade of red as the liquid that had spurted out of the chicken onto my feet.

It was dark now. We all ate, but neither Peter's wife nor the children joined us. They ate separately near the fire that had been used to cook the rice, where they'd been washing clothes earlier. Everyone was talking excitedly about various things in various languages. John was speaking with Martin, who was sat on the other side of him. Anna, sat on my other side, was busy with Cynthia, recounting the events as if they were discussing scenes from a movie they had just seen. Matt was taken up by Peter and Jacques as they admired his new scars.

"Well, that was a new sort of Christmas tradition," John said, turning to me.

"I'd say so."

"Did you speak to Fati?"

"I did."

"How did it go?"

"Oh, you know," I sighed. "I don't think she was too happy with me, but I told her I would help her and that we would try to find a way for her to finish school."

"You did the right thing. Just give her time."

"Lily, did you bring more wine?" Cynthia called to me, waving an empty box. I smiled at John.

"If you'll excuse me," I said.

As I made my way back inside, I paused for a moment. Just beyond the clay wall that surrounded the compound I could see the moon illuminating the huts, casting a blue-silver streak through the fields. There was no other light for miles. I walked over to look out into the night. It was like a painting and I wished there was a way I could capture it and keep it with me always to look at when I needed to remember nights such as this. Above me the sky was an explosion of tiny specks of light. Was it true what they said? Were we really made up of all that? The marrow in my bones and those embers burning violently up there in space, could they really be the same thing?

"Incredible, isn't it." I jumped. John was standing next to me. "Sorry."

"Did you manage to speak to Issa?"

"No, not yet. I'll keep trying, though."

"I have to tell you something. I did something. You see ..."

"You did something?"

"I—well, I may have already submitted our proposal."

"You submitted it?" he repeated.

"Yes, I just thought to hell with it. Jeremy won't know. I'm sure if there is anything to it, Issa had his reasons. You trust him, and I trust you, so to hell with it."

"Lily," John said, smiling at me. He looked as though he wanted to speak but he shook his head and laughed. He had that strange look in his eyes, the look I had caught so many times already that day. "Lily," he repeated again, leaning toward me, his hand on my face. Suddenly, his mouth was covering mine and it happened as naturally as if it had happened a thousand times before and would happen a thousand times again. But my heart, my heart knew that something was different and it leapt into my throat as I kissed him back, helplessly and happily. After a few moments I pulled away.

"We'd better go back," I said. "They'll drink all the wine."

John laughed.

"Alright," he said, pulling me toward him one more time. We kissed again and then we returned to the others, contented with our new secret.

After dinner, someone brought out a battery-operated radio. The compound quickly filled with more and more children. We sat and watched as they danced, pulling us up from time to time, beckoning us to join them. Somewhere around eleven, Cynthia went inside to sleep. Slowly the children disappeared and Martin and Jacques said their goodbyes not long after. Anna, Matt, John and I sat up with Peter for a little while longer. Peter had brought out another bottle of gin and Matt had retrieved a book on stargazing from inside. We sat, poring over it with a flashlight, trying to match the images from the book to those in the sky. The gin made it an easier task.

"I have some extra cots," Matt said, when he noticed that Anna had begun to doze off in one of the chairs.

"I may recommend bringing them outside, though, as it's pretty cramped in there." John went in to help Matt bring out the cots along with some extra *pagne* to use as blankets. Anna woke up and said she was too cold to sleep outside so she went in with Matt.

"Finally," John sighed once they had disappeared inside. "Do you think we can squeeze onto one cot?"

"Not for very long," I laughed.

"Just for a minute, then," he said and held out his arms for me to join him. "It was very sad for me, when I arrived here without you yesterday. Something was missing and at first, I wasn't sure what it was. Then I realized, Lily isn't here, and it all made sense."

I said nothing as he ran his hand through my hair. It wasn't long before we both drifted off to sleep.

I awoke before dawn and crawled back into my own cot. I was awake, wide awake, and I lay there, watching the night sky fade into early morning light. It wasn't long after dawn when the women awoke and I could hear them from across the compound, sweeping with their twig brooms and starting a fire to heat water. John was still fast asleep on the cot beside me. I waited and listened as the noises increased and more voices could be heard, and footsteps and movements, as the sun grew in strength and light. A groan came from inside. Slowly Cynthia wobbled out.

"My God, it's hot in there," she said, seeing that I was awake and rubbing her eyes to adjust to the sun. "You guys had the right idea."

"Merry Christmas!" I said cheerfully, remembering what day it was.

"Yes, merry Christmas," she said with less enthusiasm. "Say, what's the plan for the day? I think we may have drunk Matt's village dry. I thought, it being market day and all, everyone might want to head back to my place and we can cook a nice Christmas dinner there?"

"I'd be alright with that," John said, awake now.

"I'd also kill to sleep somewhere with electricity and a fan," Cynthia said, leaning back in her chair. It wasn't long before Matt and Anna appeared groggily, and Cynthia informed them of the new plan to which they happily agreed. Peter still had yet to appear from his set of rooms, but his wife and children were busy reheating the rice and sauce from the previous night. They offered us each a plate. As we were eating, John's phone buzzed. I tried to listen in casually, but he walked away so I couldn't make anything out.

"Hey, Lil," Matt said, sitting down next to me after breakfast was finished and I waited for my turn to shower, flipping through a three-month-old issue of *The Economist*. "Can I ask you something?"

"Sure," I said.

"You do a lot of work with young girls, don't you? At the school in your village?"

"Yeah, some. I have a health club there."

"I have a favor to ask you," he said. It was rare that Matt should look so serious. I set down the magazine and waited for him to continue. "There's a girl in one of my classes. I'm fairly certain she's pregnant. Another student said something about it and I've been keeping an eye on her and it's becoming pretty noticeable."

"How old is she?"

"Oh, I'd say fifteen, sixteen maybe. It's hard to say."

"Do you know if she's spoken to anyone?"

"Well, I know her family pretty well. Her father is Peter's cousin. I mentioned it to Peter, and he said that no one in the family's said anything—but he's noticed too. It's kind of strange. I don't know if they're waiting for her to say something or what. But I know there are things she should do at the *dispensaire* here. They do check-ups and that sort of thing, don't they? For pregnant women?"

"Yes, women are meant to have a blood test; wherever your nearest hospital is, she could go there. And at the *dispensaire* in my village, they do monthly prenatal check-ups. It is good to do, especially being so young."

"Right. The thing is, I don't really feel it's my place to talk to her, you know?"

"You could try, but I know what you mean. It might be very awkward for her, coming from you."

"Yeah, exactly. I was talking to Peter and I mentioned the work you do. We thought maybe you could speak to her? Explain things. What she needs to do. Peter and I want to help with the cost for any medical needs she has. I mean, I would hate for them to use it as an excuse for her to drop out. I'll talk to her family about continuing school, but…"

"Yeah, I would be happy to talk to her," I said. "I could come back next week."

"Well, I thought maybe you could speak to her now."

"Now?"

"Yes, Peter could go get her and bring her here. You could just have a quick word with her."

"Right. I guess so. Sure," I said. "She's a student of yours at the CEG?"

"Yes, she's repeating *troisième* again this year, so I've known her for a while now." I nodded. "Great. Well, I'll let Peter know. I really appreciate it."

"No problem."

Peter, who had stumbled from his rooms only moments before, nodded happily in my direction as Matt gave him the okay to go and bring the girl here. I thought of Fati. Would she ask me how to handle things that way as well? It sounded like the time for that had long since passed. Soon Peter appeared with a timid-looking young girl trailing wearily, yet obediently, behind him. Matt went up to greet her. I waited. He was motioning toward me. I smiled in their direction and Matt waved me over.

"This is Nunna," he said. "I told her about you, the work you do in your village." He was speaking French to include the girl but she looked down, only briefly meeting my eyes as she said *bonjour*. "We can set up some chairs over here," Matt said, switching to English and motioning to a quiet corner of the compound. I led the girl over as Matt went to fetch some chairs. We stood for a moment. How to begin exactly?

"So, Matt has told you of my work, then?" She nodded, still refusing to meet my gaze. Matt appeared with the chairs and then took leave of us, muttering words of thanks to me. "*Tu es enceinte?*" I blurted out the words. She looked up at me now as if seeing me for the first time and then her eyes returned quickly to the ground. She nodded again. "Does your family know?"

"*Je ne sais pas,*" she said, her voice soft, without conviction. I don't know.

"For how many months? Do you know?"

"*Cinq mois.*" She said it as if it was a question more than an answer.

"Have you been to the *dispensaire*? Have you seen anyone yet?" She shook her head. "You know, when you are pregnant, it is very important to go to see the *infirmier*. It is important to keep you and your baby safe. You must go soon, there are tests to make sure you and the baby stay healthy."

"*L'argent,*" she said.

"I think Monsieur Matthieu and Monsieur Peter will help with that. They are worried about you. They want to help you. They want you to finish school." At this she looked at me and there was a flash of Fati in the look she gave me. It said, *silly woman—how little you know*.

"*Ça ne marche pas,*" she said. It does not work.

"*L'école?*" I asked.

"*Oui,* for girls it doesn't work." I stopped for a moment. This went against every instinct I had. No, no, no. Education above all else. But here she was, sixteen maybe. She had been repeating the equivalent of fifth grade for two years now.

"You don't want to finish school?" I asked her, trying to convey my sympathy and not to sound accusing.

"*Non,*" she said, eyes in the dirt.

"What will you do, then?"

"I will go live with the father and his family," she said. "We will be married. We will farm, like my family does."

"And that is what you want?" I asked. She looked up at me as if it was a foolish question.

"*Oui, bien sur.*" She nodded anxiously.

"Well, you still must be sure to go to the *dispensaire*. I will speak with Monsieur Matthieu and Monsieur Peter. Don't worry about the money."

"How did it go?" Matt asked once she had left. I told him everything. He didn't say much. He'd already known how it would go. But he thanked me again and then went off to arrange for drivers to take us all into to town.

When we heard the sound of the engines outside the compound, we thanked Peter and his wife profusely for being such marvelous hosts, bowing our goodbyes to show our gratitude.

"Lily and I are going to stop off in Kabou on the way," John said as we all boarded our motos. We'll catch up with you there." I looked at him curiously and mouthed Issa's name. He nodded as we took off.

"He insisted you come too," John informed me once we reached the station in Kabou.

"I see."

"We're meeting him at the café behind the station. He was pretty upset about it all. He said he wanted to explain to both of us." The café was mostly empty and we spotted Issa, alone, as we entered the wooden gate.

"*Joyeux Noël,*" Issa said, as we approached. "Thank you for coming. I'm sorry to interrupt your celebrations but I wanted to see you both, to explain in person."

We sat down and Issa insisted on buying us both drinks. His demeanor was more reserved than normal but not overtly so. He didn't appear as you might expect someone in his position to: like a criminal caught in the act, full of apologies and exaggerated remorse.

"You see, several years ago, before John came here, there was another American working here and he put me into contact with someone from your organization," he said, looking to me. "The man wanted to build latrines for a village just north of Kara. It was a big project and I was happy to help him. The only problem was, he couldn't pay very much with the limited funding, but that was fine. I really wanted to help. He needed me to coordinate with the locals and the suppliers. Much like we are doing now, with this project. But then, as the project went on, he relied on me and my team more and more to transport materials and we were using our own motos. Every day for weeks going hundreds of miles, carrying heavy materials. He gave us money for the gas but it was only just enough. Then I had an accident. My moto crashed on my way to the site. I was in the hospital for a week. It wasn't bad, I was lucky. But I couldn't work and my moto was wrecked. Basically, he said sorry, but you can't work so you don't get paid. After everything I had done ..." He shook his head and shrugged at the audacity of it. "I asked him if maybe we could use some of the funding for repairs for my bike. I had bills from the hospital, not much, but it was difficult. He said it was against the rules.

"So, the project went on and they had some difficulties. They ended up needing another round of funding. He asked me to help again, to make a budget, and he put me in charge of coordinating with the suppliers and ordering the materials. I did what I had to do. I knew the amount I took, it wouldn't impact the project. It would be just enough to pay for the repairs of my moto. It seemed fair to me at the time."

"I see. I understand. But now? Why did you keep doing it?" John asked.

"You see, Naapoo, he needed some very expensive parts. If he didn't have a moto you would find someone else. He needs the money. His wife is sick and he would like to take her to see a doctor in Lomé. But it is expensive."

"But you're my friend," John said. "You could have told me. I would have found a way."

"You are right, John," Issa said. "I should have told you. I suppose I just thought it would be easier. It wasn't enough to affect the project. Just enough to help Naapoo. But still it was wrong. I hope I haven't put our project at risk."

"It sounds like whoever you were working with before was a real asshole," John said. It was obviously a good enough explanation for him. I wasn't as convinced it was all as altruistic as Issa had made it sound. But either way, what did it matter if he profited a bit? Why shouldn't he? Because someone in New York or D.C. thought you'd be able to find people to break their backs for next to nothing?

"Well, everything's been submitted. I don't think it should be a problem," I said.

"If it is I take full responsibility," Issa said. "I don't want anyone to get into any trouble for my actions."

"I don't think it will be an issue," John said. "But does Naapoo have enough to fix his bike? I'm sure we could find a way, if he needed more."

"I think it will be enough. Thank you both, for

understanding," he said. He meant it in a way I'm not sure John understood. I smiled. "Well, I don't want to keep you, you must go! Celebrate your *fête!*"

"Would you like to join us?" John offered.

"Thank you, but I'm still making my way back from Benin. It has been a long journey. I just want to go home and sleep."

"Alright then, safe travels," John said as we all stood and shook hands.

"*À vous aussi.*"

"You believe him then?" I asked once Issa was gone.

"Don't you?" John asked. His expression and tone made the question an obvious test.

"I guess, sure. I don't see why I shouldn't," I said. I had learned it was a line not worth crossing with John.

Back at Cynthia's place the celebration had continued on in full swing without us. They had decided to prepare a makeshift Tex-Mex sort of meal using beans, fried tortillas, taco seasoning Cynthia had brought back from her last trip to the States and Laughing Cow cheese. I trusted they knew what they were doing. Anna and Cynthia were just beginning to fry the tortillas and the whole house smelled of oil, like an old Chinese take-out. I should call home. What time was it there? Had they done presents yet or were they just arriving at my grandmother's? It all seemed so far away. Perhaps this was more of a home now than anything I would find back there.

Chapter Twelve

Detroit
April 15thh, 2011

I had too much time on my hands, or too little depending on how you looked at things. I signaled to the waitress to refill my coffee and lit a cigarette. They said that in another month you wouldn't be able to smoke in here anymore. It was desperately hard to imagine a Coney Island without a smoking section. The waitress came with the coffee and discreetly put the check on the table. I understood the gesture. Even my time here was running out. The lunch crowd would soon begin to slowly trickle in and she didn't want to miss out on tips from patrons that required more nourishment than someone who subsisted solely on coffee and cigarettes.

It was a little after noon. Since finishing work, I'd spent the last week checking things off my unwritten list of people to see and places to visit before I left. Yet, despite my limited time to accomplish everything, I still found myself with an overabundance of hours each day to be filled. Hours when most people are busy with work or other responsibilities. A few students and workmen trickled in with the increasingly frequent jingling of the door. I put away my books and pulled out the newspaper I had picked up on the way downtown. It was full of the usual things. Sports news, another school closing down, analysis of a month-old census, and concern that the city's population had plummeted by twenty-five percent over the last ten years. I put the paper away. More and more patrons paraded through the door. It would be the perfect afternoon to pay my last visit to the Detroit Institute of Arts for a while. When I was a student I used to go between classes sometimes, and recent encounters had renewed my interest in art. I paid my tab and left a decent tip for the waitress.

Outside, the sun was bright but the air still had a bite to it, retaining the cool freshness of early spring. It made my mind somewhat clearer as I walked the block or so down Woodward and across the outskirts of the university campus to the museum. I paid the twelve dollars and wandered on with no direct intention. Since it was a weekday afternoon, the museum was empty and quiet with only the distant sound of footsteps echoing off the cold marble walls. The bottom floor was home to the ancient ruins of Egypt and other less well-remembered civilizations. But the remnants of desecrated tombs and lives no longer lived seemed too harsh for me today. I wasn't very eager to be reminded about the impermanence of things. On the second level, I wandered through the Renaissance until, at last, I was with the Romantics and the Impressionists and the Post-Impressionists and Pre-Modernists and whatever else they were cataloged as.

Alone with Picasso and his blue lady, and my favorite, Gervex's *Café Scene in Paris*. Why did I like them the best? Just enough smoke and mirrors. Not so much that you didn't know what it was you were looking at but just enough so that it was too beautiful to find in it real life. Was this the way to ensure immortality, then? To know it wasn't all in vain. To wind up here in a frame or, maybe, in a book on shelf somewhere? There was something else, though. Something more noble than just trying to achieve permanence, something more than wanting to be remembered. What was it? A bit of truth perhaps. You could write it in a few lines on paper or replicate it as best you could with a few strokes of paint on a canvas. A truth that unites us, a beauty that ties us all together, whether you find it in a bowl of oranges or a poem by Keats. I was always searching for it. I looked for it in everything and everyone. Sometimes I found it so elusive and sometimes it came to me plain as day. When it came like that, it overwhelmed me.

I'd found it that night in Jack's paintings. He said he didn't mind so much what became of them once he handed them off. Did he really mean that? I had meant what I said: his paintings were beautiful. I could easily imagine them hanging here beside the others. Had I meant anything else that night? If I had found him months ago ... No, that wasn't true. If I had met him months ago I would not have been who I was that night. Still, I felt a bit guilty about it all. It was no excuse to have left his calls unanswered and unreturned. If he called again I would answer. I silently promised myself that as I stared up at the closest thing I could find to immortality.

When I finished at the museum, it was late into the afternoon. I was supposed to meet Sonia that evening.

The plan was we would go see her roommate Paul's band play a show in Hamtramck then head back downtown for an art exhibit. The exhibit was being held at what once had been an old automobile factory and was now slowly being taken over by artists' studios and gallery spaces. It was the sort of thing we always did, but tonight would be different because it would be the last time for who knew how long.

When I arrived at Sonia's place, she was just getting in from work.

"So what do you want to do? Grab a drink somewhere first? A bite to eat?"

"I have some vodka here if you want. I need to roll a joint before I do anything," she said, sitting down at the coffee table and opening the tin can that contained the rolling papers and pot. The house seemed empty.

"Is Paul in?"

"No."

"Well, we could go to the Stick again first. We have lots of time to kill before anything really gets going."

"Sure, if you want. It's your night after all," she said, but the tone didn't match the sentiment. Something was off. There was something in her voice, the way she said hello, offered me a drink. It was all perfectly normal and yet there was a hostility behind it that I wasn't quite sure what I had done to deserve. Perhaps she was just tired; it took a while for the day to wear off her. Hopefully that was all it was and after an hour or so she would perk up.

"Alright then, that's what we'll do. Might as well enjoy the sunshine while we've got it." I said, trying to be patient and wait it out.

It was still early and the bar was empty so we sat at some tables outside because it was just warm enough to get away with it.

"Cheers," Sonia said and I raised my glass.

"Cheers."

We sat with our drinks and I tried to think of something to say to lighten the mood. Everything eluded me. Sonia stared out at Woodward Avenue. The sidewalks were empty. There was only the constant swishing of cars past the ever-changing streetlights. Green, yellow, red, green again. The howl of the engines. I couldn't bear it anymore.

"What is it? What's going on with you? It feels like you're mad at me and I have no idea why."

"You want me to be honest with you?" she said, looking at me from behind her big orange sunglasses.

"Of course, why else would I have asked?" I waited as she lit a cigarette between her pursed red lips.

"I think you're making a mistake, Lil," she said with a directness I hadn't expected.

"And why on earth would you think that?"

"I think you're running away."

"Running away from what?" Now I was angry and I didn't care to hide it.

"You know, you like to go on about how sick of everything you are. But you don't *really* hate it here. You just like to think you do because then it makes you better than everyone else. You'll miss it. Trust me."

"Oh come on," I laughed. "That's not why I think I'm better than everyone else," I said, trying to make light of it. I didn't want to go down this road. "And give me a break, you think you're better than everyone else too. Just because I'll miss it doesn't mean I'm making a mistake."

"I'm being serious."

"Okay then. Fine. Why is it a mistake? What exactly am I running away from? You still haven't explained that part."

"I don't know exactly." I sighed loudly in frustration. "No, look, I think maybe it's a lot of things. You're having trouble with your poems. Your grandmother—"

"If you can't be supportive of me—"

"I am supportive. That's why I'm telling you this. You want more. You want excitement. And to a point, I get it. I think you want to get out. I think you should. But it just seems so sudden. Maybe there'll be a better opportunity through the paper or another paper. Something that advances your career a bit more. This just seems so extreme."

"So what you're saying is, you think I'm supposed to play the game. Wait for my turn. But I'm sick of sitting around and waiting for things to happen. You know, when I was younger, I always imagined that I wouldn't be like other people, that my life would be an adventure—"

"Oh come on, Lil! You don't think I'd like to take off, say fuck all this? I want excitement? I want an adventure? I mean, do you think I like being a shop assistant at some stupidly overpriced boutique and having to dress all these uppity assholes that come in every day? No. Of course not. And sure, I think about it too. Packing up and taking off. But then I realize, you know what? Life isn't exciting. Life isn't an adventure. Life is boring. You need to grow up, Lil. We're not nineteen anymore. The kind of life you're looking for isn't real. You're chasing phantoms. And sure, maybe it's fine for now. But in another five, ten years? What happens then? When you've thrown away your career? It's not so cute anymore."

I was quiet for a minute.

"I disagree," I said, finally. "I think you and I have a fundamentally different view on life. If that's how you feel."

"How so?"

"I don't agree that life has to be so miserable and boring. I think people settle for that sort of life because in some ways it's easier to be miserable and bored than it is to do anything about it. Do you think it's easy for me to go? To leave everything and everyone I know? Don't you think I'm terrified?"

"I don't know. Doesn't seem like it."

"Well I am." I was almost shaking. "Can I be honest with you now?"

She nodded.

"I think maybe you feel guilty for wanting to stay here. Or, maybe, even that I judge you for it. But I don't. I think if you're so miserable and bored all the time you should do something about it. If you aren't, well, I don't think there's anything wrong with being happy here either. But Sonia, the thing is, I'm not happy here. I never have been. And it's got nothing to do with anyone but me. Maybe you're right. Maybe I'll come back a huge, enormous failure. But you know what, I'd rather that happened than spend the rest of my life wondering what if? What if I'd done it? Taken the risk? And you know what? It may not seem like it but it is terrifying. I'm scared as hell that you might be right. I'm leaving a good job, people I love, all for nothing. So, what I need from you right now, as my best friend, is not to doubt me. Because I'm doing that enough already."

"Alright Lil," she said as she stamped out her cigarette on the iron railing. "I'm sorry."

"Me too. Look, I didn't want to get into it with you. I just wanted tonight to be—"

"We should go. We'll be late."

We drove to the bar in silence. When we pulled up outside the Painted Lady, the narrow streets that surrounded it were lined with cars. It looked like a full house. As soon as we entered, Sonia spotted Paul by the bar.

"You made it," he said, giving us each a quick embrace.

"Of course," Sonia said. "It's busy tonight."

"Yeah, the first band was pretty shit. You didn't miss much. We don't go on for another hour. Thanks for coming out. Let me get you guys a drink and then I'll show you where everyone is sitting."

Paul, Sonia's roommate, had been a good friend of hers for years. I'd always got the impression he would have liked to have been more, but she never let on that she felt anything but friendship for him. He guided us to a large table in the back, full of people I was mildly acquainted with. Another band had taken the stage, making it difficult to hear much of anything that wasn't being said directly to me. But it hadn't stopped Sonia. She was busy making her way into conversations that had begun long before our arrival. I was always envious of her ability to effortlessly belong to any situation she was placed in. I pretended to pay attention to what was going on around me. It was a familiar scene and it was funny the things that it both lost and gained with the knowledge of its impermanence in my life. Across the table, Sonia was making gestures in my direction. I assumed she was referring to my impending departure. She was talking to a young man in thick-rimmed glasses. I was certain I'd met him before, but I couldn't remember where or when.

"Sonia said you're leaving for Africa," the young man yelled in my direction from across the table. I was stuck. I nodded.

"Togo, to be exact." Africa could mean so many things. He asked a few more of the usual questions and I gave short, polite justifications of myself, and then he asked a question that annoyed me more than usual. "Why not just stay here and help?" He added, "This city's as bad as a third world country." Sure, it was partly a joke but one I had heard before.

"Because most places in Africa have more hope than this city," I joked back.

"That's terrible," he laughed.

"I'm only kidding," I assured him. The strum of guitars warming up took over the sound system and ended our conversation, and we made our way to the stage area to watch the band. I was still distracted by his question. And Sonia's questioning earlier. For too long I'd stayed in this city, tried to convey its struggles, to make sense of its plight. It was my turn now to make sense of my own. To save myself.

"Should we head off to the Russell, then?" Sonia asked me when the music stopped. "It will take them a while.

We can go on ahead."

"Maybe you should just go, I'm a bit tired."

"Oh come on, Lil. Please don't be angry at me for earlier."

"I'm not. I'm just tired."

"Hey, let's forget it, please? I'm sorry. I support you, okay? It's gonna be great for you. I know it. This is it, come on! You can't bail on me now."

"Okay. Fine."

I followed her out.

The factory was a massive old site. While some serious work had been done to transform it into a gallery space, it still retained an emotionless, industrial feel. The cold cement hall was wall to wall with people, with strange installations, sculptures and paintings scattered throughout. As soon as we entered the room, I wished I hadn't come. There was a band playing in the corner, some sort of psychedelic funk. I wasn't quite sure at what point Sonia was no longer at my side but suddenly I turned and there was no sign of her anywhere. Had she done it on purpose? I tried to push that idea out of my head, to find something to distract me. There was nothing. The music would have to be enough so I made my way to the back corner to get a better listen. I stood for a moment, a small crowd of bobbing heads in front of me. I felt a tap on my shoulder and turned to see a young woman with short black hair smiling insincerely.

"Excuse me, but would you mind standing over there? You're blocking my piece." I turned to see a tattered old backpack overflowing with crumpled and torn pieces of paper and pens. I'd assumed it had been left there by someone accidentally. When she failed to laugh or give way in the least, I realized she was serious. I offered a quick, confused apology and pushed my way to the side.

There was nowhere else to stand near the music, so I gave up and started to look for Sonia again. I was hoping she wouldn't mind going somewhere else, anywhere but this dystopian nightmare of an exhibition. Everything about this place was worse than even I could have anticipated. I was trying not to sulk about it but my annoyance was turning into anger as I stumbled through the crowd, weaving in and out of what little space I could find in the overcrowded mess of it all. I tried to find another empty corner to call her from but when I dialed it only rang unanswered. There was no way she would hear her phone here, anyway, above the noise.

I decided to go check down around the entrance area where people had gathered, drinking from brown paper bags and smoking cigarettes near the parking lot. I walked quickly down a flight of old metallic steps and out the heavy glass doors. There was no sign of her there, or anyone else I might recognize for that matter. I sat down on the concrete steps and lit a cigarette in defeat. This was not my scene. As much as I had entertained the idea that I had held some small place in it, I couldn't pretend anymore. There was something unsettling about it. The disorder of it all. It represented no more than a loss of meaning. I found it frightening. It made me think about a piece I had written a few months earlier for the paper on the need to attract a new 'creative class' to the city. At the time it was just one of those lovely little buzzwords invented by academics. What cities like this needed was to attract the young 'creative class' to come and breathe life into desolate old places like this. Was this what they meant by life? I sat there alone with my cigarette in silent protest against all of it, especially how the whole evening was winding up. Nothing had gone the way I wanted it to. Perhaps it was for the best. Perhaps it made it all a little easier to say goodbye.

Someone had taken their place beside me on the steps, uncomfortably invading my personal space. I turned to demonstrate my displeasure but my scowl was unexpectedly met with a familiar set of eyes.

"So, do you come around here often?"

My heart stopped. I froze.

"Oh. Hello," I fumbled awkwardly. It was Jack. Of course it was Jack. Jack whom I had avoided for the past week, whose phone calls I had left unreturned.

"Fancy seeing you here," he said, smiling at me. "I wouldn't really have pictured this as your kind of crowd."

"It isn't really. I've lost my friend. I'm actually trying to escape."

"I see. What did you think of it?"

"I think it should have stayed a factory," I said. "At least then it could have continued to make something of use."

"That bad, eh?" We both laughed.

"What are you doing here?" I asked him. "I wouldn't have guessed it was your thing either?"

"I was supposed to meet someone here about an exhibition in a few months and to see the space."

"I see."

He looked at me curiously. He seemed happy to see me and it made me feel ashamed for having avoided him, for being such a coward about it all. "I'm sorry I haven't called you back. I just—"

"No, no. I'm sorry. I think maybe it was a mistake to have moved so fast. See, the thing is, I really like you, Lily." He looked at me again. He was searching for something again. A sign. Something I couldn't give. "That night, I felt happier than I have in a very long time."

"Yes. So did I really. I wanted to call. But, see, the thing is, I never called you back because I'm actually leaving."

"Leaving? Where to?"

"I'm moving to Africa."

"It was that bad? Really?" He laughed.

"I'm serious," I said, laughing as well, hearing myself say the words, thinking how it all must sound. "I know I should have mentioned it before. I just really didn't expect to like you so much. It was all very poor timing. But you know that thing I was looking for? I'm quite determined."

"Ah, so you are serious then. Where are you going?"

"Togo. It's in West Africa." I'd got used to adding on the extra detail, before they asked.

"And how long will you be gone?"

"A little over two years."

"Two years," he repeated. "And what about your poetry? Will you still write?"

"Of course. You'd have to cut my arm off to stop me." We sat for a moment in silence as people shuffled up and down the steps. The muffled sound of music and voices from inside became louder and then softer again with each swing of the door.

"I hope you find it. Whatever it is you're looking for. I don't think you'll find it here either."

"Maybe we could keep in touch? It might be difficult by phone but we could email or Facebook?"

"I would like that," he said. "You can write to me about your adventures. I don't have Facebook but I can give you my email. Do you have a pen and some paper?"

"Of course," I said, and he scribbled down his email address.

"You're very brave, you know," he said, repeating words to me I had spoken not so long ago. It was already beginning to feel like another life. I laughed. It was all I could do.

"Oh my God, Lil!" Sonia's voice came from behind me. "I've been looking for you everywhere!" She looked as annoyed and distressed as I had been when I stumbled outside just moments earlier.

"I was looking for *you!*" I said as she made her way down the steps and finally forgot her frustrations enough to notice that I wasn't alone.

"Oh," she said, recognizing Jack. "I didn't see you there. Do you guys want to get out of here? We can get food or drinks or something somewhere else?"

"I'm afraid, once again, I'll have to turn you down," Jack said, standing up from his spot beside me on the concrete steps. "As much as I would love to, I only meant to pop in here for a moment. Another deadline looms." I didn't believe him, but I didn't try to change his mind.

"Take care," I said, standing up, both of us unsure of exactly how to part. He smiled again, hesitating. I searched those sad green eyes for a sign that I hadn't added to their tragedy. He placed his hands on my elbows and kissed gently me on the forehead.

"Take care, Lily. Good luck. And don't forget to write."

"I'm sorry, Lil," Sonia said, staring at me guiltily once Jack was out of view. "I interrupted something. Did you know he was going to be here?"

"No, no," I reassured her. "It's fine. I just ran into him. We were finished, anyway. Let's get the fuck out of this place."

"Do you want to get food?"

"I think I just want to go home, really."

"Alright," she said. The ride back to Sonia's, where I'd left my car, was full of an elusive silence. I was afraid to speak, afraid the delicate truce we'd struck might collapse once the silence was broken. But Sonia didn't mind; she was always braver about those sorts of things than I was. So she spoke first.

"What are you thinking about, Lil? Are you thinking about Jack? Was it strange to see him?" Her voice was gentle. Her earlier edge had worn off.

"Yes, a little. But that was my fault. I should have called him back, at least."

"You told him you were leaving?"

"Yes."

"Does it make you want to stay at all?"

"Because of him? No. We barely knew each other."

"Yeah, but you never know," she said sadly. I sometimes forgot that, for all of Sonia's cynicism, she was, beneath her shell, a romantic.

"No, it doesn't change anything. That show was pretty awful," I said, trying to change the subject.

"It was alright," she said and I looked at her.

"Really?"

"The music was alright."

"Yeah. The music was alright."

"Everything is going to change, Lil."

"Only a little."

"You'll be different."

"I won't be different."

"You already are."

"I disagree." I sighed.

"Look, I get it, I do. I'm sorry I gave you a hard time earlier. I do understand, believe it or not. You want to go 'into the forest' and all that. But I'm going to miss you."

"I'm going to miss you too. But it's only two years. It isn't forever."

"Two years is a long time. A lot can change."

"It's true," I said. What else could I say? "But not for us. We'll always pick right back up where we left off."

"I hope so."

"You'll write me?"

"Of course. Do you want to come in for a smoke before you go?" she asked as we pulled down the dark, tree-lined street toward my car.

"I think I should be going. It's pretty late," I said. Really I couldn't bear to drag it out any longer. She'd parked her car next to mine and we got out for a quick embrace to say goodbye.

"Alright, well, take care of yourself, Lil," she said as she squeezed me tightly.

"You too."

"Don't you forget to write either!" she called as she got back into the car.

"Never!" I called back.

When I entered the brightly lit foyer, it was just after three. It was as if the light had brought everything else crashing forward, everything I had held back so successfully all evening. For the last two months, to be more accurate. This house had too many memories. They were everywhere, every corner of every room. They were happy ones, of course, but then this also made them very sad because so much of what had made them happy was in the past. It was gone. My grandfather, my childhood, *her* even. Her health was going. It was obvious to everyone but her. What if she died while I was gone? Two years could be a very long time if you haven't all that many left. What if Sonia had been right? What if I was running away?

I stood for a moment and tried to collect myself in front of the mirrored coat closet. Was I already different? I couldn't tell. Not physically at least. And what about Jack? Why had I run into him tonight of all nights? Was it a sign? A sign I should stay?

"Who's in my house?' My eyes welled up with tears as my grandmother called out her usual greeting. What if I never heard that voice again after tonight? The tears and the sobs were threatening to overcome me. Stop it, Lily. Not now. Not yet. I took a deep breath as I walked into the living room to say hello. She was perched there, in her usual place.

"Well, darling," she said. "This is it. Are you nervous?"

"No," I said. "Well, no more than you would expect."

"Are you having second thoughts?"

"No, no. I just…"

"You can tell me."

"Well, I worry about whether I'm doing the right thing."

"Why wouldn't it be the right thing?"

"For one thing, I worry about you. And Sonia said something tonight, that she thinks I'm running away and I—"

"Okay, listen here, kiddo. First off, don't worry about me. I'm tough. I'll be fine." Her tone was somehow kind and harsh at once. "I'll miss you of course, more than anything. But I'll be alright. And we'll see each other again soon." She had prepared herself for this night better than I had. It was then that the tears came and I couldn't stop them. She held me in her arms, a grip I'd known for my entire life. How easy it was to disappear in the safety and comfort of it.

"Listen, honey," she said after she'd let me have my cry. "It's okay to be nervous. It's normal. You should be. But let me tell you something," she said, her eyes narrowing. "Of all my grandchildren I always knew you'd be different, do something different. You do what you need to do. Don't worry about what anyone else thinks. This is what *you* want. You can't live your life for other people. You just have to promise me one thing, though. Don't give up on your writing. You have a way of saying things. Just promise me you won't give up on that."

"I promise," I said. Perking up.

"You know, when my dad came over here he was probably about your age. We didn't talk about it much.

You just didn't back then. You left the old life behind you. But you know what he said to me? He said, 'Always be kind to people, never take yourself too seriously and smile. Everyone will love you.' And boy did they love him! A little too much if you ask me. It used to drive my mom crazy." She shook her head, smiling at the memories. "But anyway, he was right, Lily. They're going to love you."

"You think so?"

"I know so."

"Thank you."

"So, you haven't changed your mind then?" she asked me again, teasing.

"No, no, I haven't changed my mind."

"Well, damn. I guess I'm going to miss you terribly then. But don't you worry. We'll all be fine. Like we said before, two years will fly."

That night I dreamed of my grandfather. I dreamed that he was leading me to a room and there was an overwhelming light coming from it, brilliant and gold, and I could hear voices and laughing and I knew inside that room was the past and it was so bright, the happiness that was in there, radiating from the room. The joy of everything that had once been, the memories, the love. All of the love had gotten me this far in my life. I wanted so badly to go into the room, but somehow I knew I wouldn't, I couldn't enter the room. We paused just outside the door, and he smiled at me and disappeared inside. He was handsome and strong, the way I wanted to remember him, and I woke up just before I could follow him. I awoke full of happiness, glowing like the room, and I felt myself begin to cry, for I understood finally that it was time to go.

Chapter Thirteen

Togo
January 3, 2012

Things were slow in village. The *infirmier* had yet to return from his holiday. There would be no club until the following week and the few meetings and talks I had were scarcely attended as everyone recovered from their New Year's celebrations. The only thing that distracted me from the boredom was the thought that soon I would see John again. We'd agreed to spend the weekend after New Year's together. The first sort of arrangement that wasn't centered around work. I had planned to leave on Friday but there would be no baby-weighing for me to attend, so I could leave on Thursday afternoon. There was little for me to do here. I sent John a text asking for his thoughts.

"Why not leave tonight?" he responded immediately.

"I'll leave first thing in the morning," I sent back. That night I drifted off to sleep happily dreaming of what the next few days and nights might have in store for me.

Somewhere around three in the morning I awoke, startled. I thought it had been a dream. A voice coming from beyond my window, shouting my name. Almost a whisper. "Lily," the voice had cried, and I awoke in confusion, fumbling to find my phone to check the time. But then I heard it. A quiet tapping at my door. My heart jumped. A strange feeling of dread came over me. It wasn't a dream. Someone had been calling to me from outside my window and was now at the front door. I sat up slowly. The tapping persisted. I wrapped myself in *pagne* and carefully opened my bedroom door. I was afraid to turn on the lights, uncertain of who this strange visitor might be at such an ominous hour. Another knock and then the voice from my dreams: "Lily," it whispered, the voice of a young girl. Fati? I turned the switch to fumble with the key. Adiza stood opposite me in the darkness.

"Lily!" she cried, breathless. "You must come quickly. It's Fati. She took the medicine." The terror in her eyes overtook me. I dressed quickly and followed her into the night.

As we walked the short distance to her compound, my heart raced wildly, unsure of what was unfolding. Adiza led me to the rooms in which the family slept, rooms where I'd never before set foot. There was no light other than the erratic beams of our flashlights. I could see Fati sitting naked atop a large bucket. Usman and Jean were lying on mats in the corner, asleep. Fati looked up at me and said nothing, her face contorted in pain as she held one hand over her bare stomach.

"Where is your mother?" I asked. What was I supposed to do?

"*Au champ*," Adiza answered. The field.

"When will she be back?"

"Tomorrow."

"Does it hurt?" Fati nodded silently, her eyes closed.

"She is bleeding," Adiza said, motioning to the bucket. "There is a lot of blood, Lily." There was fear in her voice. I was trying desperately to not to make it worse by showing the terror that was rising in me.

"Fati," I said, trying to keep my voice low and calm, "can you stand up, just for a second?"

I wanted to see how much blood, exactly, she might have lost. She nodded and stood a moment as I shone my light into the bucket. I couldn't stifle the gasp that escaped me. I quickly gestured for her to sit again. It was almost a third full, and there seemed to be pieces in it, clots of some kind. Was she hemorrhaging? I had no idea. How much was too much blood?

"Okay," I said. "Adiza, do you know where the *matron* lives?" She nodded. "You must go, tell her what's happening." I looked at Fati. "How is the pain?"

"It's getting better," she said, but her face betrayed her.

"Lily—" Adiza was still standing there. Why wasn't she running to help her sister?

"What? You have to go! Hurry!" I snapped.

"Lily, but—" There were tears now, which filled her eyes, mixed with fear. "You must come with me. She won't listen to me, if I go alone. Please, Lily …" She was right. A fifteen-year-old girl, banging on doors in the middle of the night. At best they'd only send her away with a scolding.

"Alright. We will go quickly," I assured Fati. Adiza and I ran through the houses to the *matron's*. When we arrived, I knocked at the door and after a few minutes she appeared, wrapped in *pagne*, her tired face a mixture of surprise and concern. I quickly apologized for waking her and told Adiza to explain the situation in the local language to save time. The *matron* listened sternly and when the frightened girl had finished, breathless in her attempts, the *matron* turned to me and said simply, "Lily, it is an abortion. There is nothing I can do. She must go to the hospital."

"How can I get her there?" I asked. How was I supposed to get Fati to a hospital in the middle of the night? It was at least four miles away.

"Oh, you must wait until morning. But you cannot go with her!" she said, struck suddenly by a new thought. "They will think you helped her."

I looked at Adiza and then at the *matron* and no one said anything. I don't know what I had expected her to do. More than that, at least, but she wanted no part in any of it. I apologized again and we left, quickly making our way back.

When we returned, we found Fati, wrapped in *pagne*, sitting on the floor, leaning against the wall, her eyes barely open.

"I think the bleeding has stopped a little," she said when she saw us. It was now after four in the morning and the sun would soon be rising. Adiza knelt down beside her and whispered. I imagined she was informing her of our conversation with the *matron*.

"When will your mother return from the fields?" I asked.

"Eight o'clock. Seven, maybe," Adiza said.

"When she returns, she must take you to the hospital," I said and Fati nodded.

"I'm tired, Lily, I think I should lie down." Fati said, closing her eyes and leaning back against the wall. Blood was beginning to show through the *pagne*.

"Try to stay awake, Fati," I pleaded. "I'm going to take you to the hospital now."

"Lily," Adiza said. I shook my head and stepped outside.

My first two calls went unanswered but the third time my usual driver, Mubarak, awoke, his voice still coarse with sleep. I explained it was an emergency and he agreed to leave right away.

"We're going to get you help. It won't be long now," I said, re-entering the room and sitting down beside Fati. She closed her eyes and leaned her head on my shoulder. Her forehead was hot with sweat. How had she gotten the stuff?

"Where is it, Fati," I said, shaking her gently. "What did you take? Do you still have the packet?" She opened her eyes wearily but I didn't know if she heard or understood what I was saying. Usman stirred in the corner. "Adiza, what did she take? Was it a pill? Do you know where the medicine is that she took? The bag or the packet, so I can show them at the hospital, so they know?"

She shook her head. I didn't know if it was out of fear of Fati getting in trouble or if she really didn't know. The engine of a moto growled outside.

"You must ask him to help me carry her," I instructed.

Adiza returned with Mubarak and we placed Fati between him and me on the moto. We wrapped *pagne* around Fati and Mubarak to hold her securely.

"She is very ill," I explained. He nodded, asking no

questions. He sped down the empty dirt road just as dawn was breaking. When we reached the hospital, he helped me to carry Fati inside. She was barely conscious now. A member of staff saw us and came over to help.

"What is it? An accident?" he asked, looking to Mubarak, then to me.

"She is sick. There is much blood," I said. The man helped Mubarak carry Fati into a room filled with patients in bed. They laid Fati down. The *pagne* around her waist was now covered in deep red stains. I caught the man's face as he realized what was happening.

"I will get the doctor," he said. Mubarak was still standing beside me, but I had no purse or money, nothing with me.

"I'm so sorry," I explained, almost in tears, searching through my pockets for change. All I had with me was my phone. "I forgot my purse."

"*Non, non,*" he assured me. He was looking past me, at Fati on the bed. Her eyes were closed but I could still see the steep rise and fall of her chest. Where did that man go? Where was the doctor? "Would you like me to take you back?" Mubarak offered. I shook my head. "*Courage,*" he said. "Please, let me know if you need anything."

I was alone. A few of the other patients had looked upon us with mild curiosity when we first entered, but now they had remembered their own misfortunes and they were still, uninterested in ours. I went back out into the main hall to look for help.

"The girl needs a doctor," I said when I spotted the man who had helped us.

"The *sage femme* has been called," he said. "She is coming."

"But she needs help now!"

"She is coming. Please, calm down," he said firmly.

"But she's still bleeding. She needs fluids. Can't you do anything?" I yelled.

"She is coming. You must wait. It is still early." I went back to Fati, frustrated. It was now half past five. I tried to shake Fati. If I kept her awake maybe it would help. She barely moved and only let out a slight moan. I decided to try to phone the *infirmier*. Perhaps he could call one of the doctors here and get them to help us. There was no answer. My mind raced. Who could help me? I called Cynthia.

"Hello?"

"Can you come by the hospital? Something's happened to Fati. She took something. No one is helping her. No one is listening to me."

"I'm coming. I'll be right there," she said. I shook Fati again. The woman in the bed next to her was watching me. The tears were welling up. The woman's eyes had that defeated look of having suffered for too long. She shook her head at me. I looked away. I took Fati's hand and placed my other hand on her forehead.

"It will be okay," I whispered. "Just hang on." I waited. For how long, I don't know. It seemed as though time had stopped. I let go of Fati's hand and went back out into the hall. The doctor was talking to a woman in a white coat. When he saw me, he pointed her in my direction and they walked over to me.

"It is an abortion?" she said, addressing me.

"She took something," I said. "I don't know what it was. She has lost a lot of blood."

The woman nodded. "Wait here," she said and went into the room where Fati lay. It was nearly seven-thirty. Gladys would be back soon. Poor Adiza. She must be so worried. I sat down on the bench in the hall. I was staring blindly at the doorway when a familiar figure entered, walking toward me quickly. It was Gladys.

"Where is she?" she said, her voice loud, almost hysterical. "Where have they taken my daughter?"

"The *sage femme* is with her, I'm not sure—"

"Lily, I didn't know," she said almost in tears. "I didn't know what she was going to do."

"I know," I said. The man came out of the room and as I looked over, Gladys's eyes followed mine. "She's in that room," I said, and immediately she charged down the hall toward him. She said something in in the local language and then went past him, waving him off into the room. I waited. At first it was silent and then I heard it. But I didn't hear it, not really. I felt it. In my stomach and down to my toes and then up through my chest so that I couldn't breathe and I began to shake. I closed my eyes. Please God, don't let this be happening. The man followed Gladys into the room, as he heard that primal wail. She was yelling something in her language and he in French. I put my head in my hands. There were only voices now, hers full of grief and anger, his cold and detached. I didn't want to see, to know for sure. Gladys was sobbing as the man walked out.

"The girl has died," he said simply, now standing before me again. "You must take her mother home. You must take her to her husband." I stared at him the way that he had stared at me when I begged him to help her barely an hour before. When Fati was still breathing. When she still had a chance. "Please, she is upsetting the other patients," he continued, but I turned my head. The man continued speaking in French, but it wasn't to me. Cynthia had appeared and the man pleaded with her. She appeased him somehow, and he went away.

"She's dead," I said, looking up at her.

"I'm so sorry," she said.

"He wants to get Gladys out of there."

"I'll go," she said. "It's fine, just wait here." She walked calmly into the room where Gladys sat with Fati's lifeless body. After a few minutes the wailing from inside the room stopped and Cynthia reappeared. "I think maybe you should go back to my place," she said softly. "I'll make sure Gladys gets home. It might be better for you if I go back first, just to see."

I sat there, unable to decide what to do. I understood what she was saying: she wanted to be sure no one blamed me, no one would think I had helped her. I agreed. There was nothing I could do for Gladys right now. I just wanted to disappear. Cynthia gave me her keys and I left. I walked in a daze down the street. I got to Cynthia's and sat down and started to cry. After a few moments I realized my phone had been vibrating in my hand since I arrived. John had called several times. I answered.

"There you are, did I wake you? You were meant to leave first thing, remember?" he teased, his voice light and happy.

"Something's happened," I said.

"What's happened? Are you alright?"

"Fati, I was with her at the hospital. She's …" I couldn't say the words because they made it real again. I couldn't stop the sobs.

"Where are you now? Lily?"

"I'm at Cynthia's. She came to the hospital. She's taken Gladys home," I managed to explain.

"Look, I'm going to come to you. I'm leaving now. I'm on my way," he said.

"Alright."

"I'll be there as soon as I can." I hung up the phone. What was happening with Gladys? I should have gone with them. I hadn't been thinking straight. Now there was nothing for me to do but wait. I don't know how long I was sat there before Cynthia returned.

"How is she?" I asked as she approached.

"She's okay. Still shaken."

"I should have gone with you."

"There was nothing you could have done and I wanted to be sure no one thought it was you that gave her whatever it was. But her sister confessed everything, that Fati had kept it a secret from everyone. She said you were the only one that would help her, that you tried to save her. They are going in search of the man who sold her the medicine."

"They left her there for so long," I said. "After I brought her in. It was like they were punishing her."

"You did everything you could," she said. "I spoke to John as well. He called me as I was leaving. He's on his way here. Why don't you go and lie down? You must be exhausted."

"I don't think I could sleep."

"Hold on," she said. She went inside and returned quickly again with a glass of wine. "Here."

I drank it and my head was suddenly heavy. I decided to lie down in her spare room. I didn't remember falling asleep. When I awoke, the sun was strong and the heat was stifling. Slowly the memories came back to me. Voices were coming from the living room. John had arrived. I went out and saw the two of them sitting at the table. John got up to embrace me.

"Oh Lily, I'm so sorry," he said, holding me close. "Are you alright?"

"I'm fine." I sat down. "Thank you for coming. And thank you for everything this morning," I said, turning to Cynthia.

"Of course. It was nothing."

"I suppose I should go back now."

"You should eat something," John offered. "Why don't we get some food and then head back?"

"No, I'm not hungry."

"Alright." John and I said goodbye to Cynthia and flagged down a couple of moto drivers on the main road to take us to my village.

When we entered my compound, the two old women were sitting solemnly outside. They muttered hellos but it was there in their eyes, the way one looks upon a wounded animal, full of sorrow and pity. I didn't know if I should go to Gladys or not. Cynthia said that no one blamed me, but part of me was afraid that she might hold me responsible. Perhaps she would have been right to.

"I should go to her," I said to John once we were inside.

"You don't have to right now. You can go tomorrow."

"No," I said. "I should go to her. Just wait here."

I went slowly outside and back out the gates around to Fati's compound. A few women were outside, but there was no sign of Gladys or Adiza. One of the women came forward and offered to show me inside. Inside the room where I had sat with Fati just hours earlier, Gladys now sat with Adiza and the children, huddled and grieving. When I walked in she stood up, her face swollen from all the crying. She took both my hands.

"Thank you," she said, her voice full of grief. "Adiza has told me what you have done. Thank you," she repeated with difficulty. Adiza sat quietly, her eyes exhausted and frightened and still wet with tears.

"I wish I could have done more." My eyes welled up again.

"She is with God now," she said. "She will rest in peace with God." I nodded.

"I will leave you with your family," I said. "I'm so very sorry." I left and walked quickly past the women, my cheeks running wet with tears. Inside, I broke down again as John came and took me again in his arms. I sobbed uncontrollably.

"You need to rest," he offered. "Why don't you lie down. I'll go look for something to eat." I didn't argue this time. When he was gone I decided to have a shower and the cold water shocked my aching body into awareness. I put on some fresh clothes and sat on my bed, waiting for John to return. When I heard him knock I half expected it to be Fati and the children coming for their evening visit.

"I got some eggs and bread and wine," he said, placing

the black plastic bags on the table. "I'm going to make us some egg sandwiches." He poured two glasses from the box of wine and placed one before me.

"Do you want to talk about it?" he asked gently.

"Her sister had come to me in the middle of the night," I began and then it poured forth, the tiny details I would never forget. The color of her *pagne*, the way the *matron* had said, 'Lily, it's an abortion. There's nothing to be done.' The way she'd been left at the hospital for almost an hour without being seen by anyone, without any help. The way I had watched the rise and fall of her chest for comfort, for hope. John listened. When I was finished he took my hand.

"You did everything you could have done," he said. Everyone kept saying that. Did it matter? What difference had it made? He said he'd heard from people in town there would be a small funeral tomorrow. A few hours after the sun had set, the funeral drums began to beat loudly. We could still hear them from my bedroom window when we went to bed. Listening to their solemn rhythm, we lay together in one another's arms, and gently, he began to kiss me and I let him, willing to be lost in his kisses, in his hands, and I tried to remember to come up for air until I couldn't anymore and finally there was nothing to remember and there was nothing to forget, there was just us and the drums and I thought about a line I heard from somewhere about making love to forget about death and I had almost forgotten when the relief of sleep found me.

John stayed with me for almost a week following Fati's death. There was a small funeral that lasted a few days but it wasn't the extravagant affair it is in less tragic cases, such as the passing of an elder, when the ceremony is a celebration of their lives. This affair was quiet and quick. If Fati's parents were ashamed of her, of the reasons for her death, they did not show it. They arranged everything as it would have been if she'd died in a car accident or of malaria or one of the million other tragedies that befall a small village in Togo too often to take much note of. There seemed to be no blame placed on anyone. It simply happened sometimes, these things, and she was with God now, as Gladys had said and someday so would everyone else. This life was not all there was—how could it be? Many of the girls from my club were there. Some of them looked on at the crowd and the drums and the dancing with tears in their eyes and others only stared expressionless, unyielding. Did they see themselves in Fati's tragedy at all? Did they think: that could have been me? Or: I will not let that be me? Or was that the same to them as saying, I will not die of malaria or cancer, and so just as pointless? There was no lesson to be learned. Death is not the great teacher, that is life. Death only turns us to dust.

I was thankful to have John with me, to distract me from myself. I was thankful that he was with me to make an appearance at the funeral and he was there to say it was okay to leave, when I just wanted to be alone with him and away from the chaos. Gladys and her husband and the children stayed inside for the most part. People went inside the compound to give their condolences. I went once again to see Gladys but I felt that it was difficult for her to see me and I did not stay long.

I saw Adiza once, near the other schoolgirls. Her eyes

were the eyes of a mourner: red and swollen. I asked her how she was doing. "*Ça va?*" I asked, knowing the answer.

"*Bien,*" she replied, as if it was a memorized response and there was no other way to answer my question.

A few days after the funeral, John and I went into town to have a drink at Petit Baobab. We were sitting quietly, gazing over the mountain and the sunset. There was something that he wanted to ask me, but was trying to find the right way to do it. I knew what his question would be, but I didn't know if I had an answer, so I waited for him to ask it. To see what I might say.

"You'll have to be getting back soon," I said, interrupting the silence. "I know I can't keep you here forever, but it has been nice. Thank you."

"I thought maybe you could come up to Kara for the weekend. If you wanted to."

"Yes," I said, thinking it over. "Maybe I will."

We sat again in silence and his question hung there, still unasked.

"Do you think you'll stay, then?" he asked finally. "I understand it must be difficult. It's just that—"

"I know," I interrupted. "The project."

"It isn't anything you need to decide right now, but we should find out about the grant soon and—"

"Yes, well, then I should stay," I said.

"I know it will be hard." He smiled and took my hand. "But I'll be here with you."

Chapter Fourteen

Togo
September 15, 2012

About a month after the funeral I got an email from Jeremy:

Congratulations, you got the money. Takes a few weeks to clear the account. I'll be in touch. Best of luck! Keep up the good work!

Part of me was relieved, but there had also been a part of me that had considered the possibility that not getting the money would have given me the perfect excuse to pack up and go home. Even after knowing I wouldn't be given the option of a graceful exit, I still entertained the thought that once the project was over I could go and, hopefully, no one would blame me for wanting to. So, I marked the days on the calendar with an eye that perhaps saw the end somewhere around September. The end of a charade I was no longer interested in participating in.

As my weeks filled with meetings, working out logistics with John and Issa, hiring mechanics and locals from each village to do most of the work, I realized that this was my real work. Everything else was just folly. The club, my work at the *dispensaire*. That was all done for my sake. To keep me busy. To make me feel as though I held some importance. In the months that followed Fati's death, I lost something. I had lost Fati, yes, but I had also lost the last remnants of the illusion I'd had up to that point, which had allowed me to think my work here held any meaning greater than my own selfish desires.

So much of the time that passed was simply me going through the motions required to complete each day, and all the while I could feel this intolerable anger building up inside me. Everything agitated me. The way the *matron* was incapable of spelling the names right on the *carnets* and her paralyzing devotion to bureaucratic details over efficiency. The girls at my club, the way they still laughed at my accent and failed to see beyond our differences so that I could reach them, so that they could hear me, my lessons, my warnings, to see past the color of my skin, my funny look. To understand that I was providing them with information that was powerful, that could help them. Gladys and Adiza avoided me. I worried they blamed me for everything somehow. The boys came by alone sometimes. For the most part my evenings were quiet.

I was honest with John about my indeterminate future. I promised I would stay for the completion of the project but that was the most I could guarantee.

"I understand why you would want to go, Lily," he said one evening, as we sat together under the stars after a long day of meetings. "But I think that, eventually, you would regret it if you left."

"Maybe. I guess we'll see."

Luckily there wasn't much time to dwell on my decision. By April the project was in full swing. We visited each site when the work commenced, making sure everything was in order and offering to make runs for food and water. We were always on hand should any problem arise, though they rarely did. And while there wasn't much we could do to help the locals with the actual installations, we took advantage of the crowds we drew to give impromptu talks on health and hygiene, throwing in bits of information on gender equity, financial skills and gardening, too, where we could. We hoped to do most of the work over five months' time, expecting pauses due to the rainy season. According to Issa and Naapoo, it seemed that every year the rains came later and later. By the time June arrived we had yet to see a downpour, so we were able to complete the first three installations quickly and without any delays.

July got off to a decent start but we were unable to complete the last village we had scheduled for that month because finally the rains came. There was a sense of relief among the farmers. They hoped it would continue and we hoped it would hold off just long enough to finish the week's work. It became apparent the timeline would be unpredictable. We worked when we could, in between torrential bouts of rain that came and went, leaving little trace of their violence, as the sun and the heat quickly cleared up any evidence of the strength and fury with which they passed. We continued.

Some of the villages greeted us with celebrations. They held elaborate ceremonies with dancing and singing and *tchuk*. Others accepted our aid with a quiet sort of dignity, where the hierarchy of elders came and said a few words of thanks and offered us a chicken or two. I came to dread these displays of gratitude, as it was usually left to John or me to have to carry the poor squawking animals all the way to Kara on the back of a moto, tied at the feet and very rightfully fearing for their lives.

There was one village whose reception was unlike the others'. When Issa and Naapoo had finished the work and John and I had said our piece, one of the elders took his turn to speak.

"He says they are very grateful to you for bringing them water," Issa translated for us as usual. They were familiar words, but as the man carried on talking, Issa's expression changed. The old man continued before pausing long enough for Issa to reveal his message to us. But instead of addressing us, Issa addressed the old man, his eyes hard and his words harsh. John and I sat uncomfortably as the two exchanged words we didn't understand and the man, unrelenting, urged Issa to fill us in on what was happening.

"He says they are very grateful for what you have done," Issa said with an exhausted sigh. "But they also need a school," he began. The old man nodded in satisfaction, most likely recognizing the words in French. "There are no schools around for the children to attend."

"He also said we need a hospital," one of the younger men chimed in, in French, not trusting Issa to convey everything.

"Yes," Issa said, scowling. "A school and a hospital. But I told him that it takes time and besides, he should be grateful enough for the pump! I told him that the work you do here is difficult. You must leave your family and come here to help people you do not know. I told him it is rude to ask more." John smiled with amusement and I struggled to reassure the old man that we were not offended.

"We understand," I said. But that wasn't true. We didn't really understand. I, for one, had never lived in a place without schools, a hospital or water. "The problem is, there is only so much money we can get each year." Issa repeated my words but with more authority and less kindness. "I'm very sorry. This is all we can do for now."

The man nodded with a smirk, as if that was what he had expected us to say. He bowed again and we were off. We stopped for a drink in town when we had finished. The customary end to a long day's work.

"The people of that village were ungrateful," Issa said as we sat down, obviously still angry with the old man for having the nerve to ask us for more.

"*Oui*," John nodded and I shot him a surprised look.

"He didn't mean anything by it. You can't blame a guy for asking," I said.

"Yes, but after everything you've done," Issa said, shaking his head. "It is not good. It is not nice."

"*Oui*," John agreed again.

"So next week, we'll come with you on Monday when you begin the next one? Which one is that again?" I asked, wanting to change the subject.

"I forget the name. It's farther west but it's not as far as the last one," Issa said.

"I hope the weather holds up."

"*Oui*."

"If not, we'll have to try again on Tuesday," John said.

When we finished, Issa and Naapoo offered to give us a lift back to my place, but we declined, opting instead to stay for another round.

"Issa was laying it on a bit thick, don't you think?" I said, once they had left.

"No. He's just defensive of us. Of our work. Like he said, we do give up a lot to be here."

"I don't see the correlation, but alright."

"Look, Lily," he said, agitated. "You don't have to be such a martyr all the time. He didn't mean anything by it."

"A martyr, really? Is that what you think I'm going for?"

"I don't know what you're going for. I know it's been hard on you, but I really can't get inside your head anymore. Issa thought the guy was being disrespectful and I agreed with him."

"I think you might not worry so much about being disrespectful if you needed things like clean water, a hospital, schools," I pressed on.

"Oh, come on," he said. "This is what I'm talking about—you think it's just so terrible here. Is it? Is it so awful? Sure, it's hard but I look around and I see people that are happy. I see people spending time with their families and not in some useless office job, nine-to-five bullshit just to own a home, a car, a TV. I see kids playing outside, not sitting in front of a computer screen. I see people taking care of one another, looking out for one another, in ways I've never experienced back in the States. It's not all bad, you know? Nothing is. Try to see the good once in a while, Jesus Christ."

I sat for a moment, speechless. It was the first time he'd ever lashed out at me so harshly. But slowly, with each word, I grew more and more angry. It wasn't just the way he spoke. Equally disturbing were the things he was saying. He had a sort of glorification of this way of life I couldn't share, I didn't agree with. It made me worry that the same idealism that I resented in him made him skeptical of me. Was I a self-proclaimed martyr, then? No better than his savior complex? Two sides of the same coin?

"I'm sorry. Look, I've been thinking," he said, his tone gentler, trying to change the mood. "I was thinking when we're done here, maybe you and I could go away for a few days? Maybe to Cape Coast? Ouagadougou even? I think we deserve a vacation."

"Hmmm." I looked out across the balcony. It was almost dusk. The street was growing quiet. "It depends when we finish things and when the school year starts up again."

"So, you're sticking around, then?" he said smiling, reading too much into my words, words I hadn't given much weight to.

"I don't know."

"Alright, then. Well, think about the vacation idea. It might be just what you need."

We finished the final installation just before September. There were strikes again and a delayed school year was inevitable. I was still allowing myself to entertain the idea of leaving but something stopped me from fully committing myself to it. I decided to take John up on the idea of a vacation. Getting away for a few days might help to make up my mind. We decided to spend a week in Ghana. A little oceanside get away. The fresh salty air. Perhaps the sea would be calming. Perhaps it would do us both some good.

The journey to Cape Coast was long but there were no bush taxis, just regular little buses, so it felt much more bearable and time passed more quickly without the discomfort of being squashed and elbowed for hours on end. The streets of Cape Coast were different from anywhere I'd been in Togo. A strange combination of European influence and West African scruff. After we checked into our hotel, we went out for a wander and spotted a touristy little hostel and bar combination that sat right on the edge of the ocean. It was a strange time of day. Too early for dinner and too late for anything else. We chose one of the dozen or so empty tables right near the edge, overlooking the sea.

We sat for a while without speaking. Too busy staring out into the expanse of the endless blue ocean. It somehow seemed more inviting, gentler than the violent waves of Lomé's shores. Both were mesmerizing with their slow hypnotic rhythms but there was a tranquility in these waves I had never experienced in Togo's capital. Perhaps it was me who was more calm, being so far away from the things that failed to give me peace. The sun hung low in the sky. Its light was growing weaker but had yet to lose its brilliance. I felt a terrible sadness welling up in me. The sort of sad you feel that isn't sadness at all, just a sort of overwhelming of the senses. I simply felt too much. It reminded me of a line from a book I read once, about needing to drink because you felt things too deeply. The author needed to numb the overwhelming sensations of living. What a lovely excuse that was, I thought as we ordered a drink. John was looking at me, looking at the sea. I pretended not to notice because there were things he had wanted to discuss with me. Things I had, up until this moment, wanted to discuss as well, but now they all felt useless and I was afraid they would spoil the moment.

"So," he said as the waitress arrived with our beer and we took the first fresh sips. "What are you thinking about, Lily?"

"Honestly? I'm thinking about a line from a book I read about how the narrator has to drink because he feels things too deeply and he can't cope with it," I said. "I was thinking maybe that's my problem, because it's the best reason I can find so far."

"It is a good one," he said, smiling, but I couldn't help but feel the sentiment was lost on him. "And what is it that you're feeling so deeply about?"

"It isn't any one thing," I said, though it was useless to try to explain. "The point is that it's everything and that's what makes it overwhelming. Look, it's silly. Just forget it."

"I know that it's been hard for you," he said, trying to make my abstract ramblings cohere into some sort of concrete problem he could identify and solve. It wasn't the way. I couldn't convince him.

"Oh, it isn't about that," I snapped.

"Well, what's it about, then? I'm trying to understand you," he said, almost pleading. His patience was even more infuriating.

"Oh, I don't even know what it's about," I said,

giving up. "Look, there's nothing to understand. I'm not explaining things right, anyway. Let's just enjoy ourselves. I was only trying to make conversation."

I had spoiled things now. John sulked in his seat across from me and I couldn't muster the words or the desire to console him. We ordered some food because, despite our misery, we were still famished from our travels. After we ate I started to feel bad about the way I had behaved. It was such a nice evening. It would have been a shame to start things off on such a sour note.

"I'm sorry, I didn't mean to be crabby. I think I'm just tired from all the traveling. Forgive me?" I asked.

John took my hand. All was forgiven. It was almost too easy.

When sun set we went back to the hotel, too tired to make much else out of the night. The internet speed at the hotel was like nothing I'd experienced in over a year. John dozed off early and I decided to take the opportunity to catch up on the news for the first time in months. But, as my tired eyes read over the headlines on the cold blue screen, I knew instantly it had been a mistake. A shooting at a university in Texas. At least thirty civilians killed in a bombing in Syria. Drone strikes in Pakistan. I closed the laptop. I would be better off getting a good night's sleep. After that, everything would look better in the morning.

The next day we decided to tour Cape Coast Castle. It had always felt wrong to me to make tourist sites out of the tragedies of mankind. Like monuments to the great failures of humanity. I never understood the sort of people who visit Anne Frank's house or Auschwitz, but, then again, I felt equally bad about turning a blind eye. And John had insisted, "It's history." So I went along with it.

As we made our way into town, a gray mist hung over the colorful shops and houses. The early morning sky of a seaside town. The scent of salt mixed with each breath. As we neared we could begin to make out the ominous outline of the castle through the fog. It wouldn't have looked out of place in Europe, with its high stone walls, perched warily against the crashing waves. But here its foreignness was over-exaggerated. An imposing and hostile reminder of imperialism and conquest.

Inside the main entrance, there was already a large group of tourists lined up in front of us. It was funny to hear the sound of Americans again. They were young, teenagers by the looks of it. It must have been one of those group trips schools organize from time to time. When we got to the ticket counter the woman told us we could either join the group for the guided tour or go it alone with the map. I was never very fond of guided tours, but John was keen and I was trying to be more amiable. We joined the group of fifteen or so American teenagers and an older German couple.

The guide took us from room to room, and, with an unsettling detachment, he relayed to us the brutality that had taken place here. Rooms upon rooms where so many hundreds of thousands of people lost their lives, their homes, their families, their humanity. When we reached The Door of No Return, where the slave ships set off for the Americas, one of the Americans spoke up, without invitation, to enquire as to why no one had stopped it from happening.

"Didn't anyone know?" he asked in disbelief.

John and I exchanged a look. I felt sorry for the guide to have to politely answer such an alarmingly ignorant statement. If I was him I would have said, "You're American, for God's sake. What did you think the Civil War was over?" But the guide was more reserved. He seemed better acclimated to such ignorance. Calmly, he gave a rehearsed answer, carefully avoiding too much placement of responsibility on one group of people or another.

The tour ended at the plaque Michelle Obama, who'd traced her heritage back to this castle, had placed there a few years earlier. It read:

In everlasting memory of the anguish of our ancestors. May those who died rest in peace. May those who return find their roots. May humanity never again perpetrate such injustice against humanity. We the living uphold this.

Moving as it was, I didn't think 'We the Living' were doing a very good job of it, but I was sure it must have made the other Americans feel better.

The rest of the day we walked around the small port town. The sun came out and lifted off some of the morning's heaviness, but it still hung around and clouded our thoughts, and we said little as we explored the rest of the city. That evening we went back to the little restaurant we had been to the night before, and managed to have dinner without the previous evening's unpleasantness. I had become complacent. I couldn't see much use in it anymore.

Afterwards, we stumbled upon a little bar that was blasting Rasta music and decided to have a look. Inside it was dark with red lamps and strange tapestries decorating the walls. There were a few young backpackers at the long picnic-style tables, smoking cigarettes and what smelled like weed.

We took a seat and a man with large dreadlocks and bloodshot eyes took our order. I was staring off into the eyes of Haile Selassie, which looked back at me from one of the tapestries, when the man returned with our beers.

"Smoke?" He offered what was obviously a joint.

"Oh, well, sure," I said taking a puff and passing it to John, who did the same.

"You are American?" he asked.

"Yes," John answered. "But we live in Togo."

"Togo," the man nodded. "How long you live there?"

"Almost four years now for me."

"Wow." He shook his head, laughing. "It is a long time. You like it there? It is good, it is like here?"

"Yes," John said. "But Ghana is, well— You have better roads, better cars, better everything."

The man laughed again and passed us the joint once more. "It is not so different when you leave the city," he assured us. "In the north it is the same. You will go to the north?"

"No," I said. "We don't have time."

"Maybe next time then," he said and left us to our beers. Immediately, I could feel the weed. It had been ages since I'd smoked. Instantly, everything took on a warm, fuzzy glow.

"Well, that was a pleasant surprise," John said.

"Very pleasant," I said.

"It's much better than that dirt they try to pass off as weed in Togo."

"Yeah, definitely."

"You know what you were saying yesterday," said John, "about feeling too much? I think I get what you meant."

"Yeah?"

"Yeah, I guess it's just different for me."

"It's different for everyone."

"Sure."

"I think for me right now, I just feel a bit lost, you know? And it isn't about Fati, either. I mean, in a way it is, but even if she hadn't died, even if she would have lived that night, I still think I would feel the same in a way."

"And how's that?"

"Well, I guess it's like… I used to call myself a Romantic," I said, taking a sip of my drink. "Not in the lovey-dovey sense, but I believed in mankind. I believed in the idea that man is capable of greatness. I don't think I believe it anymore. I think I've been proven wrong."

"That's quite a tragic statement," he said, shaking his head. "Do you really believe that?"

"I'm afraid I do."

"And what about people like you and me? Those who want to do good in the world?"

"It's a nice sentiment, but I don't know that it adds up to too much in the bigger picture," I said. "We're too few in number. It's too much that we're up against. Didn't you feel it today? We still haven't learned anything from the past. Look at all the wars, famine, poverty, rapes, torture—all the injustice that goes on all over the world every day. And what do we do about it? Put up a plaque and move on to the next tragedy. It's just an endless cycle of destroy and forget. You were right that day. I gave people too much credit. You were right about it all. If God doesn't exist then everything is permissible. The best and the worst of it. Mainly the worst."

John looked at me, his eyes narrow. He said nothing. He had no apparent argument to try to convince me otherwise.

"Can I tell you something really embarrassing?" I continued, lighting a cigarette. It felt good, to finally say out loud all the terrible thoughts that had been building up inside me. "I used to want to be a poet. I used to think that by scribbling a few words down on some paper, I could make a difference in the world. It could mean something. Could change things. How silly it all seems now. How terribly naïve." I shook my head with a sad laugh. "I came here mainly for myself. Because of what this kind of experience could do for *me*. I took it for granted that just by being here I would be able to help people. I would do good work. That's really how I failed Fati. I thought I could make the world right for her. Me, in the face of all this? How arrogant that must have seemed. If I had been able to see just how much she was up against, then maybe I would have realized how much she was willing to risk."

"Lily, I don't know how many times I have to say it. You can't keep going on like this. It isn't good. It doesn't lead to anything."

We were both silent for a moment.

"I have to tell you something," John said, his voice quiet against the strange rhythms of the music. "They're closing down my NGO here at the end of the year. I've suspected it for a while now, but I got the final word a few weeks ago. I wanted to find the right moment—"

"The right moment?"

"I know. I—"

"At the end of the year?"

"Yeah, but they've actually offered me another post. It's at the head office in Dakar. It's a fairly impressive promotion, really. I'll be overseeing most of their work in West Africa."

"Well, it's good that that's all worked out for you, then."

"Lily," he said, softly. "Maybe you could come with me. Maybe it would be good for you, to go somewhere else. I could put in a word for you. You've got the experience. I don't see why they wouldn't…"

"Why didn't you—"

"I should have said something sooner. I didn't know if it mattered, honestly. You weren't sure if you were going to stay and—" He stopped and looked up at me strangely. "You know, I thought you might have known already."

"How would I have known?"

"I don't know." He shook his head. "Sometimes it's the way you look at me, your eyes. It frightens me sometimes, the way they seem to see me, read my thoughts maybe. I'm sorry. I'm stoned …" He shook his head and paused a moment before he continued. "But really, think about it. You could still do good work there, but it would be a fresh start."

"Maybe. I don't know …"

"Just think about it," he said. "There's no need to know right this second."

"Alright. I'll think about it."

That night I couldn't sleep. For hours I stared up into the darkness. John's body was silhouetted in the moonlight, his breathing slow and steady. John was leaving and he was giving me exactly what I had been wanting so badly since Fati's death. An excuse to go.

Finally I got up and walked outside to smoke a cigarette on the balcony. The night was quiet, save for a few small lizards that scurried into the bushes as I sat down in one of the old wicker chairs. For some reason my mind kept wandering back to the plaque on the old castle walls. How it haunted me now in the quiet morning hours. Why? Because I used to believe in 'We the Living'. That was what I had been trying to tell John earlier. That I used to believe that we could hold the weight of the world on our shoulders and still prop it up. We could make it better. Through strength. Through perseverance.

I went inside just as the gentle blue dawn came intruding into the quiet, dark hotel room. I sat down on the bed. John rolled over beside me and opened his eyes.

"You're awake?" he said. "What time is it?"

"I can't go with you, John."

"Look, you don't need to know for certain yet."

"But I do know," I insisted.

"So, what will you do then? Go back to the U.S.? You'll

be miserable. You'll regret not coming with me."

"No, no. I'm not going back to the States. You were right in what you were saying earlier. I have to stop going in circles about it all. Fati's dead and it isn't fair but the only way I can atone for that fact, even just a little bit, is to stay. To finish what I started. But wiser. With a better understanding. With more compassion. I have to stay, John. You were right in the first place, that leaving here, that's what I would regret the most."

"Lily..." His eyes were serious as they examined mine. "I don't want to leave you."

I put my hands on his face and he kissed me and I let him. And we made love in a sad sort of way. In a hopeless, messy way. And I felt something I hadn't felt for a long time. I felt at peace with myself. I felt relieved that it was over. Even so, I knew that eventually I would miss him, once he really was gone. I would miss him terribly.

Chapter Fifteen

The rest of the trip went by as if nothing had happened and I let it go that way, even though everything had changed. Maybe John believed that I might change my mind or that perhaps, once he actually had left, I might decide to follow him. Once I'd really felt the loss of him.

When we parted ways at the station, we made no plans to see each other again. I found a moto driver and made the last leg of my journey back. I had arranged to meet Cynthia for a drink in town before heading all the way back to village. She'd been texting me incessantly since we'd gotten into Lomé to find out exactly when I'd be back. I assumed due to boredom from the strikes. When I arrived at Petit Baobab, I ordered a much-needed beer and climbed the staircase. Cynthia was waiting alone. She smiled at me, but I could see instantly something was amiss.

"Welcome back," she said, lighting a cigarette. "How was your romantic getaway?"

"Not so romantic." I took a seat. "I think it's over between us."

"What? How did that happen? Did you have a fight?"

she said, sitting up in her chair in surprise.

"He's moving to Senegal. They're closing his office here, so he doesn't have much of a choice."

"And he waited until you were on vacation to tell you?"

"Well, he did ask me to go with him. But I said no."

Cynthia paused for a moment, looking down at her cigarette. I suspected she was trying to decide between consoling me and advising me to reconsider.

"So, what'd I miss? Are the strikes over yet?" I asked.

"School started back up on Wednesday."

There was something else, but she was hesitating. I said nothing. I wasn't in the mood for guessing games.

"Well, there's other news I'm afraid," she sighed, unable to resist. She lit another cigarette.

"It's not good, I'm guessing?"

"No. It's Matt. He's leaving as well. But the circumstances are less pleasant."

"Did something happen?"

"I haven't really spoken to him. Anna knows more, but there was an incident with one of the teachers at his school. Apparently one of the girls accused the teacher of forcing the girls to sleep with him for good marks last year. Matt went after him. I guess the girl was also a student of his. It was bad. The guy was not in good shape after. Anna said that if they hadn't pulled him away when they did …"

"Jesus. Well, he deserved it," I said, taking one of her cigarettes.

"Yes, but he really could have gotten himself into some trouble. Apparently, the chief of the village was reasonable. Everyone there liked Matt. He was lucky. He gave Matt a day to pack and be gone."

"And the other guy?"

"I don't know," she said. "I just…"

She didn't finish her thought. I could see she was upset. It was an awful thing. The kind of thing I heard about often but hadn't ever actually encountered.

"Are you alright?" I asked.

"Yes, I just … I gave some bad advice, I think," she said. "I saw Matt the week before in Kara. We went out for drinks and he told me what the girls were saying. I told him he had to do something."

"You didn't tell him to almost beat a man to death, did you?"

"No, but he seemed so out of it. He was really having a hard time with things." She continued her story, but she was no longer telling me. She was just saying these things out loud because she had to, to whoever might be there. She had to hear herself say them. "I knew he was in trouble."

"What do you mean, 'in trouble'?" I said, taking a sip of my drink. I'd need another one soon the way things were going.

"You've been busy with your project. You haven't been around much, but for the last few weeks I saw things were, well—something was off."

"Off? How so?"

"He was drinking a lot. I mean, we all drink, but this was different. I even mentioned it to Anna. She noticed too, but we just figured that, you know, it's difficult here. Sometimes you go through phases of feeling it more than others. We thought it was a phase. Perhaps we could have talked to him about it, maybe then …"

"Look, I don't think there was anything you could have done," I said. "Where is he now? Has he left for Lomé?"

"Yes, apparently. Anna went to meet him in Kara. He was in a bad way. She went with him down to Lomé. I offered, but it's difficult with classes starting."

"Is he going back to the States?"

"Yes, I think so. Surely they won't let him teach here anymore."

"Wow," I said. I took another cigarette and sat back. Neither of us said anything for a moment.

"I think this will be my last year teaching here," she said, as if she had only just thought of it. "Three years is a long time. It's long enough. You know, I think I know what was getting to him. It gets to me, too, but I try not to think about it. You spend all this time teaching these kids English and at the end of the day, you can't help but think: for what? How many of them go on to university, the Lycée even? Why does it matter?" She was choking back tears now. "How much do I remember from high school Spanish, anyway? I don't blame them. But who can I blame, though? Because it should matter. I used to think: I believe in education, that no matter what, knowledge enriches your life. But does it? Or have I just told them these things because it was true for me? But what if it isn't true for them? I say you can do anything you put your mind to, if you work hard enough, but that's not true. Not if your father dies and you have to quit school to work or you're sick with malaria all the time and miss months of class. What if all I've done is trick them, like some cheap salesman of the American dream? What if I've done more harm than good?"

"Oh, Cynthia," I said. "I felt the same way after Fati died. But you're doing your best. That's all you can do, in the end."

"I know. But it just doesn't feel like enough sometimes." She wiped her tears and looked at me and sighed. "So," she asked cautiously. "What about you?"

"What about me?"

"Your project's done. John's leaving. What have you got left, anyway? Six, seven months? No one would blame you, you know? If you decided to go with him."

"I would blame me. No. I've decided to stay. I want to finish what I started here." I smiled. I felt sorry for Cynthia. A lot was changing in a short amount of time. "It's been a rough week," I offered.

"How about one more for the road?" she asked, and I nodded. "On me," she said and disappeared down the stairs.

I thought of what Matt had said about her that night he was trying to categorize us. Cynthia was a believer. Funny he should be the one to test her faith. When she returned to the table she looked more relaxed.

"So, you and John. That's it?" she asked, lighting a cigarette.

"Yes, and you know what? I feel as though it should upset me more than it does."

"Well, that tells you everything right there," she said. "You know, I think something was going on between Anna and Matt."

"Really?"

"Yeah, but I never got a chance to ask Anna and now, well …"

We were quiet for a moment. I looked out at the mountain. Slowly the green was fading into red. A gust of wind swept across the terrace. Harmattan would soon be upon us.

"What will you do, then, if you leave here? Teach somewhere else?"

"No," she said firmly, then thought for a minute. "Maybe I'll go back to school."

I returned home that night just before dark. I was drained. It was an awful mixture of physical and emotional exhaustion, and I felt that as soon as my head hit the pillow I might sleep for days. First, though, it was necessary to shower. I dropped my bags to the floor and quickly gathered my bucket, resisting the temptation of the bed, knowing how worthwhile it would be once I was clean and cuddled up in its sheets. When I emerged from the cement shower there was a figure outside my door. Instantly came a rush of annoyance. All I wanted was my bed, and it was so awkward to greet people soaking wet, wrapped in *pagne*. Then I realized it was Adiza. She looked down as I approached.

"*Bonsoir,* Lily," she said, giving a slight bow. I had barely seen her since that night. This was the first time she had come to me on her own, without having to fetch the boys.

"*Ça va?*" I asked, concerned, as I opened the door and motioned for her to enter.

"*Oui*," she said. I invited her to sit down and went quickly into my room to change. When I came out she was sitting on the couch, with her arms folded and her eyes down. She had lost some of her swagger since first I met her. That childish giggle, that teenage conceit, it had all disappeared.

"You went away?" she asked, as I sat down beside her.

"*Oui*, I went to Ghana for a few days," I said.

"I thought maybe you had gone," she said. "Maybe you would not come back."

"No, I came back." I searched for Fati in her face. I used to think they were so different that they could hardly be sisters. Now her eyes, so sad and serious. She looked much more like her sister than she used to.

"How is your mother?" I asked.

"Good, good," she said. "My mother she still cries sometimes, but it is less."

"And how are you?" She shook her head.

"Lily," she asked suddenly, ignoring my question. "Will you start your club again?"

"Yes," I said. "Next week we will begin. Will you come again this year?"

"Yes," she said, then paused a moment. "Maybe I can help you? Like Fati did," she asked carefully.

"I would be very happy if you would help me," I said, and she flashed a smile that reminded me of her old smiles.

"I started at the Lycée this year," she said proudly.

"Wow," I said. "You're very smart. Just like your sister. I bet your mother is very proud." She beamed again, satisfied with herself.

"Lily," she said, growing more serious. "You should go and see her. I think she thinks that you blame her. For what happened to my sister."

"That I blame her?" I looked at her, startled. Adiza nodded and I could see she was unsure if she had done the right thing in telling me. How strange that Gladys thought that. I had been so certain that it had been the other way around.

"Lily, really it's my fault because I knew that Fatima had the medicine, but I didn't tell anyone. I knew she was going to take it," she said, and I could feel her pain. Adiza, Gladys and I were all suffering in our own ways. How much guilt we had all been harboring.

"Oh, Adiza," I said, putting my hand on her shoulder. "It isn't your fault. Please, you did everything you could to help her. And I would never blame your mother. I blame myself sometimes."

"But you tried to help her. You were the only one." Her eyes were wet as she struggled against her tears.

"We all feel guilty because we loved her, but it was no one's fault. Not yours or mine or your mother's or Fati's. Please believe that." She nodded. "Tomorrow I will go to see your mother. I'm so sorry, I didn't know. I will go first thing," I promised and Adiza nodded again.

"*Merci*, Lily," she said, getting up to go. "Maybe tomorrow I will come in the evening to help you for the club." I smiled. I wanted to hug her but that sort of thing wasn't really done here.

"Yes please, if you don't have too much homework," I said.

"*Bonne nuit*, Lily."

"*Bonne nuit*, Adiza."

And with that she was gone.

When I ultimately lay down in bed I could not sleep. I kept going over everything that had happened. How much could happen in a day? It felt like a lifetime ago that I had said goodbye to John at the station. And Cynthia, poor Cynthia. I'd always suspected she held a little flame for Matt. No wonder she was so upset. And Adiza. My heart broke for Adiza. How happy I was that she had come to me. How much I reprimanded myself for not going to Gladys. I had been afraid. Afraid she had blamed me for not finding another way out for Fati. How foolish I was. What a coward. I should have gone to her months ago. I would go in the morning.

I fell asleep that night a bit lighter than I had for some time. It was as if the weight of grief had lessened just a bit because I had finally shared it with them and we had found how foolish we had all been bearing the burden alone, taking all the blame and responsibility. I hoped I could remove some of the weight from Gladys's shoulders, as Adiza had done for me and hopefully I had done for her.

The next morning, I awoke early, remembering where I was again. Alone in bed, not with John in some crummy hotel room in Ghana. I remembered Adiza. I had to go to Gladys. I got up and made my coffee. I went through the usual morning routine and for the first time in a long time I felt happy to be there. I felt at home.

Once I was sure the children had left for school, I made my way over to Gladys's house. She was in the courtyard, finishing the last of the breakfast dishes in a bucket of water. When she looked up and saw me, she smiled brightly.

"Good morning, Lily. How are you?" she said, with her thick Ghanaian accent.

"I am good, how are you?"

"I am fine, I am fine," she said smiling. "Please, sit down, I will get a chair." She disappeared into the house and came back with two plastic lawn chairs, arranging them next to one another. We both sat down. "How was your trip?"

"Oh, it was very nice. Ghana is a beautiful country."

"Yes, I think someday I would like to go back there. It is better there. You have seen. Not like this place, these people." She said the last bit with a sense of bitterness I had not heard in her before. "But you did not go to the north, where I come from?"

"No, only Cape Coast."

"The north is not like the city," she said. "But still, it is better than this place. Adiza didn't think you would come back. She was crying. Oh, this girl!" She rolled her eyes with the frustrations of a mother with a teenager. I laughed.

"Yes, she came to see me last night. I want to tell you," I said, hesitantly, "I'm sorry that I haven't come to see you more since ... I was just afraid. I thought maybe you didn't want to see me. Maybe it made you sad or maybe you thought I could have done more to help."

"Oh, Lily!" she cried, taking my hands. Her eyes were glistening with emotion. "Oh, Lily," she repeated and shook her head. "It is good for you to come see me," she said. She took a deep breath. "I do not know how she got the medicine. When you said it is dangerous, I told her no. But she is a very stubborn girl."

"I know," I said. It seemed as if it was a relief for her to speak to me.

"She said to me, 'I have to finish school,' but how did she get the money? At first, I thought maybe the boy, he gave it to her," she said, shaking her head. "I told him, 'You did this!' But he is just crying and crying. He tells me, 'No, I didn't know.' I felt very bad. I think he is telling the truth. He was so sad." She shook from the memory, her eyes full of pain as if she was still speaking to Kpante now. "And this man who gives her the medicine! He go to jail! He cannot hurt other girls now." She was growing angry and I could see how much pain there was still in her. How much pain there would always be. She stopped herself and looked at me, obviously catching herself at my concerned expression, and she smiled sadly, softening a bit. "But you, you were her friend. You tried to help her. I say to you thank you." She reached for my hand again. "I still cry sometimes. But she is with God now. We will meet again." I nodded. I was happy that she could take comfort in that.

"I miss her very much," I said.

"You will meet again," she repeated. "Lily, I want Adiza to have the injection. She said you talked about it at your club? I told her, do not be like your sister, you see what can happen? But still I am afraid."

"I will go with her if you want, to the *dispensaire*," I offered. "She must go back every three months." Gladys nodded.

"I think I will go, too. I want to get the injection, too," she said firmly and then she laughed. "Oh, Lily, it was good for you to come."

It was good. A great relief. We said our goodbyes and just as I turned to leave she called out to me.

"But Lily, what did you bring me from your trip? Where is my bread?" I laughed. All was right between us now.

"Oh! I will bring it tomorrow!" I called back, and she laughed again, waving me off.

It was a long time before I heard from John again after our trip. At first it had been difficult. I missed the excitement of looking forward to long weekends together, either here or in Kara. I missed having someone to text when funny little things happened around me or when I read a book he might like or came across an article that made me think of him. What made things even more difficult was that he did not attempt to contact me either. For the first few days, I thought he was just trying to give me time, but when a week passed I found it more difficult to make excuses. Perhaps I had been wrong about him holding out hope I would change my mind. Perhaps his invitation to Senegal itself had been an empty gesture. Perhaps I would never know. It hurt me at first, though it had no right to, for I didn't try to call or text him either. Still, it was a bit of a blow to my pride, though I tried not to dwell too deeply on it.

Luckily, I didn't have the time. My days were full of work; I started a boys' club along with my girls' club, aided by Monsieur Robert. I gave talks at the *dispensaire* twice a week and still aided in the baby-weighing sessions every Friday. I began to plan a strategy for conducting home visits with the *matron* to go and speak to the villagers on family planning and other things we deemed important together, with advice from the *infirmier*. In the evenings, Adiza came over, sometimes with her brothers and sometimes alone. We discussed topics and lesson plans for the clubs, and she also used the time to study as Fati had.

Sometimes I caught myself almost calling her by her sister's name, or glimpsing her out of the corner of my eye and mistaking her for Fati. Her favorite subject was English, and we practiced together. Her lesson plans were most amusing. One of her reading comprehension exercises dealt explicitly on how to identify sorcerers. I wasn't sure if it was hyperbole or not. Life carried on.

I was meeting Cynthia for a post-market drink one Saturday, just a few weeks before Christmas, when she told me John was leaving that weekend.

"He's having a little going-away party in Kara," she said, hesitantly. We hadn't spoken much about it since the day I returned. I assumed she still spoke to him from time to time, but I didn't ask and she didn't offer.

"Oh?" I responded. There had to be a reason for her to bring it up now. I tried to sound uninterested.

"Yes, he'd like you to come, but I think he's nervous to ask you. I saw him last week. I had to do some banking and we met for a drink. He says he feels bad that you two haven't spoken since your trip. I think he'd like to make amends before he leaves," she explained.

"There's nothing really to amend. We didn't exactly part on bad terms or anything."

"I know, but … Well, I think you should go. I think you'll regret it if you don't," she said.

"I'm not sure about that."

"I know you, I know your pride. Even if you don't care, it's better to go and show there's no harm done."

"Well, if he wants me to go, he'll have to invite me."

"He will," Cynthia said. "I'm sure he will."

"Anna's going too, then?" I asked, and Cynthia gave me a strange look.

"You haven't heard?"

"What?"

"She left. Just a few days ago. She called me from Lomé. I wasn't sure if you spoke to her as well."

"No," I said, surprised. "Why?"

"I think it had something to do with Matt. It was very hard for her."

"So, it's just you and me then?" I said, looking at her, shaking my head.

"Yup, I'm all you got," she teased.

I didn't know if Cynthia had relayed our conversation to John, but the next day I got a phone call. For the first time in months his name flashed across my screen and I resisted the temptation not to answer.

"Hello?"

"Hello, Lily." His voice made my heart beat a bit faster as the memory of him came to life again. "How are you? It's been a while."

"It has, yes. I'm doing well. How are you?"

"Good. Just wrapping things up, saying my goodbyes and all that."

"Is this your goodbye phone call, then?" I said and then instantly regretted it. I sounded bitter. Still, he was a little full of himself to think I should have wanted that.

"No, no," he said quickly. "No, I wanted to, I just … I'm sorry I never called or anything, after we got back."

"No need to be sorry," I said, my tone gentler. "I never did either."

"This is true," he laughed.

"When are you off, then?" I asked, wanting to move the conversation away from the past.

"Next week."

"Are you going straight there?"

"No, I'm going back to Morocco for the holidays, to catch up with some old friends."

"That should be nice."

"Yes, I'm looking forward to it. It's been a long time since I was back there." He sounded relieved that we were now speaking of things that I surely had no interest in. They were the kinds of things you ask acquaintances out of politeness. To make conversation, to fill the air. "I wanted to ask, you know, I'm having a small gathering next weekend to say goodbye. It would be nice if you could come."

"Right, when is it?"

"Saturday."

"Yes, possibly. I'll try."

"Yeah, please do. Issa will be there. I know he'd like to see you."

"Well, good luck packing and all that. Hopefully I'll make it."

"I hope you do."

After hanging up the phone, I sat for a moment. What had I expected? If there was any doubt in my mind about how he felt, it was now removed. And it was only then that I really felt the loss of him. The weight of what we had shared. How much we had experienced together. It was then that I realized that perhaps it had been more than I had wanted to admit. It was then that I realized how alone I was.

I ended up going to the party. Cynthia and I booked a room at a hotel nearby. She convinced me that we should go only to make an appearance and then we could treat ourselves to a nice dinner and lots of wine from bottles, not boxes. It was a convivial scene, but it was difficult to be back in that house again. It was filled with ghosts. As I wandered from room to room, I felt Matt and Anna's absence heavily. And John's too, though he was still there. I missed the way it used to be. Catching each other's eye across the table and stealing kisses on the balcony. I tried to give the impression that I was happy to be there. I made polite conversation with people I knew, only vaguely, through my work with John. Pretending to listen, searching desperately for things to say. Cynthia stayed close for the most part. John was the guest of honor and in high demand. I started to wonder if I would even get a chance to say hello. Or goodbye, for that matter.

After an hour had passed, I wanted to leave. We'd made enough of an appearance and it seemed John would have sought me out if he'd wanted to. If he'd had anything to say to me. I was beginning to feel foolish for listening to Cynthia. It would have been better to have stayed away. I went to grab Cynthia but she was caught in a conversation with an earnest-looking Togolese official. The minister of transport or something. All I knew was that he was too important to interrupt with the intention of stealing her away and I had no desire to join in their conversation.

"Lily, I'm happy you came!" Issa's voice rang from behind me.

"Oh, hello there," I said. It made me sad to see him. His warm smile. His kind, bright eyes.

"It is good. I know it has been difficult for you and John. He told me you are staying here?" I nodded. "I think it is the right thing for you."

"Really?" I asked, surprised.

"Yes, really," he laughed. "You know, I think maybe you are better than John in this work. Never tell him I said that, though, you promise?"

"I promise." I laughed as well, even more surprised. "But I don't know if I'd agree with you there."

"No, no, it's true. You are like me, Lily. You see things for what they are. And still, you don't let it stop you. In the end, we won't be disappointed because we always knew we were fighting an uphill battle. People like John, they need their illusions to continue. But, for us, even knowing what we know, we could never do otherwise. For John this will be a good thing. A big promotion in a big office, full of people and their illusions. It's people like us that need to be here on the ground."

"Thank you, it means a lot," I said. Though I wondered

if he was trying to comfort me or himself. "What will you do now? Do you have anything else lined up?"

"Oh no. Hopefully whoever they replace him with will want me to stay on."

"Replace him with? I thought—" I felt a shallow pain in my chest. Issa's eyes flashed with regret as he realized what he had done. "I would have found out eventually," I offered.

"It is better this way," he said.

I looked over at Cynthia, still locked in conversation. I glared, willing her to notice me. Nothing. "I'm sorry, if you'll excuse me," I said to Issa and he put his hand on my shoulder.

"*Courage,* Lily. I'm sorry."

"*You've* nothing to be sorry for." I smiled because it was the only way not to cry and made my way past him out onto the empty porch for a cigarette. So, John had not been ousted; he had chosen to leave. Was he trying to get away? But then, why had he asked me to go with him? Did he assume I would say no? How could I make sense of it?

"I'm glad you came." I looked up to see John standing in the doorway. He was alone. "I wasn't sure if you would."

"Neither was I. But here I am."

"I saw you speaking to Issa." He hesitated and I looked up at him, unable to hide my anger. My hurt. "Look, they just decided to keep the office open. It was our project that did it really. They were so impressed with what we accomplished. What I told you in Ghana, that was the truth. I really thought—"

"Did they give you the option then? To stay on here?"

He sat down next to me on the wooden bench, just far enough so that the cold gap that hung between us could not be filled by the warmth of his presence. "I'm sorry, Lily. That things didn't work out between us. I've been doing a lot of thinking the last couple of months. Remember what you said to me in Cape Coast? About losing faith in humanity?"

"Was I that dramatic about it?"

"Yes," he smiled. "You were. You are. But that's not the point. Can I tell you something? Can I be honest with you?"

"Please do," I said.

"I know you haven't had the easiest time here. And trust me, I'm not doubting your loss. I know you cared a lot about Fati. But honestly? I think maybe you use this hopeless, 'all is lost' attitude as a means of excusing yourself from responsibility. If everything really is as futile as you say it is, then you don't risk anything. It takes the burden of responsibility off you. It's easier that way. If the whole country is just one big mess of ineptitude, then you don't really have to try to change anything."

"I'm sorry? I don't have to try? What the fuck have I been doing the last year and a half of my life? The club, the talks, the project? That's why I'm still here. In spite of everything. *I* decided to stay. You've got a lot of fucking nerve –"

"Look, don't go crazy, I'm only trying to help you—"

"Help me? Ha!" I was almost yelling. John kept glancing nervously inside, hoping no one would hear, or worse, wander out to join us. I didn't care who heard me. "Okay, let me return the favor then," I shot back.

"Lily, I'm sorry. Maybe I shouldn't have—"

"Yes, but you did. At least I'm not delusional. You think this place is so perfect—"

"I never said that."

"It was a choice for you, to be here. And it was a choice for you to leave. It will be the same in Senegal. I doubt you'd love it so much if it wasn't."

The door opened behind me and I saw the relieved look on John's face when Cynthia appeared from inside.

"Hey, am I interrupting?"

"No," I said, standing up from the bench. "I was just going to find you, are you ready?"

"Sure," she said, giving us both an uneasy glance. Then she went to give John a hug and I stood back, waiting. "Good luck, take care."

"Thanks," John said, his eyes still on me as they embraced.

"Yeah, good luck," I said, coldly, not moving from where I stood.

"Lily, I'm sorry. I really am. I shouldn't have said those things. It wasn't the time…" He looked as though he wanted some sort of sign that I understood. That I accepted his apology. Perhaps an embrace, a kind smile. I turned to leave.

"Have a safe trip," Cynthia called out as she followed behind me. "You okay?" she asked once we were through the gate. I couldn't help it: the second I was free I couldn't stop the tears. "Hey, oh no. Lily, I'm so sorry I said you should go tonight."

"No. I'm glad you did," I said. She began trying to flag down a moto off the main road. "Let's just walk for a bit?"

"Sure, whatever you want." It was nearly dusk and there was almost a breeze, enough to make the heat more tolerable. "What did he say?"

"What didn't he say. Did you know he didn't have to go?"

"What?"

"Issa told me, he chose to leave. They aren't closing the NGO down."

"No, I had no idea." She was quiet for a moment. "He's a real asshole, you know? I guess I gave him more credit than he deserved. He asked me if you would go and I thought that—"

"No, it's fine. I'm glad, in a way. Now I know I'll never wonder what might have been." I let out a sad chuckle. "There were so many things I should have said. Oh, I just get so angry thinking about it. All his idolizing of this place, this work, this life. Then he picks up and leaves for some fancy new post in Dakar. You know what he said once? He told me he preferred it here to back home."

"Of course he did," Cynthia laughed. "He'd probably have two wives. Maybe even three. Makes perfect sense. Don't listen to him. Don't let him get to you. I'm sorry. I should never have made you come to his thing."

"No, don't worry. In a strange way, you were actually right. It did give me closure." I thought of what Issa had said. "I'm glad I came." We walked on and I felt the anger begin to dissipate. "You know, when I came to Africa, I was looking for something. I think I finally found it. But it isn't what I thought it was."

"Isn't that always the way." She shook her head. "So, what is it that you've found?"

"I guess it's less of a thing. It's more of a realization that I'll never stop looking. Never stop trying to find a way to do something meaningful. I don't know if what I'm doing here is the best way to have an impact, to do good. But I'll finish what I started and I'll take what I've learned, and if it isn't I'll keep trying to find another way. And really that's all you can do in the end."

"Amen sister."

Chapter Sixteen

Detroit
May 25th, 2013

"So, you didn't write anything?" Sonia repeated as we sat at the bar sipping our drinks. "Like nothing? Not a poem, not a word for the whole two years?" She had a look of what was either disbelief or disdain, I wasn't sure.

"I did a bit in the beginning, you know, but it was difficult."

"Why?" she asked. "Didn't you have time?"

"It wasn't that, it was just ... Everything was different from what I expected."

"But different how?" It sounded more like an accusation than a question.

"Oh Jesus, I don't know," I said. "I mean, how do you think? It was hard to see people live like that and I just felt, well, I felt it was silly. Everything I was working on up to then was silly."

She said nothing. I had offended her. But did she worry about offending me?

"Should we head off then?" I asked.

She put her drink to her red painted lips and

swallowed the last of its clear contents, harshly returning the glass to the counter so that the ice clanked in echo of her annoyance. She threw some money on the counter and I did the same.

"I just thought you might want to talk about it," she said, unlocking the car door.

"Well, it felt like you were attacking me."

"I was just surprised, is all." She began to dig around for the joint we'd been smoking on the way downtown. It wasn't a kind thing to say. I had disappointed her somehow. But what right did she have to be disappointed in me? That took some nerve. Out the window, there was the familiar blur of storefronts and streetlights. Try to forget it, I told myself. Let it pass. It was always bound to be difficult, coming back. Even though I had known this, it was still hard to take.

It wasn't far to the Scarab Club. We arrived quickly without a word having been spoken between us. The lot was only half full and there were small groups of people making their way inside.

"Let's have a cigarette before we go in," I said as a sort of peace offering. We stood for a moment outside the entrance. "Look, I'm just a bit sensitive about it, alright."

"Okay, well, I didn't mean to sound like I was attacking you, I just—Oh, hey, it's Will! Hey Will!" She waved to a tall, dark figure approaching from the lot.

"Hey!" Will replied, giving Sonia a quick embrace.

"Will, this is my friend Lily. She's the one I was telling you about. She just got back, she's been living in Africa for the last two years."

"Right, nice to meet you Lily," he smiled. "You guys been inside yet?"

"No, we just got here too."

"I think Tim's inside."

"I was telling Lil about him."

"Yeah, he's got a few pieces up tonight. Should be interesting. Glad you guys could make it out."

"We used to do this stuff all the time, Lily and me. We were always going to shows, galleries. Got to get Lil back into the swing of things. You ready, Lil?"

I flicked my cigarette into the empty street. It was me, I realized. I was on the defense. I had to stop it. I followed the two of them in, curious as to whether this was anything serious or if Will was simply another one of Sonia's many platonic admirers.

The gallery inside was small, bright and stuffy. People stood in clusters around the room. Like most openings, it was more about seeing and being seen than viewing the actual art.

Purposefully, I went the other way from Sonia and Will, pretending to be intrigued by some framed collage of colors across the room. They carried on without me. I found myself scanning each frame, almost without being fully aware of my intentions. I was looking for something. A particular style. A memorable assortment of colors. A fluff of black hair under a fedora hat. I walked slowly and silently past each image. Some were impressive in their distinctness, but none was what I was looking for. It had been so long, anyway. Would I even recognize his work anymore? Sonia and Will were standing near the small bar that had been set up opposite the entrance.

"What do you think, Lil?" Sonia asked, as I approached them.

"I think it's much better than that last exhibition we went to."

"Which one was that?" She didn't remember. It was a night I had thought about so often.

"At the Russell."

"Oh, God, yes! That was awful."

"What was this?" Will asked.

"Oh, just some terrible thing we went to before Lily left. I remember you told me that story about the girl and the pile of garbage that you almost stepped on. It was actually her 'piece' for the show."

"Oh, one of those, yeah," Will nodded. "No, no. Trust me, I wouldn't take you to one of those. I should introduce you to my friend Tim," he said, focusing his eyes on me. "He's around here somewhere. His work's there, toward the back."

"He's cute, Lil. And we know how you have a soft spot for artists," Sonia said. I rolled my eyes at her. The last thing I had wanted this evening was to be pushed off onto someone. "Let's go have a look," she said, dragging me.

Again, I followed behind them. Tim's work was quite generic, more like prints than paintings, but I tried to pretend, to take my time, to see them.

"I like them!" Sonia said. I wondered if she meant it or if she was just trying to be nice.

"Yes, interesting."

"There you are," Will called out from behind us. "We were admiring your work."

"Good to see someone is," Tim laughed. He gave Sonia a hug.

"This is my friend, Lily," she said. "She's the friend I was telling you about. The one that was living in Africa."

"Right, welcome back," Tim said.

"Yes, well done on the paintings," I said.

"Thank you. You know, if you guys can hang out for an hour I'd be happy to get away soon. Maybe grab some food or something?"

"I think we can manage to keep ourselves entertained for an hour or so," Sonia said.

"Great."

"He's cute, isn't he, Lil?" Sonia asked once Tim had disappeared back into the crowd.

"Yeah," I said. "I think I'll go get a drink. Want anything?"

"We've already got some, thanks," Will said, raising his plastic cup.

Back at the bar, I couldn't shake the feeling that it emanated from my pores, how obviously uncomfortable I was. How out of place. I waited as the bartender poured me a glass of wine from the endless supply of bottles that lined the white linen table behind her. So many bottles, such excess. I sighed heavily, and my eyes fell unexpectedly on two paintings just beyond the bar. Before my mind could even process what I was seeing, I felt it. A sharp jolt to the chest. I almost gasped as the bartender handed me my wine. How had I not noticed them before? They stood out so strongly against the rest. I walked through the crowd. One was of a woman staring out of a diner window. She had dark hair and sad eyes. Her eyes reflected the rain just beyond the glass. Who was she? I suffered a strange sort of envy of her. The other was of a building. Dilapidated. An old storefront, overrun with graffiti. I recognized the street. I had walked past it one night. Lifetimes ago.

"You like these?" I turned to see Tim standing next to me.

"Yes," I said.

"They are captivating, aren't they?"

"Do you know who the artist is?"

"Yeah he's a local guy. Jack Mason."

"Is he here tonight?"

"Do you know him?"

"Sort of, I met him once. Just before I left."

"No, he isn't here. I heard he was leaving town just before the opening. He was going to New York, I think it was? Where they all go, trying to 'make it.' You're disappointed?"

I looked at him. I didn't like the way he said it. We had only just met and I had been unwittingly dragged into this set-up.

"A bit," I said. "*C'est la vie.*" I searched the room desperately for Sonia and Will.

"Well, I think I've done enough schmoozing for now. Shall we find the others and get out of here?" he said.

"Sure."

We found Sonia and Will and made our way through the crowd. Tim was making a show of it, saying his goodbyes and muttering things like, 'Oh that's so-and-so from the *News*' or some blog I'd never heard of. We decided to take one car to the restaurant. The place was only a block or so away. It was a new place that had just opened. Inside it was dark and crowded and overpriced.

Over the course of dinner, I watched Sonia and Will. It was serious. Why hadn't she mentioned him? Of course, we'd only spoken a handful of times over the last two years. I was paying the price now for all those broken promises. The distance between us was no longer physical. It cut more deeply than that now.

Tim had studied art, obviously. He did some freelance design work. He was a typical Detroit renaissance man. He knew how to hustle. Sonia could tell I didn't like him. At first, she tried to help it along. She told stories of our past escapades, but they sounded contrived and she lost interest. She didn't introduce me as The Poet anymore. Now I was Lily That Lived In Africa. No one asked about Africa. It wasn't until the end that Will turned to me with a question, not about the past, but concerning the future.

"What will you do now?" he asked.

"Are you going to try to go back to the paper?" Sonia asked.

"No," I said.

"Will you stay in Detroit?" Tim asked. "Things are really getting going, you know. Even just over the last two years. It's a pretty exciting time."

"No, I don't think I will, actually." I hesitated. I hadn't planned on giving my little announcement like this but there seemed no point in pretending. "I've actually been talking to a woman from an NGO in London. She's doing some research there that's related to some of the work I was doing in Togo. She's invited me to come out, to help with some of it."

"Like a job?" Sonia asked.

"Yes, just for a few months I think. But it will take a while to get the paperwork going. I need to get a temporary work visa."

"When would you go?"

"I probably wouldn't leave for another month at least."

"Well, congrats," Will offered.

"Yeah, London's a pretty cool city. Think I'd still prefer Detroit, though," Tim added.

After the dinner, we drove back to get our cars. No one tried to make the night continue. I was relieved.

"So, you're moving to London then?" Sonia asked again once we were alone in her car. Did it bother her that I hadn't mentioned it earlier? Or maybe that sort of thing didn't matter as much as it once had to our friendship.

"If it all works out."

"Isn't it expensive, though? Like one of the most expensive cities in the world to live in?" I smiled. London was as expensive as Africa had been dangerous.

"Maybe. I think all cities are. But people do it somehow."

We both were silent.

"You aren't coming back then, are you?"

"From London?"

"From anywhere."

"I don't know. I'm sorry I didn't write you back," I said, and she smiled and shook her head, staring out at the road ahead, not at me.

"You know, at first I thought they got lost in the mail, coming all the way from Africa and all. But I get it." She didn't get it, but I hoped she at least had some sympathy.

"Is it serious with you and Will?"

"I'm not sure yet. I do like him. But we'll see. You didn't like Tim, then?"

"No, I'm sorry if I spoiled your plans. Do you remember the artist I met just before I left?"

"Yeah," she said, looking over at me.

"I saw some of his paintings in the gallery tonight."

"Really? Was he there?"

"No. Tim knows him. He said he had just left for New York, or something." Like all the rest of them, he had said. I smiled. No, not like all the rest. If New York was where he was going, it wouldn't be to 'make it'.

"Oh, that's too bad," she said, but it was an automated response. "You know, Lil, Tim's not so bad once you get to know him. I mean you're leaving again, anyway. You could have a little fun with him before you go."

I rolled my eyes. Some things never change, and yet, you can't go home again. How can both things ring so true? She dropped me off and we said goodbye. Inside the old oak doors my grandmother was waiting.

"How are you doing, honey?" She lit a cigarette.

"I'm alright," I said, pouring a glass of wine in the kitchen. I sat down across from her. She was looking at me now; she knew it was a lie. "It's funny being back," I began carefully.

"I bet," she said, swirling her drink. Letting me take my time with it. She looked thinner. Her face was more gaunt. Her shoulders more hunched. I saw the physical effects of two years on her face and body. Still, she smiled as she always had, with a glow and warmth that time could not diminish.

"How was tonight? Did you have a good time, at least?"

"It was alright," I repeated the words.

"Just alright?"

"I told Sonia about London," I said.

"Was she sad you're leaving again?"

"No, I don't think she was. I think she's gotten used to me not being around. I think tonight was sort of a disappointment for both of us."

"I'm sure that's not true," she said.

I hesitated. It had changed for us as well. In the same way that Sonia had, my grandmother had gotten used to life without me. Where once I had been such a standard feature in their lives, now I felt like an outsider trying to get back in. It was a hard revelation. The fact that I had attributed so much importance to myself, and yet it had all gone along smoothly for them without me. New habits became routines and old habits, while they might die hard, with enough time they do die. Since I had returned, I'd told my grandmother about Fati and Gladys. About Cynthia and John. About my work. But there was still something I couldn't convey with words. Something about the experience that made me feel as though I was looking at the world through a sharper lens and nothing that I left behind was what I thought it was.

"You know how many times in Togo I thought about nights like these? I couldn't wait to be doing all this again. Going out with Sonia to galleries and shows and everything we used to do? And now that I'm here, it just isn't the same. She's not the same. I'm not the same. Nothing's the same," I said.

"You know what I think, honey? It's going to take some adjustment being back. After everything you've gone through. You need to give yourself some time to settle in."

"I just feel so lost," I said. "Like I don't belong anywhere anymore. I'm afraid I've changed. Too much maybe." I realized how sad it made me to think it, once I heard myself say it. Once I heard the grief in my voice. My grandmother looked at me and her eyes grew wide with surprise and she pursed her lips in soft amusement.

"Well, of course you've changed. How can you not have changed?" It was not so much her words that surprised me as the simplicity with which she spoke them. "But not that much," she assured me. "You're still my Lily."

"Am I?"

"Of course you are," she laughed. "Who else would you be? You need to go easy on yourself, honey. Remember, when you left you didn't feel like you belonged here either. Don't forget that. I mean, it's understandable, you're feeling a bit sentimental, being home again and all. But listen, you have to stop this now. Don't dwell on things. Think of London. How exciting it will be. Think of what you'll be able to do with all you've learned, everything you've experienced. Be excited, honey. Your life is just beginning. Going away and coming back, well, it's always going to be difficult. And of course it's going to change you. If it didn't, I'd be worried." She laughed a little and I smiled. "But not too much. You'll always be my Lily. No matter where you go or however long you're gone for. Don't you worry about that."

Suddenly I felt myself begin to laugh through my

tears. "Oh, you're right. You're always right. It's me. I'm taking it all too personally."

Tonight, with Sonia, it had felt as if a great distance lay between us, unmanageable lengths. Months and years. Oceans and continents. And yet how many times over the past two years had I summoned her spirit, and thought what would she have done if she were here now, and tried to emulate her courage, her lack of respect for convention? I had done the same with my grandmother and I had heard words she could not speak to me but would have said all the same when I needed them. The two of them were with me always, even if they seemed farther away from me now than they had been when I was in need of them in some little village all the way in Africa. Life goes on, as it did after Fati's death, and yet Fati too was always there. In everything I thought and felt and lived. I smiled at my grandmother thankfully. She made me see it now as she had always done. Though one thing still bothered me.

"I didn't write," I said sadly. "I don't want to now. I worry that Sonia was right in a way ... Perhaps it had been a mistake to think leaving here would help. I'm afraid it's done the opposite ..." I waited and her eyes became serious. She was thinking it over carefully, what she should say.

"You know," she said finally. "Sometimes I think that it's better to experience things and then let them settle a bit. It will come back to you. I'm sure it will. It's better not to rush it. Just give yourself time, Lily. Be patient."

"Yes," I said, though I wasn't sure I believed her. But there might have been some truth to what she was saying. After all, I still had work to do. At least that much I was sure of.

Chapter Seventeen

Togo
April 25, 2013

I had not dreamed of Fati since her death and then one night she came to me. It happened just a few days before my departure. It was the kind of dream that felt indistinguishable from waking life. We sat in my living room just as we used to, and at first everything went on as it always had. Fati sat with her notebooks and I with mine. Then, I suddenly remembered that she was dead. At first it was almost as if perhaps her death had been the dream and really, she was alive. But then the memory of the grief returned and I realized I had it all turned around and this was the dream, and I began to cry. Fati came to where I sat and took my hand. She smiled and said, "*Ça va*, Lily." Her smile was the same smile that used to say 'Oh, Lily. How little you know', but this time there was a joy in it that hadn't been there before. It filled me with a sense of peace. I awoke in the night, sobbing. It felt as though she had really come to me. I thought perhaps it was just the stress of leaving and returning home, but it stayed with me like the warmth of a memory that had actually been lived.

I mentioned it to Cynthia, but she was unimpressed.

"I have strange dreams all the time here," was all she'd said.

Cynthia was leaving, too, but not until the school year ended. She often chided me for abandoning her, but there would be little more than a month that she'd need to go without me. We met for drinks every market day until my departure, as we always had, but now I tried desperately to hold on to each minute of my walks into town. The children no longer chanted *anasara* but 'Lily' as they ran up to greet me. The groups of women along the dusty road, dressed in their beautiful *pagne*, smiling at me. The mountain, full of its sorcerers and magic. I wanted to remember that walk forever.

"Any plans for when you get back?" Cynthia asked me on our last day together. She had asked me before but I had no answer. I still didn't have much of one.

"No," I said. "Enjoying the good life for a while. You know, indoor plumbing and all that. Then who knows? Maybe I'll go back to school as well."

"You should apply somewhere in New York. We could be roommates!" Cynthia had been accepted to a teaching program at Columbia. She was very pleased with herself and I was happy for her, though a bit jealous that she at least had a plan. "You'll figure it out. Just take your time. It's difficult, you know, the first time you go back."

"I imagine," I said. "What was difficult for you the first time you went home?"

"Well, you'll have changed. Everyone else, not so much," she said, mixing her sachet of gin into her glass of tonic water. "So, you're heading down to Lomé on Monday, then?"

"Yes, this is it," I sighed.

"Can you believe it's been two years?" she asked, shaking her head.

"No," I laughed.

"What will I do without you for the next few weeks?"

"Oh, you'll be fine. I'll see you in New York in a few months, anyway," I teased.

"It goes so fast, doesn't it? I feel sometimes I just got here yesterday. But it's been three years."

"Now that it's over, it seems that way. But that's always how it goes."

"Do you want me to help you pack?"

"No, it's done. I'm supposed to be having dinner with Gladys and her family tonight. You can come if you want."

"Actually I have my own packing to do. A year more's worth than you. I suppose it's almost that time, then," she said sadly, gazing off into the distance.

"Yes," I said. "I suppose it is."

We walked down the cement steps and out onto the busy street.

"Good luck with your last few weeks."

"Have a safe trip back."

"You too," I said as she embraced me.

"See you on the other side," she called as she disappeared into the town center and I wondered when I would see her again. If I would see her again.

Gladys came to see me the following morning to pick up the bags I had filled with things I could not take with me but would be useful to her: cooking utensils, clothes and leftover school supplies from my club. I was giving her my furniture too, but she had not wanted to take anything before I was gone, afraid to leave me in such an empty place alone.

"Lily," she said carefully as she collected the first round of bags to take with her. "I want to take you today, to see my husband's brother. He can give something to you for your journey. To keep you safe. Will you come?" she asked eagerly. It didn't sound like the kind of invitation that could be refused. She said she would return in a few hours, before the sun began to set. Around four that afternoon, Adiza appeared at my door to enquire if I was ready to go and we met Gladys on the road outside my compound.

"We will walk. It is not far," she said.

We followed her until she turned down a hidden path just before the Lycée. We carried on as the houses became sparse and the fields gave way to forest. I had seen the trees from a distance, but I had never walked through them and I regretted not exploring these mysterious little roads before now. How much beauty had I missed in my short time here? How many different paths had I passed by, never noticing them?

We reached a clearing and there was a compound a short distance ahead of us. A man was sitting on a bench near the entrance and he stood to greet us when he saw us approaching. He seemed to have been expecting us, as he stood with his hands in his faded gray shorts and greeted Gladys with some familiarity. I greeted him in the local language and his face lit up with great pleasure as I spoke.

"*Anasara habla Bassar!*" he laughed, shaking his head at the outrageousness of such a sight. He led us inside the compound to a few scattered chairs. He continued to speak to Gladys and motioned for us all to have a seat.

"My husband's brother is busy now with another man. This man is his assistant. When he is finished, he will see you," she explained. "He is there." She pointed to one of the little huts that rested apart from all the others. I looked over but it was too dark and far away to see anything. There was a flash of the night we had all gone with Matt to see the *féticheur* and it all came back to me, Fati telling me once that her uncle was a *féticheur*. We sat quietly and watched as another man emerged from the strange little hut and the assistant walked over to speak to him. They exchanged a few words and then our host ran quickly around to the side of the building and re-emerged with a small brown pygmy goat with a rope tied around its neck. He handed the goat to the man and the man went back into the tent. A few moments later we heard the cry of the poor condemned animal and shortly after the man left the tent with the lifeless body in his hands. They tied the body onto his moto and then he was off. Finally, the assistant signaled for us to enter the hut.

Inside, the smell of fresh blood hit me, as my eyes adjusted to the darkness. I noticed a rock in the center of a small shrine, covered in the fresh crimson liquid. In the corner a man sat and he grinned toothlessly at us when our eyes found him in the dim room. He stood to greet me and we shook hands, bowing to one another. I had never seen this man before, but he had a look about him that seemed familiar to me. There was something in his eyes, dark and serious. Suddenly I realized that they were Fati's eyes.

"Lily, this is my husband's brother," Gladys explained as we sat opposite the smiling old man who had Fati's eyes. "He is going to make a blessing. Maybe he will tell you something for your future. He says it is better if you buy a chicken to make an offering. It is okay?" she asked. I nodded. "Good. He has a chicken here for us. Don't worry." She negotiated the price of our sacrifice and I handed the man a few thousand CFA. "He will bring it after," she explained.

The man prepared a pile of shells and coins with the practiced ritual of preparing a holy sacrament. He picked up the bottle of gin and poured some into a small shot glass and drank from it. He refilled the glass and passed it to Gladys, who drank. He then filled it again and gave it to me. I took a sip and quickly realized it was not gin but *sodobe*, a homemade substance reminiscent of moonshine. I offered the glass to Adiza, but she refused.

The man poured some *sodobe* over the rock. He gathered his shells and coins and spoke to them, then to the rock. He chanted as he shook the shells and coins in his hands like dice and threw them on the cement floor. Then he repeated the gesture, his voice rising and falling in intensity. I looked over at Gladys to see if perhaps she might translate but she ignored me, her eyes intensely focused on the fetish. Was it a prayer? A question? Perhaps it was nothing more than the gibberish it sounded to be. When he was satisfied with whatever answers he heard, he stopped and sat quietly for a moment. He looked down and nodded, as if to someone in conversation, but whatever voice he heard was not discernible to us. Finally, he looked up at me and smiled. I returned the smile because it was warm and bright and I found it instinctive to answer his smile with my own. He spoke to Gladys. She listened for a moment and then signaled for him to pause so she could translate for me.

"He said there is something the fetish told him that he wants to tell you. He said the dead have come to you in your dreams but that you should not be frightened. He said they will protect you because there are still many places you must go." She paused a moment and the man continued. "He said you have done good here, but he said that you are right and it is time to leave." She paused again and I could see she was having trouble with the last part and I waited to hear more. "He said…" She turned to ask the man again and he spoke readily, with his hands, trying to convey his message. Gladys nodded, leaning toward the man as if it might help her to translate, though she heard him clearly. "He said the work you have done here is good, but you have not begun your *real* work yet." She looked at me questioningly and the man nodded along as she spoke. "You understand?"

"Yes," I said. Somehow, I understood exactly what the stranger meant.

"He wants to give you something, so you can be safe, so you won't get sick. So you have protection," she explained. The man continued. "But first we will get the chicken and then he will give you the—" She paused, unable to find the word in English.

"*Charbon*," Adiza offered in French.

I nodded.

"He will put it here," she said, pointing to the outside of my wrists.

As we discussed it, the old man called out into the courtyard. Soon his associate appeared with the chicken flapping in his hands. Again, we were offered the *sodobe*. Then the *féticheur* took a large knife and quickly slit the bird's throat. They shouted at the bird as it flapped about helplessly until it gave up and lay still in defeat. The man looked up and clapped cheerfully.

"It is good," Gladys said. "They have accepted your offer."

The *féticheur* then crushed charcoal onto a stone slab. He gave a bit to each of us. "You must eat it," Gladys instructed, though I was already familiar with the ritual and put the metallic-tasting substance to my lips. "Now he will cut you," she said. I laughed nervously.

"Are they new razors?" I asked. There were certain lines I would not cross. I only trusted the gods so much.

"There is a shop next door. Adiza will go," Gladys said.

I gave Adiza a few hundred CFA. We waited as the *féticheur* continued to prepare the charcoal and his associate disappeared with our offering. Soon, Adiza returned with a fresh packet of razor blades. The man walked over with the rock of gray dust. He motioned for Gladys to make the incisions. She made three quick slits on the outside of my wrist. Then the old man rubbed the charcoal into the cuts. Then again on my left wrist. It was a quick pain, like a paper cut. "You must not wash it, until tomorrow," she instructed. The ceremony had finished. The old man smiled at me with Fati's eyes one last time, shaking my hand as we got up to leave. Adiza and I waited for a moment outside the compound while Gladys said her goodbyes.

"He is your uncle?" I asked. "*Vrai oncle?*" She nodded. I wondered if she saw the resemblance I had seen. "Can a woman be a *féticheur?*" I asked, already knowing the answer.

"*Non.*"

When Gladys appeared, we began the journey home. "It is good," was all she said, and we walked the rest of the road in silence. I wondered about the dreams. Was it a funny coincidence? How many people dreamed of such things? It had to be quite common. But I used to believe more easily in such mysteries. That was the point, wasn't it, after all? The mysteries. To know that not everything was settled. Not everything was decided. Wasn't it more foolish to think that it was?

The morning I left Lomé, I gave my exit interview. I had had little contact with Jeremy since we had been awarded the grant money. He asked the questions he was meant to ask, and I gave the answers I was meant to give.

"You did a lot of good work here, Lily," he said, going over my final report. "Your work in promoting women's health. I'm sure you've made a lasting impact. Say, that reminds me, whatever happened to that girl? The one you had mentioned when you were down here last year?"

"The girl?" I repeated. "What girl?" It took me a moment to realize he was speaking of Fati. The girl. Some girl in some village somewhere. A dime a dozen they were. "She died," I said. "She got a hold of something she thought would end the pregnancy and she took it and she died."

"I'm sorry to hear that," Jeremy said. He paused, taking a deep breath. The pause was just long enough to give the effect of empathy before continuing. "So, what are your plans, then? After you get back to the States?"

"I figure I'll take a few months and see what comes along," I said.

"You know, that reminds me. I have a contact in London. She's at an organization there whose research is very closely related to your field of experience here. She's based in London but they have organizations all over the world promoting women's health initiatives. I met her at a conference in Dakar last summer. I could give you her contact details, if you're interested. If nothing else, she may have some leads."

"Sure, thanks," I said.

"Great, I'll email you her details. It's good to have things lined up."

"Yes, I suppose I should have thought more about it. The end always felt so far away. Somehow I didn't really think it would come."

He looked at me strangely, then he picked up his papers and gave them a pointless shuffle on the desk to signify that we had finished.

"Well, good luck then. You fly out tonight?"

"Yes."

"Take care."

"You too."

Back at Galion, I packed up my room and went to have one last drink on the terrace. The place was empty. I was alone. I thought of the first time I had been here with John. It had been so exciting. Would I ever feel as much excitement as I had felt here? Would the world ever be so strange and yet so wonderful? Now it would all be over, and this would only be memories. This place. Would I ever return? But I knew that even if I did, it would not be the same.

Chapter Eighteen

**London
November 21, 2013**

I spotted Marion and Liza as soon as I entered the café. Marion smiled as we made eye contact, but Liza seemed not to notice. I made my way through the maze of café tables and customers to where they were seated. Neither had any drinks before them, so I took a seat.

"You found it alright?" Marion asked as I removed my coat and scarf.

"Yes, yes, it was easy enough. I just got a bit turned around outside the station. Were you waiting long?" I asked.

"No, not at all. I'll go get the drinks. What would you like?"

"Oh, just a regular black coffee I guess, but you don't have to," I said, uncomfortable with the idea of Marion paying for everyone.

"I don't mind. An Americano then? Liza?"

"Just tea for me," Liza said.

I was still getting used to things. There was no such thing as regular coffee; it was an Americano. Here, you needed to specify. Tea, on the other hand, usually only meant one thing. Silly little opposites. I took a deep breath and tried not to regret my decision to meet them so quickly, though I wished they'd have picked a pub instead of a coffee house chain like I expected real revolutionaries to do.

"So, I just finished *State and Revolution*," I said, unable to bear the silence anymore.

"Yes. We should wait for Marion to come back before we get into it," Liza said. She had an accent I couldn't place. She was probably my age, maybe a bit older, but I could tell she thought that I was much younger. I gave up on trying to make conversation. She didn't seem to notice. We waited for Marion.

"I brought you some sugar," Marion said, relieving the tension, as she set our drinks down on the table.

"Oh, thanks," I said, and she resumed her place across from me. "I was telling Liza that I had just finished *State and Revolution*."

"What did you think?" Marion said.

"I thought it was brilliant."

"What did you like about it?" Marion asked, while Liza sat next to her, silently, both of their eyes on me.

"What I find most interesting is the impermanence that all of it was supposed to have. Communism, the way most people imagine it, was a temporary state, according to Lenin. But, well, it's just sort of difficult now to know how to apply it to today's world. I mean, is it still possible to imagine something like bringing about the dissolution of the State?"

"Well, we have to start by studying the past," Marion said. It was an obvious statement.

"Right, well, no doubt it is important. I just wonder sometimes what we can actually *do* with it all. How we actually change things once we've studied the mistakes of the past?"

"We are doing something," Liza jumped in. "We're educating people on what Marxism is, what socialism means."

"I understand, I do. But most of the time don't you just find yourself preaching to the converted?" I hadn't meant it as an attack, but I could see from Liza's expression my words did not sit well with her.

"Do you think *your* work has really helped people, though? Aid work? You think that's the way to *do* something? All those organizations just help to proliferate the imperialist agendas. It's neocolonialism."

This was Liza's favorite argument and she never missed the opportunity to remind me of how much damage I had done by assisting the enemy while living in Togo.

"Well, yes, that's true." I always agreed because it confused her and she lost her excuse to continue the lecture. I did agree with her on some level, but it was an oversimplified argument at best.

"That reminds me, I have a book I want to give you," Marion said. "It's by a man who used to work for the Red Cross. It's quite revealing, the ways in which aid is used to manipulate conflicts. I think you'd find it interesting."

"It sounds interesting," I said. I liked Marion. She was an American, as well, but I knew little else about her. How she wound up here and what she did outside of editing their little Red Paper. I'd attended two of their meetings so far. The discussion points and the readings were interesting, but these little coffee dates felt kind of like attempts at initiation into a cult. Still, they did fill up the empty weekend afternoons.

"Are you coming tonight to the talk?" Marion asked, ignoring my earlier dissent. She still believed strongly that I could be converted, despite my hesitations.

"Yes," I said.

"Good, I think you'll enjoy it. How is your research going?"

"Oh, it's alright. To be honest it's pretty difficult. I feel like I'm playing a bit of catch-up right now. It's like, even though I spent two years of my life actually doing the work, I'm still not well-versed enough on the theoretical side to be taken seriously here. And you know, the more I learn about 'behavior change models' and concepts of 'sustainable development', the less I think it actually matters. Wherever they came up with this stuff, it definitely wasn't in some little village in a country like Togo," I sighed. "But I guess that's why they wanted me. So I could have an influence and bring my experiences to the front."

"Yes, I'm sure you will," she said a little too cheerfully. I detected a hint of either condescension or pity. Perhaps both. "I'll bring that book for you tonight."

"Great," I said. We'd nearly finished our coffees. "Well, I should be off. I have a bit of work to do beforehand."

"See you tonight," Marion called. Liza said nothing, only smiled without much effort as I headed off. I wondered what they would say about me once I was gone.

I wasn't lying about the work, but somehow I couldn't bring myself to go back. I passed an old used bookshop and unthinkingly wandered in. The familiar scent of stale, stained and dusty pages drifted through the rows of old pulp fiction, heaving bosoms and redundant detective stories. In the very back, there was a small shelf, hidden away, labeled Poetry. I spotted a raggedy old copy of Pablo Neruda's *Residence on Earth*. Perhaps because of the Marxists, I was drawn to it. Or perhaps it was simply because I remembered a few lines from a poem of Neruda's I had heard once, and though I couldn't remember what they were, the sentiment stuck. So, I rescued him from his forgotten exile in a London bookshop. Three pounds fifty and he was mine. I got another coffee and sat for a while reading.

Around five, I left for the talk. At the Tube station, the train took ages to arrive and when it finally did, it was so jammed full of people that I barely got on. We only made it two more stops before we were delayed again. A crushing panic was beginning to set in. I wondered: which is worse? Being packed in an overcrowded minivan that should have ceased to run twenty years ago, in the sweltering heat? Or being shoved around in claustrophobic conditions miles under the earth in a metal tube? I was coming to the conclusion that they were both equally uncomfortable, and perhaps equally dangerous in a soul-crushing sort of sense.

At Knightsbridge, the crowd in the station was a mass of anxious travelers trying in vain to board the already full compartments. Unable to take the lack of air and pressure of bodies practically piled onto one another, I fought my way toward the open doors through the crowds and out of the station. It was after six. I could hail a cab, but it seemed everyone had the same idea. I started walking.

When I arrived at the venue, it was nearly seven. I found the room and snuck in quietly, taking a seat in the back. The talk had already begun. I wasn't sure how much I had missed. There was a panel of three, and a middle-aged woman in the middle was speaking with an American accent. She was in the midst of a story about getting harassed on a flight back into the U.S. Her tone, her clothes—it all reminded me of something out of a Woody Allen movie. A typical New York intellectual.

"You see, this sort of harassment is nothing new to the old left, people that have aligned themselves with the Communist Party or similar 'radical' movements. We are constantly under surveillance; our names are on lists. It's only getting worse," she said.

The rest of the panel nodded in agreement. They continued with their stories and anecdotes. I tried to follow but I had already missed most of the background. When the talk finished, I found Marion. She was near the front with her husband and Liza and a few other people I recognized from previous group meetings.

"You made it," she said as I approached.

"Yes. What a nightmare it was out there."

"Lots of people were late. They did try to wait, but one of the panelists had to catch a flight out and they couldn't really postpone it for very long."

"Well, at least I caught a bit of it."

"Look, there's going to be a small gathering at Liza's for Rebecca, the American panelist. We're going there now. Can you join us? It isn't far."

"Sure," I said. We waited a few moments for the others

The Ardent Witness

to assemble. "How did you find it then?"

"Very interesting," she said. "Well, we can go. The rest of them will come around shortly."

Her husband, Simon, and another older gentleman appeared by her side, and we left the building and stepped out into the cool November air.

Liza's flat was only a few blocks away. I wondered if she worked or studied there but I didn't ask because it didn't seem appropriate. It was all about the politics, not the personal. Though I had offered various bits of information about myself since I'd begun attending their meetings, no one else seemed so eager.

"I hope you get a chance to speak with Rebecca," Marion said as we walked. "She's a very interesting woman. She attended the trial of Chelsea Manning. I think you missed the beginning when she was talking about it."

"Really?" I asked, impressed.

"Yes. She wrote about it for one of our publications in the U.S. You should ask her about it. You used to work in journalism, didn't you?"

"Yes. I would love to hear about it."

Once we arrived at Liza's flat, everyone busied themselves with bottles and glasses. Soon the others poured in with the constant buzzing of the bell and before long the tiny flat was overflowing with people and conversation. I got myself a glass of wine and Marion made a few introductions for me to some of the people that were just arriving. Eventually, I made my way into the living area. Rebecca was seated on the floor in the middle of the room, holding court.

"Come, I'll introduce you," Marion said, appearing

beside me. "This is Lillian. She's just recently begun to attend our meetings here in London." Rebecca smiled, feigning interest. I was most likely the least important person at the party. "She missed the beginning of the talk, but I thought maybe you could tell her a little about the trial. She used to be a journalist in Detroit."

"I remember watching the verdict while I was in the States this summer," I said. "You know, Al Jazeera America was the only news channel to have it live."

"That doesn't surprise me," Rebecca said. "They were absolutely terrible to the media, anyway."

"How did you get in?" I asked.

"Pure luck. I showed up at three in the morning and waited in line. They were admitting a very small number of people from the general public. Somehow I was one of them."

"You flirted with the guards, then?" said one of the older men that was sitting near us teasingly. Rebecca rolled her eyes.

"Oh, shut up, Fred. Anyway," she began, now she had the interest of the room. "They had her separated from the rest of the courtroom by a disproportionate amount of armed guards. She wasn't even allowed to turn her head to see the rest of the room. Ellsberg was there, and I'll never forget, he tried to reach out to her as she was escorted to the front of the room and these armed guards leapt at him, tackling this little eighty-year-old man to the ground. It was unbelievable. And then the judge, it was positively Orwellian. You know, they only allowed sixteen people from the general public in. There were dozens of activists outside they'd kept out, and the judge just kept asking if everyone that had wanted to get in had gotten in. Like he was so concerned, knowing full well how impossible they had made it …"

She recounted the ordeal in a disorganized fashion, the way it tends to go for one who's witnessed history and is eager to share what they've seen, especially when it's of such great and unacknowledged significance. I was envious of her. She had been there and where had I been? I was always a step behind. Still, the need to 'be there' was diminishing. She had been there to play witness and that was important. But she'd filed her story and then it would be forgotten by most. And what would the rest of us do? What could we do? Here I was drowning in powerlessness again.

"Lily?" I turned to see Simon, Marion's husband, addressing me. "I wanted to introduce you to Sean and Louis. I was just telling them about your time in Togo and your interest in our studies."

"Hello," I said, turning to see two young men I vaguely recognized from previous meetings.

"How are you finding things in London, then?" Louis asked. He had a thick French accent.

"Well, you know how it is in a new place. I'm still finding my way around but, you know, it's getting easier."

"How did you hear about us?" Sean asked.

"Oh, it was quite random actually. Marion had a booth near one of the campuses I was taking a walk through and I noticed some pamphlets on anarchism. We got to talking and she invited me to come along to a meeting."

"Marion is one of our best recruiters. She got Louis and I involved, how long ago was it now?"

"Oh, too long ago to remember," Louis laughed. "And how are you enjoying the meetings so far?"

"I've found it very interesting. I think in some ways it has helped me to make sense of many of my experiences in Togo. The disparity, the lack of development."

"I'm sure it has," Louis said. "What brought you to London?"

"I'm working here now, doing some research for an NGO whose focus is on women's health in developing countries. Their main offices are here in London but they run all sorts of programs in developing countries, mainly in Africa. They're looking for new approaches, ways to improve their services and beneficiary outcomes in order to try to have more of an impact. My job is to have a look at what other, similar organizations are doing and, also, to apply some of my ground-level knowledge to give some suggestions. So your talks and readings have been interesting for me as I try to frame some of my arguments, you know?"

"I can imagine," Sean said. "Though I'm not sure how eager they'll be there, to hear our kinds of arguments."

"The director, she's really encouraged me to use my own personal experiences. So hopefully that will also help to convince them."

"I've never been to Africa. Though I spent a few months in India when I was younger. I imagine it would be similar. In terms of the level of poverty. It's criminal. I'm intrigued," Sean continued, staring at me with a quizzical look. "How would you say we're helping you with your thesis, if you don't mind my asking?"

"You see, in my case, as a health worker, a lot of what

I did there operated on the assumption that what people need in a place like Togo is information. That we have to arm them with the knowledge they need to make more informed decisions about their health and therefore, they'll lead better lives, practice safe sex, know how to prevent diseases. But soon after I got there I realized: most people are very aware of what they need to do, but if they don't have the medicine, the hospital staff, the roads, just the basic material necessities, how can you expect things to change?"

"You can't—you're just shifting the responsibilities on to people, blaming them for things out of their control and alleviating the responsibility from the people whose hands it's really in," Sean said.

"Exactly," I said. "Basically most NGO's, mine included, operate under the same false premise."

"And you think your report is going to change all of that?" Sean asked, smirking.

"No," I said, embarrassed. "I'm not saying that I think that I—Well, I hope it helps at least."

"Don't take him too personally, Lily," Louis said. "It's good what you're trying to do. It's just that one of the main components of our ideology is the idea that reform can't come from within the current capitalist constructs."

"I see," I said, but I didn't. Actually I was more confused. "So, what do you do then? To change things?"

"We study history and we educate people with our publications and our talks," Louis said. "So when the time comes, we'll be ready."

"When the time comes? So, what you're calling for is an all-out revolution then?" I meant it partly as a joke.

Louis smiled but Sean didn't look amused.

"You could look at it that way," he said. He seemed annoyed that I was trying to peg him down with it.

"So then, how does one go about such a task directly?" I asked. I knew I was egging them on, but I couldn't help myself.

"It doesn't quite work like that," Sean said, with a tone that suggested it would be a waste of time to explain it all to someone like me. Louis was not so easily discouraged.

"We attend protests and marches, and like I said, we publish our paper, hold our meetings and try to recruit people, like you," Louis said.

I nodded. So you wait, I almost asked, but I stopped myself.

"Well, hopefully we'll see you at the next meeting," Louis offered. Sean raised his glass and I left them to refill mine.

In the kitchen, Marion was sitting at the table with Fred, who had obviously drunk a fair amount. His eyes were glassy, but his words were steel as he recounted injustices as old as time and his equally aged struggle against them. Marion invited me to sit with them and my arrival encouraged Fred's enthusiasm. Perhaps I was the only member in attendance that had not heard his stories a million times over.

The night progressed, and the wine was flowing full and steady. There was a lot of talk of the good old days. The labor unions, the party activities, the vigor of movements that were now only shadows of their former selves. Gutted shells of resistance. So, I sat listening to stories that went unfinished, but it didn't in any way diminish their importance. They were real in a sense that only things that had been lived and felt so deeply could be real. In a time and a place that no longer existed except after too many glasses of red wine late into an autumn evening. That was fine. I didn't mind lending my eager ears to imaginary pasts. At the moment, they seemed so much more pleasant than the present.

"Please, have a seat," Emily said as I entered her office. When she'd called the meeting, I hadn't thought much of it. It was the first formal review of my report so far and it had seemed the natural next step after I had emailed her the first draft of my work. Now, it struck me that perhaps it had been strange she had offered no other feedback, no comments. She'd only suggested we set a time to 'talk things through'. I took a seat across from her and waited for her to begin. Her smile gave nothing away. She was always ridiculously polite. She never seemed to be frustrated or tired, nor showed any trace of the emotion that a human being in a stressful nine-to-five job should feel. She had that British sense of style that I was slowly developing an appreciation for. Quirky chic. Always well made up but without looking as though she wore any makeup at all. I guessed she was in her early forties. I liked her. Or, at least, I wanted to.

"Well," she said in a deep, breathless voice. "I've read it all. You're a really fabulous writer, you know? And there's so much information here."

First rule of management: Start with the positives then slowly build the attack. If that was the only positive she could find in the thirty-odd pages on her desk, I was in trouble. She paused, still smiling, and again I waited.

"First off, Lily," she said with faint undertones of sympathy in her voice. "I just want to say that I appreciate all the work you've put into this. It's obvious you've really buried yourself in the research and I know how daunting this sort of thing can be." She paused again and I suddenly got the impression she was waiting for me to speak. To defend myself? But I had nothing to say aside from what was written there in unembellished black and white. "It's just that the overall tone is ... Well, to be honest, it isn't really the direction I imagined we would take."

"I see," I said. "Well, I—I do think the evidence is there to support the conclusions I've drawn."

"Yes, well, it's a bit too critical, I think. I mean, some criticism, I understand, sure. But, basically, you're saying that, essentially, the work we do is pointless." She said the last bit with an air of disbelief that matched the absurdity of the smile she still wore as she said it.

"I'm not saying that it's *all* pointless." I tried to redeem myself. "It's just that I think the way you're currently going about it doesn't take certain things into consideration. So much of it relies so heavily on theories, but in practice it doesn't work. Take your use of the behavior change model. How can people be expected to modify their behavior if there is no social or economic support for it? You wanted me to come at it from my own experience and this is what I've seen firsthand. And I have the facts and figures to back it up."

"Lily, we've launched a good deal of successful programs across the world, impacting hundreds of lives—"

"And I do take that into account but—"

"I'm sorry, Lily, but we can't use this." The smile finally disappeared from her face. I was quiet. I searched for something to say. An apology of sorts. But I didn't want to apologize. Why should I?

"Look," she said after a moment. She'd mistaken my anger for distress. It softened her again. "I think that perhaps it's all still a little too fresh for you. Why don't you take some time to think about it? I'll be gone for the next two weeks, take some time to think things over. You do have a lot of good information here, if we can just reframe things differently … Then maybe we can even see it published somewhere. That would be very good for your career. I'll send you some examples of other reports that are more in line with what we're looking for."

She was no longer speaking to me directly. She was trying to find a way to salvage the mess I'd made, unwilling to admit she'd made a mistake in trusting me with any of it. She seemed to have convinced herself that I might still come through for her. Of course, I was young and idealistic. Of course, I still needed to learn the way these things work. She'd help me to cope with the slow corrosion of principles needed to survive in this line of work. That was the offer she was making to me now. I couldn't accept it, I knew that. But I also couldn't turn her down too quickly. I had to at least make it appear as though I would struggle with it some.

"Yes," I said. "Maybe you're right."

"Don't worry about it." She had expected no less than complete compliance and this irked me a bit, but I decided to keep quiet. "Okay, great. I'll send you those other reports. Like I said, I'll be gone over the next few weeks, but you can email me if you need anything."

"Thank you … Where are you off to then?" I asked, trying to be cordial.

"I'm going to a conference in Uganda. We're launching a new online training course to offer to some of our sister organizations there," she answered, still smiling.

"Well, good luck," I said and stood up to leave.

"Lily, you did well, you know," she called as I left, trying to reassure me. "It's just…"

"I know," I smiled back.

"See you in a few weeks!" she called as I left her office.

I wondered if she really believed I would be back.

That evening, the pub was relatively quiet. There was a young bartender behind the old oak counters. I ordered a glass of wine and found the faded carpet staircase that led up to the meeting room. Marion waved to me from her place at the table. I waved back. There were a few empty seats across from her and Simon, so I sat down.

"I'm glad you could make it," she said. "It's been a while since we've seen you. But I know you've been very busy with work."

"Yes, I have. Actually, I finished my report this week," I said.

"Well, congratulations!" Marion said. "What are you working on next?"

"I'm not sure," I said.

She didn't ask any more questions. The room was almost full. Sean was at the end and Louis sat near the front. He would be giving the talk this evening. Fred and

Liza were also in attendance and a few others I had never seen before.

Louis cleared his throat. A signal that the time was upon us. Tonight's talk was on Engels and his views on the family. I hadn't read any of the material. For the first few moments, I tried to listen, but then my mind began to wander. It was all very interesting in theory, sure. It always was. But what to do with it all practically, I still had no idea and I doubted Louis was going to enlighten us in his talk tonight.

"How did you find it?" Marion asked when it was over.

"Oh, it was very interesting," I lied.

Sean came up. "Hey there, you alright? You both enjoy the talk?"

"Yes, very much," Marion said.

"Will you stick around for a drink afterwards?"

"No, I think Simon and I will be going."

"Lillian?" He turned to me and I hesitated. "Come on, have a pint," he urged.

"Oh, alright," I said. "I never was one to turn down an invitation to have a drink."

"Why start now?" he smiled, satisfied, and went off to convince the others.

Slowly everyone drifted to the downstairs bar and I ordered another glass of wine. Liza, Louis and Fred had also stayed on. I sat with them for a while as they banged on about the usual topics. But soon I realized I wasn't interested in most of what they said. I simply didn't want to be alone. I got another drink and when I returned to the table the subject had turned to religion, a favorite whipping boy for all of them. I sat quietly as they carried on. How could they be so cynical? So sure of everything? Finally the wine and their words forced me to speak.

"It's kind of arrogant, isn't it? The way you're all talking."

They stopped and looked over at me, and I could see the surprise in different measures on each of their faces.

"Arrogant?" Liza repeated. She seemed the least startled, perhaps even pleased by my sudden impulse to join in their conversation. "How do you mean?"

"You assume everyone who believes in anything is an imbecile. Is it really as simple as all that to you?"

"We don't think *everyone* is an imbecile," Louis said, offering his ever patient and kind attempts at understanding.

"Don't you?" I asked. Perhaps he didn't, but I doubted that he spoke for the rest of them.

"You're joking. You're surely not defending religion?" Sean looked at me, shaking his head.

"Were you raised in a religious family?" Liza asked, her voice patronizing.

"No, not particularly. My parents did raise me as a Catholic, but they were never very serious about it," I said. "But still there were things about it that moved me as a child."

"But there's so many things in the Bible that are contradictory. You surely can't say that it's worth anything," Sean said stubbornly.

"There are many things in life that are contradictory, and besides, the Bible isn't all there is," I retorted, annoyed.

"Oh, like what? Islam? The fundamentalist Hindus

in India? Religion does nothing but breed ignorance and violence." Sean stopped just short of banging his fist on the table.

"Listen," I said. "I don't disagree on the point that religion can be manipulated in ways that make people who are in desperate situations look to blame others and commit atrocities. I'm not arguing with that. All I'm saying is that when I read *Bhagavad Gita* or the Sermon on the Mount, I read it the same way I would read Keats or Hemingway or any other piece of literature. And for me, in certain points in my life, I've found truth in them, I've recognized something of myself in the words beyond whatever anyone else says they mean." They remained unconvinced. I doubted any of them had even listened. They simply sat there thinking of the next argument to make.

"Doesn't it all just boil down to an idea that there is something greater than ourselves to live for?" I asked.

"Humanity. Isn't that enough? Why do you need religion?" Sean almost shouted.

"Suppose it's the same thing?" I asked.

"It stands in the way of science! Of social progress!"

"But it doesn't have to," I argued. "Do you really think if we abolished religion, people wouldn't find new reasons to fight wars and cause senseless violence? It would be nationalism or something else. They'd just find a new name for it! You could very well replace religion with a great many other things that aren't fundamentally bad, but can be used to make people justify doing awful things. So many things done in the name of religion are really done because people are desperate, because their basic needs as human beings aren't being met and they need a reason for it because it makes no sense! That some should have so much and others so little? All by chance? By luck? And this desperation can be easily manipulated by people who are greedy, people who have power and they say, 'This is why you are so unfortunate.' Yes, there is a lot of violence done in the name of religion but it is because of inequality. You'd think as Marxists you'd realize that."

"It's just superstition. Charlatanism," Liza said. I looked down at my wrists, rubbing the faded charcoal marks.

"Well, what's so wrong with a bit of mystery?" I sighed. "Perhaps there are things out there that can't be explained. Why does that frighten you all so?"

"It doesn't frighten us," Louis laughed but I could see I had struck a nerve. "We just believe in science."

The rest nodded and grumbled a few words. It was late into the evening and the table was filled with empty pints and wineglasses.

"Well," Sean said, looking up with glassy eyes and laughing, "Well done for being a good sport about it. I suppose we ganged up on you a bit."

"No harm done," I said.

It was getting late and I didn't want to miss the last Tube. I liked them all, I thought, as I made my way back home, but I couldn't share their dogmatism. I couldn't belong so resolutely to one thing or another. Perhaps I made a poor revolutionary for it. Yet at the same time, I still wasn't convinced that they were much better at it.

When I got home, I sat down on my bed, feeling

the sudden urge to cry. You failed again, you fool. And it was no wonder. You've actually managed to fall into the trap of everything you were meant to be escaping. You've wound up so very far from where you started. What had become of her, the girl I had been that night, in a crummy little studio in downtown Detroit? A night that felt like lifetimes ago. So brave and so sure. And what had become of him? I remembered sitting on those cold cement steps when he told me that he hadn't felt that happy in a long time. Was he happy now? Maybe he had lost it, too? Maybe he really was in New York trying to 'make it'. I took a deep breath and tried to concentrate on my breathing, to calm myself down. I poured a glass of wine and went over to my desk. I pulled out the tattered old notebook, stained with coffee and wine and a faint coating of sub-Saharan dust. I flipped through until I saw it, the handwriting that wasn't mine. It was foolish, but it was all I could do. I opened up my laptop and began to type.

Dear Jack,

Perhaps you don't remember me, but I often think of that night. I wonder if my memories are as true as the reality of it, or if they have become a bit like your paintings. An over-idealized picture of a time, a place and person that never really existed. Or never as perfectly as I wanted it to.

I saw some of your paintings when I was in Detroit over the summer. I recognized them instantly. I often think of what you said about them, that once they were done and hung up somewhere, you didn't worry about what people thought of them, whether they mattered to anyone or meant anything.

My problem was that I did. I desperately wanted my words to matter, to mean something. The fear that they might not was paralyzing. I suppose that's my tragedy. I don't know why I'm telling you all this, except I think you might be the only person that I can say these things to who might understand them.

Anyway, the paintings were beautiful. At least I remembered that much about that night perfectly.

Yours,
Lily (the poet)

The next morning, I awoke with a pounding head and a feeling of dread as I thought back to what I had done. But then there it was.

To The Poet,

You can't believe how happy I am to hear from you. Somehow, I always held out hope we might find each other again. Somehow I almost knew for certain that we would. I, too, often think of that night. I think your memories perhaps hold more truth in them than the reality. But then, I think the same thing about my paintings.

Your letter reminded me of something I read recently. It was a book on Romanticism. I was reminded of you. But the part that stayed with me was that they had the idea that art was a new religion. That it could replace all the mysticism that the Enlightenment had taken away from us.

So they built museums and opera houses to rival the most magnificent cathedrals all across Europe.

What I mean is, I don't think your tragedy is that you want it to matter and it doesn't. I think your tragedy is that it does mean something, but you don't see it. Think of your poems as a type of prayer, an offering, a meditation. Whatever you want to call it. But write. It's the only way to keep the fire burning, regardless of what comes of it otherwise. Your words are beautiful. I'll never forget the way they moved me that night.

Yours,
Jack

P.S. Where are you now? What are you up to these days?

That afternoon I decided to go worship at my designated temple.

All museums are mazes, but on different scales. As I wandered through each congested room of the National Gallery, I wondered if anyone even looked at paintings anymore, or if they simply took photos of them as proof that they existed and that they'd seen them in the flesh. Or 'in the paint' would be more appropriate. No. That's rather harsh of me. Some people do look and see. A few at least. But they get lost in the crowds. I never had to fight the crowds at the DIA. Oftentimes I wondered if I was the only person in the whole building. Oftentimes I might have been. I skipped over the Renaissance, like in the old days. I even went past Michelangelo this time. I stopped myself when I got to the wall of Turners, that old

English master and his descent into abstraction. In his later works was something of the sea that he could not have captured otherwise. But when I eventually moved into the next room, the crowds were overwhelming. On one wall hung Monet's greatest hits, but there was no hope of getting close enough to see if they held any more magic in them than the countless reproductions. My eye was instantly caught by something else from across the room. It was Pissarro's *The Boulevard Montmartre at Night*. I walked over to it through the crowds. Was there more truth hanging in that little frame than anything I might find outside of it? I stared at the little flecks of paint that made up the streets, the cars, the sentimental streetlights. I felt the sad, sudden pain of joy swell up into my chest. I left the gallery to find a quiet place to get a drink.

I sat alone in the dark pub and thought about my afternoons in Detroit. My old place downtown. The brightly lit booths of Coney Island. I missed them terribly but it was with a longing that made them more alive and more beautiful and more true than they could ever be to me now, in reality. Like Pissarro's Montmartre. Or Jack's Detroit. It wasn't really a place that I longed for. It was a moment in time. A feeling. A part of me. A part that I searched for and found and lost and found again. In galleries and diners and dusty mountain roads. In a sub-Saharan sunrise and in others like me that never stopped looking for it. I picked up my pen and began to write,

> *I used to search for it in the eyes of strangers.*
> *A spark of hope*
> *That burns with the rarity*
> *Of such mad desires.*

Author's Note

I never intended to write about my experiences in Togo. The book began as a way to cope with the loss of such a profound and important time in my life that was suddenly over with. It was a way for me to make sense of the experience, and also, to remember it. At first, I wrote about things as they had actually occurred, but soon I realized that I could not fully convey what had happened by simply recounting it. It would leave too many things unsaid. Too many things I would not be able to put into words otherwise. The people and events I write about in this book are fictitious, but still I hope that I have done my best to honor the place and period in my life that inspired them.

About the Author

Originally from Sterling Heights, Michigan, Danielle Maisano has been unintentionally settled in London for over half a decade. She has a BA in journalism from Wayne State University and during her time in Detroit, she worked as a journalist in both print and broadcast. In 2011 she joined the United States Peace Corps and where she served from 2011-2013 in Togo, West Africa.

In 2013 she moved to London to pursue her MA in International Relations and Diplomacy from the School of Oriental and African Studies. She has divided her professional career between stints as a freelance writer and work within London's charity sector. In 2016, she traveled with her husband, Alex, to explore his Chilean roots in the port town of Valparaiso. They settled there for over six months and during that time she was able to concentrate on writing her first novel, *The Ardent Witness*.

Acknowledgements

I would like to thank editor Carrie O'Grady, publisher Consuelo Rivera-Fuentes, friend and artist Lauren French, professor and mentor Jack Lessenberry, and all of the friends and colleagues I met and had the honor of working with during my time in Togo, without whose kindness, support and generosity I would not have lasted two weeks, let alone two years. I also want to thank my husband, Alex, my mom and grandma Elaine for their unwavering belief in the power of dreams, and all my family and friends whose love and encouragement over many years has given me the confidence to keep putting pen to paper. Words cannot express my gratitude.

Victorina Press Publications

Fiction

My Beautiful Imperial (2017)
Rhiannon Lewis

The Marsh People (2018)
M. Valentine Williams

Blind Witness (2018)
Vicki Goldie

The Secret Letters from X to A (2018)
Nasrin Parvaz

Mi Querido Imperial
(Spanish Translation of *My Beautiful Imperial,* 2018)
Rhiannon Lewis

Children's Books

Songo (For Children and Families) (2018)
Rachel Pantin & Mauricio Venegas-Astorga

*Songo (For Children, Early years settings
& practitioners)* (2018)
Rachel Pantin & Mauricio Venegas-Astorga

I am Adila from Gaza (2018)
Mabel Encinas-Sánchez

Non-Fiction

One Woman's Struggle in Iran: A Prison Memoir (2018)
Nasrin Parvaz

Violeta Walks on Foreign Lands ~ Violeta Anda en Tierras Extrañas (Bilingual Spanish-English, 2018)
Edited by ~ Editado por Odette Magnet & Consuelo Rivera-Fuentes

Forthcoming in 2019/20

Fiction

An Artists Muse
Deborah Wilson

Dirt Clean
Judith Amanthis

The String Games
Gail Aldwin

Vengeance has Landed
Manfredo Zaverpi

The Bomb on the Winnipeg
Adam Feinstein

The Nobody Man
Steve Jenkins

Redención (Spanish)
Paloma Zozaya

Non-Fiction

Fountain of Creativity: Ways to Nourish your Writing
Bethany Rivers

Just Gill: Saving Soi Dogs
Barbara Young & John Dalley